Spring at Brookfield

'John,' said his brother, 'if you want Doris, you're going to have to flatten me first, y'know that?'

'Any time, mate!'

'Now,' said Dan. 'Tonight. And winner takes all.'

John stared at him, surprise overriding his mounting anger. 'You serious? The farm as well?'

'The lot,' said Dan grimly, unbuttoning his coat.

John followed suit, more slowly. 'What about the loser, then?' he demanded, narrow-eyed.

'He gets out, don't he,' stated Dan. 'Right out, clear out of Ambridge. For good. Brookfield wouldn't hold both of us.'

'Done!' rapped John, then laughed. 'You bloody fool. . . .'

'In here,' gritted Dan, and led the way into the barn.

Another novel of the Archers of Ambridge in Tander

AMBRIDGE SUMMER Keith Miles

Spring at Brookfield

Brian Hayles

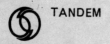 TANDEM

First published in Great Britain by
Allan Wingate (Publishers) Ltd in 1975

Published by Tandem Publishing Ltd, 1975

Copyright © Brian Hayles 1975

The Archers series © The British Broadcasting Corporation
1951–1975

By arrangement with the British Broadcasting Corporation

Tandem Books are published by Tandem Publishing Ltd
14 Gloucester Road, London SW7
A Howard & Wyndham Company

Printed in Great Britain by litho by The Anchor Press Ltd
and bound by Wm Brendon & Son Ltd
both of Tiptree, Essex

CHAPTER ONE

WITH AN easy roll of his shoulders, the ploughman tilted the blade from the furrow, shifted its balance on to the landwheel, and eased plough and horses round on to the headland with a jingle of chains and harness.

'Hyup, Badger! Whoa, Jacko . . .! Whoa there, beauties!' The two shires stood massively still, the only sound now the champ of teeth on bit, with Badger blowing and nodding his broad-blazed muzzle. As they lowered their blinkered heads to grass, the farmer stretched his aching back, slowly. Half an acre ploughed and nearly half the day gone; the thin November sunlight sifted gently across the corduroy-true lines of the furrows, their moist cleave gleaming under the pale sky. A flurry of lapwings blanketed the turned soil at the lower end of the field where it fell away toward the misted outbuildings of Brookfield Farm, and as the rattle of distant gunshots carried across from the woodlands beyond the village, the piebald wings scattered half-heartedly, almost instantly resettling to their eager scavenging. Wiping his forehead across his sleeve, the ploughman stared impassively toward the sound of the now spasmodic guns. The beaters would be moving steadily forward through the bracken, heading the scuttering pheasant towards the guns of the Squire and his guests waiting to end the clattering call of the cocks in a fall of bright feathers; a fine day's sport, for some.

He'd been a beater many a day himself as a lad, years back. It was hard work for few pennies even then, but it had its pleasures, not the least of which was the beer and cheese and pickles given in great helpings at midday. For the gentry, of course, there was something more elegant; the afternoon shoot was always said to improve by the number of glasses of port drunk by the guns at luncheon. But thinking about the privileges of a landowner wouldn't get these acres finished; the ploughman took up the smooth leather traces, and gave voice.

'Yup, my beauties! Yup now, steady . . .!'

A few lapwings fluttered idly upward at his call. Badger and Jacko took the strain, and with a deft thrust of his burly shoulders, the bright blade bit deep into the soil once more, cleaving its inevitable way.

His gun loaded, Randolph Lawson-Hope rested it, butt on thigh, and casually scanned the lie of the land behind him; plenty of clear cover there for shooting on the turn, if necessary. It was his especial skill; even now at the age of fifty-five he had a reputation as a fine shot, and it was a rare bird that got past him. As a youngster in his father's day, he would often walk as flanking gun to the beaters, taking those birds turning away from the line of guns they found themselves being driven into; a choice placing that he was quick to take up if the allotted gun was too aged or otherwise disinclined to walk the flank all day long. Now the estate was his, however, his place was in the line facing the oncoming drive. As host gun he would call the difficult shots, even though today's guests were all experienced guns, many of them having extensive shooting estates of their own. This made the challenge even sharper, for their appraisal of the day's sport would be unrelentingly critical, though good-humoured. But already the day was going badly. Reggie Hardisty, on his left flank at number 6, had hardly had a bird rise to him all morning, and he'd make no bones about it over lunch. The shoot could well end as a total disaster, and the thought of failure ached in Lawson-Hope's very bones. He looked along the line of guns; they were still, relaxed and waiting, ears tuned keenly for the first sounds of the distant unseen beaters due to advance through Bramble Wood. A frown gathered behind the Squire's narrowed eyes and his face tightened bleakly at the fact that so far less than 200 birds were hanging in the gamecart. The

6

bag for this drive had better be good – or his head keeper would get a tongue lashing he'd never forget!

The under-keepers, Henry Adsall, Bill Forrest and his eldest boy Ted, had the beaters already strung out, ready and waiting for George Nugent's signal when he returned from the line of guns. The head keeper looked all along the line to left and right, sharp eyes missing nothing, before turning back to face Henry's quizzical stare.

'Fit to be tied, he is,' growled Nugent. Then with a sweep of his arm and a piercing whistle, he set the line of beaters in motion. 'If anything goes wrong this time,' he added, 'the Squire'll have my guts for garters . . .' He was moving forward with the line now, watching its progress with fierce eyes. 'So God help anyone who lets me down, that's all!' There was no need to say more; beaters and keepers alike knew that George Nugent's temper didn't stop at words, as would the Squire. Even at sixty years he could strike a younger man down with one blow from those massive fists, and few men chose to take an argument further than that without good reason; it went without saying that George Nugent was well-respected, especially with several pints under his belt of a Saturday. While he ruled the line it moved steadily and without flagging or racing; even Walter Gabriel didn't try any of his usual tricks, having tasted the head keeper's knuckles only two weeks back and still bearing the marks to show for it.

The chill breeze brought the sound of the beaters to Lawson-Hope's keen ears, and he tensed, judging their distance. They moved steadily closer, their quiet advance punctuated by the sharper rattle of their sticks on treetrunks, stumps and saplings. They were still half a mile away; there'd be minutes to wait yet. Again he looked down the line, his pale eyes squinting keenly. Charles and Digby were chatting quietly to their ladies, a situation that Lawson-Hope reluctantly tolerated; his own wife, Lady Hester, would never dream of accompanying the guns however fashionable it might become, for which he thanked God. And then his eye fell on Anthony. The Squire had kept his son at the stand to his immediate right for both of the morning's drives, not out of a sense of pride but as a goad. He looked at the slender boy and coldly tried to assess the sum of those eighteen years. The face was Hester's, especially the eyes; slightly too bright, almost feverish, ready to dissolve from laughter into sadness at the downturn of that soft, sensitive mouth, in her so moving, in the son so weak. So too the lank fall of hair on to the pallid forehead—'quite romantic, like the times' as Hester so fondly put it as she presented Anthony to her salon jackals. That was his place, at the town house in Chester Square among the city set. His presence here was like salt rubbed into an open wound : *Dear God*, prayed Lawson-Hope agonisingly, *why couldn't it be his brothers here instead* ! Shamed in the same instant by his own weakness, he glowered curtly at Anthony only to find that the boy wasn't even aware of his father's intense stare. Languidly watching the trees ahead, the boy smiled slightly at a red squirrel skipping from branch to branch; it paused, apparently surveying the elegant death-trap below, then disappeared into the bole of a half-dead oak. Lawson-Hope swung his gaze to his front; all else was swept from his mind as he concentrated on the approaching moment of the kill.

Anthony threw a sidelong glance at his father and saw only the stone-eyed statue of the man who, five years before, had laughed so good humouredly at Anthony's first ungainly efforts to land a trout. Now, his reflexes triggered only by the seasons and their sports, Father lived for horse, gun and rod as though seeking a personal tally against Nature. It had been so different before Sarajevo. . . .

'Mark over !'

The Squire's sharp cry of warning brought Anthony abruptly back to the present, but the first lone bird was not for him. He watched the pheasant glide forty feet above the nearly vertical twin barrels of Digby Wentworth's gun, then cartwheel from its line of flight in a disjointed tangle of limbs and feathers, finally falling into the bracken behind him. A split second later came the crisp sound of Digby's shots. The row of guns were fully alert now; from inside the spinney fronting them came the click-clack of the beaters' sticks, a steady metronome moving relentlessly closer and closer.

'Woodcock, Reggie!'

Lawson-Hope's call rang out almost before the swiftly zig-zagging bird had broken from the cover of the trees towards the flanking gun; Reggie took it with his second shot, ejecting his empty shells and reloading in one fluid movement, ready at once for the next sighting. Of the next birds to rise, the first was the Squire's himself; he took it high to the front and right and it fell barely eight feet past Anthony's stand. The boy glanced back into the bracken to note the position of its fall, but was jerked back to the alert by his father's voice, harsh as a ripsaw.

'What in God's name are they up to!'

What his experienced ears had told him soon struck home to the other guns; the line of sound moving towards them was no longer balanced and level – several voices were closer, too close, and added to this, the excited darting of a loose dog could be seen.

'Dammit, what are they doing! They've lost control completely . . . !'

There were no shades of grey in the Squire's snap judgement, and within seconds his apprehension was proved right. In a cloud of wings, a hundred or more pheasant broke cover all at once, storming over the guns and giving them no chance at all to pick their targets as they should from a properly controlled flow of birds. The leader, a cockbird, came low and fast between Anthony and his father.

'Anthony!' bawled the Squire; but his son, confused at being given the shot, delayed.

'Too close!' howled Lawson-Hope, sighting and firing at the higher birds rising to his stand. But Anthony's trigger reflex, once committed to action, couldn't be checked. At ten feet the tight blast of fierce pellets disintegrated the bird into a spelter of blood and feathers, its velocity carrying the shredded gobbets of fine flesh spattering against Anthony's face and hands. Sickened and half-blinded by the glutinous flurry, he could

9

only turn away – but there by his side was his father, shooting cleanly and savagely at the now continuous flow of birds being put up by the beaters. Deft fingers reloading, sighting, firing, again and again – butt into shoulder tight and hard, sighting, firing, reloading – and all the time those blazing eyes seeing only enemies, and glorying in the illusion that Harry and Andrew were there on either side, sharing his triumphant, bloody tally.

Suddenly, it was over. Further down the line the last bird was put up and missed, miraculously; the beaters, now out of the spinney, stopped at Bill Forrest's quiet command and stood nervously in casual groups, barely six feet from the guns. Old Herbert lit his clay pipe, turning his weather-creased face away from the wind to mutter a dry aside, heard only by the man next to him.

'Somebody's going to be for it . . .' he muttered, between draws on the thin stem. 'Jest lookit the Squire, eh?' But the nod of his grizzled head indicated the young keeper at the end of the line, apparently intent on making his unwilling Labrador sit by his left boot; it did so reluctantly, still restless with the excitement of the drive. Ted looked up from the dog to see his father standing before him; the older man's eyes were as flinty as his voice.

'Bit late for that, in't it.'

'He's still learning,' offered Ted defensively.

'He's no right here then!' was the sharp retort; but it went unheard, for Ted's ears were pricked towards the gamecart, where Keeper Nugent and Henry Adsall were swiftly counting the hung tally, strung and looped in fours. The head keeper, hands bloodied from the feather corpses, turned to face the Squire, striding purposefully towards him. Ted saw Nugent touch his hatbrim, but couldn't hear what was said, however hard he strained. It was the ripple of relief that showed along the straggled line of beaters that told him what he wanted to know, and the thin smile on the Squire's face as he indicated the gamecart to his fellow-guns confirmed it. He wouldn't get off scot free, he knew that; but the bag was good enough to please the Squire, and that would be enough to save Ted's skin this once.

'That's more like it, eh, Reggie . . .?' Lawson-Hope grestured brusquely at the trophy-laden gamecart with the barrel of the gun broken over his right forearm, then waved the other members of the shoot towards him.

'Lunch, everyone . . .!' he called, crisply. For a moment his face darkened; Anthony waited for the inevitable razor-cut of judgement, but he was ignored. He realised that his father's stare was directed past him, towards the figure of Ted Forrest standing discreetly at the rear of the beaters, his disgraced dog by his side. But in that brief moment, Digby Wentworth had strolled all unknowing into the Squire's line of sight, and broke the building tension with a jovial compliment, emphasised with a hand on his host's shoulder.

'Grand mornin's sport, Randolph!' he declared, then moving on, continued, 'Good recovery by the chaps, too, eh?' It was enough to turn Lawson-Hope's anger from its customary fury, into a chilling, magisterial rebuke. He wheeled towards his head keeper, voice keen as a whiplash.

'Nugent! If I see that boy's damned dog running loose again, I'll put it down myself – d'y'hear!'

It hadn't been a bad day, Dan Archer acknowledged to himself as he made his way across the yard to the farmhouse scullery. The ploughing finished before dusk, and the horses put away and fed, he was satisfied; but this was no way to end the day, trudging out of a chill evening into a lonely house. Easing off his muddy boots, Dan let memories sieve through his mind. As a lad, until the day his mother died, there had never been a time when the kitchen wasn't warm and welcoming with the rich smells of food cooking in the oven or on the hob. It was the special moments that Dan could recall most easily – the fresh-baked bread still warm beneath the crackled brown crust; the great iron pot bubbling with blackberries for jam; and the suet dumplings bobbing so temptingly in the thick mutton stew. With the very taste and smell of comfort coming back to him from those otherwise lean days, the disappointment on entering the now-tepid kitchen was all the worse for the sight of the grimly familiar black stockpot and its eternally simmering potato soup. Dan had learned to tolerate brother John's simple cooking as a necessary break in the day's routine; they even managed to enjoy a blunt camaraderie made all the more pointed by John's habit of always eating from his ex-army billycan, and using his army issue tin mug to drink the grimy brown tea that he refused to let Dan brew.

'I've ate already,' grunted John without looking up from what he was doing. 'Tea's not long made. Help y'self.'

'Fair enough,' was Dan's equally curt reply.

The welcome was typically dour, another sad contrast to the old days. Ignoring Dan as he helped himself to food and sat at the scrubbed table to eat, John hunched in the old Windsor chair by the glowing firegrate, boning his best Sunday boots, army style, with the heated handle-tip of a worn spoon. Dan dipped a hunk of bread into the piping hot soup and munched it stolidly, his shrewd eyes watching the easy rhythm of John's hand working the gloss of the polished leather. Dapper though John always kept himself, this extra demonstration of spit and polish was out of the ordinary. Normally, on those days when John chose to pick up casual work away from Brookfield, he would end the day's stint with an evening's drinking at The Bull with Walter, leaving Dan to his own devices. Tonight, then, was going to be different. Dan's unease grew from the fact that he knew John had been out beating for the shoot earlier that day – which meant he'd had the chance to hang about the servants' kitchen at the Hall . . . and Doris was there. Thoughts stumbling clumsily, Dan's face was impassive as he spoke.

'The shoot went off all right then, did it . . .?' A carefully controlled spray of fine spittle fell on to the near-perfect black mirror that was John's right toecap; he regarded it closely, making no reply. Dan knew better than to push for answers that weren't easily forthcoming; with John, you had to know how to wait, when he was so inclined. Taking his time, Dan mopped his plate clean and slowly chewed the last mouthful of bread. But there was something that he couldn't let rest between them; he had to know about Doris. He turned in his chair to face John, but it was the younger man who spoke first.

'Your pal Ted got an earful, this midday. Nearly spoiled the Squire's sport, he did.'

'How come?' frowned Dan. 'He knows his job well enough . . .'

'Mebbe. But that dog of his don't.'

Another pause, and still no way of finding out what he had to know, short of making a fool of himself. Resigned to being patient, Dan continued to watch the increasing perfection of the polished boot. John, well aware of the mystery he was creating, at last looked up in answer to Dan's unspoken question, brandishing his handiwork proudly.

'Had an invitation,' he remarked, brightly. 'Got to look the part, haven't I – all spick and span, eh?' Dreading the reply, Dan forced himself to comment, studying his brother over the rim of his steaming mug of tea.

'Courting tonight, then . . .'

'Not in these boots, son!' John pulled a wry face. 'Not even for Polly Harper . . .' There were few men in the district who didn't know Polly Harper. You didn't have to dress up to tumble her behind a hedge.

'So what's it in aid of?' demanded Dan.

John put the right boot down and took up the left, studying it critically. Suddenly he wasn't smiling any more.

'The Squire. Says I'm to be at the Hall first thing in the morning.' He paused, then added bitterly, 'About the ceremony . . .'

'Ceremony?' puzzled Dan, wondering at the edge of anger in his brother's voice.

'Reckons I'm going to lead his bloody church parade for Armistice Day, don't he . . .' He flicked a sullen glare at Dan, then continued bluntly, '. . . Well, he's in for a flaming disappointment, that's what!'

Chapter Two

Few things could make Lady Hester remove herself from the company of her guests, even after dinner; for one thing it simply wasn't done, and for the other, luxuriating in her undoubted and acknowledged skills as hostess gave a frisson of rare power to her already almost sensuous delight in the social event, one that she was loath to relinquish easily. This brittle pleasure was all the more triumphant when it involved entertaining Randolph's sporting guests to dinner after a shoot, for his friends were rarely hers; and gracious though the setting of Arkwright Hall was, it had neither the sophistication of the house in Chester Square nor the panache of the visitors there. The form was essentially the same, but whereas in town one hoped and even looked for the unexpected but outrageous moment of brilliance, in the solid Georgian dignity of Randolph's family home tradition inevitably took precedence over Lady Hester's attitude of fashionable whimsy. Here, intuitively avoiding the direct challenge, she was content to win her own small victories – not the least of which was enjoying the barely-restrained envy she aroused among these ladies whose ways were less sensitively in tune with the London season. Without her, Randolph was a shrewd landowner, a skilled sportsman, and a generous but stolid host. It had to be acknowledged, even if reluctantly by some, that Lady Hester was a delightful social asset, albeit an expensive one.

This evening, her skills had been taxed to the full. There was an unmistakable quality of unease in the gathering, that she couldn't yet identify. Conversation at dinner had come and gone in fits and starts; even the magpie chatter of the ladies after withdrawing to leave the men to their port, had been strained, with Mollie Wentworth apparently determined to ride the subject of the local Hunt into the ground. It was only after the gentlemen had rejoined them that Lady Hester noticed the subtle change of atmosphere, a heightened joviality not entirely due to the men's port or the ladies' indulgence in scandal. As Stokes the butler supervised the serving of coffee, a quick glance around the drawing room brought the realisation that one person was no longer present : Anthony. A silent look of appeal brought no response from Randolph, who blandly and yet pointedly continued to listen to Reggie giving a pungent assessment of his latest hunter.

'Splendid conformation. But the very devil when it comes to taking a fence!'

Acutely aware that at any other time Randolph would have been the first to notice his son's absence and mark the event with a suitably caustic tag, Lady Hester waited, bright-eyed and patient, for the appropriate chance to excuse herself. But beneath her thoughtfully charming responses to the intricate barrage of riding talk, there lay a growing apprehension : something was wrong and Anthony needed her.

She found him, at last, in the billiards room. She had paused in the corridor outside, only just able to hear the muted sound of the soft kiss of ball on ivory ball. Moments before, she had found the music room deserted, but with a Mendelssohn sonata set open on the piano there; Anthony was the only person in the house who would play such a piece, and it said something for his state of mind that he had left it unfinished. There were few other sanctuaries personal to him left, other than his own bedroom. Having made the discovery, his mother hesitated before entering this quiet haven of masculinity, once the sole preserve of Randolph and his sons, now rarely if ever used by him at all. Harry and Andrew had been his constant and eager challengers, even as boys; ever since that last summer it had remained immaculate but deserted, one of innumerable small monuments to Randolph's grief. She herself had ceased to suffer openly – or so she thought. Were there memories in the room before her that could tear her soul apart once more by raising the spectres of those two golden boys, smiling, arrogant . . . and lost?

The breathless moment was scattered by the sharp, double-click of ivory. Opening the door quietly, she stood quite still, forced to adjust her eyes to the stark contrast of bright-lit baize against the deep shadow all about the table. A polished cue rested on the table edge, while the half-seen figure holding it silently considered the placing of the red and white spheres set upon the fine-textured green. The hands gripping the cue so lightly yet so dexterously were Anthony's, but his mother barely recognised the tight-throated voice that met her as she entered and closed the door behind her.

'Out of bounds, Mother . . .'

She couldn't bring herself to reply for the surge of feeling that swept over her at the echo of pain in his voice; the phrase wasn't a warning, but a plea to be left alone. Resolute, she made no move to retreat, and faced with this silent impasse, the boy bent forward to lean over the cue now resting on the bridge formed by his arched fingers on the table's surface. Now she could see his face, deep-shadowed by the light above, intent upon this private moment of the game, using it to avoid the face-to-face confrontation that he knew she wanted. She stayed quite still even after the stroke was played, watching the blood-red ball ricochet from cushion to cushion in a diminishing trajectory until it rolled slowly and finally to a stop. Then, with a rustle of skirts, she sat down. The tan leather of the banquette that encompassed the perimeter of the room held a strangely masculine smell that at once intrigued and yet made her uncomfortably aware of being out of place. Nevertheless, explanations were due. By sitting down, she hoped she had made it clear that she expected Anthony to provide them, frankly and honestly. She could see him more fully now, standing facing her across the vivid brilliance of the baize, his hands lightly clenched together on the upright cue like a guardsman flanking a funeral bier. The canopy of the light hanging low over the table hid his face and shoulders, but she sensed he was watching her, hoping that she would go without drawing the truth from him. Straight-backed, graceful and determined, she sat and waited.

'I'm listening, Anthony,' she said.

Mother was no help, Anthony reflected; but as he looked through the blaze of light at the petite, doe-eyed beauty sitting so incongruously on the buttoned-leather settle, he warmed to her in spite of himself. That gracious face, looking a full ten years younger than her true age, the trim, proud figure that still turned men's heads – it was as though she had the power to make the past stand still. No wonder she carried on her lifestyle as though royal Edward was still crown prince of sport whether in town or country, and no one dared to tell her otherwise. Father observed her sweet extravagances with a pained affability, but would not interfere; with Harry and Andrew no more than copperplate entries on the vellum flyleaf of the family bible, husbandry of beast, community or land had less importance than keeping Hester happy.

But though Mother played her part gaily to the hilt, Anthony was well aware of the reason for her private tears – not for her lost sons so much as for a husband lost to everything but a proud and cruel memory. She too had loved but never understood her sons; now, nothing she could do would ever bridge the gulf between Father and Anthony, the survivor. Neither would anything be gained by parading old scars, least of all those that still remained unhealed. Today's small incident was nothing. There were deeper, more desperate memories that his mother must never know.

'Anthony . . . I'm still waiting . . .'

Her clear, limpidly insistent voice offered no reproach, but he couldn't yet bring himself to reply. Those dark memories hung between them just as tangibly as the shadows about the table at which he stood. Tensely, he fingered cueball and red, spinning each in turn, his mind trapped by their hypnotic gleam. A gallery of shadows, came the grim thought, but only ever the two timeless faces . . . a sudden decisive gesture stopped each ball dead as the mental echo thrust a searing image fiercely into focus. The last portait of Harry in his uniform had been hung opposite the foot of the great stairs; an academic likeness that caught only the mask of those sharp eyes and the lean, polite smile. On the night of the Armistice, Anthony, hidden by the turn of the upper stair, had looked down the slow spiral to see Father raise his glass − a fine-cut crystal tumbler threequarters full of whisky − to the portrait. In the half-light, Anthony saw for the last time that special smile that only ever passed between Father and Harry: then, tensely, he realised that Father was speaking aloud to the painted, lifeless face. The words, half-whispered, drifted up the open swirl of the great stair, reached Anthony, and choked him with remembrance of that idyllic University summer when Harry had led in his victorious team to be met by Father − jovial, immensely proud, and laughing like the undergrad he once was himself.

'We won, Harry . . . we won!'

The proud whisper died. Impulsively, seeing only those sad hunched shoulders, Anthony found himself running headlong down the stairs. The nightmare of that downward flight had never left him; at first unheard by Father, he had seen the glass shatter into fragments at the foot of the portrait, and he froze, frightened and dismayed by that futile, violent gesture. Then Father had wheeled about and saw him there, poised and clinging to the banister, his young face soft with tears. Neither moved; the look between them lasted an eternity, frozen and uncomprehending. It was broken at last by the dismissive command that ignored whatever had gone immediately before.

'Have this mess cleared up − quickly!' And with that, Father had strode away, his face cold and rejecting, leaving the numbed boy to pick up the pieces of glass, alone.

'It was nothing, Mother,' he said crisply, moving to replace the cue in its rack, and then sitting by her, open-faced and apologetic. 'Just that I made rather a mess of things at the shoot this morning.'

He was aware of those lustrous, soul-embracing eyes turned on him, studying him intently. Spare her the details, he thought urgently; she hates death, even the death of animals. She'll live the moment I describe and be sickened by it – and still she won't understand.

'Upset Father, I'm afraid,' he added quickly, '– letting him down in front of the other guns like that. I'm sorry . . .' With relief, he saw that his simplistic answer was enough; the question in his mother's eyes withdrew, overshadowed by a drawn but sympathetic smile, and she rested a cool and fragrant hand on his.

'Thank you, my dear . . .' she murmured.

The thought fleetingly crossed his mind that her gratitude was offered not only for the confession and his apology, but also for his decision to avoid giving her pain. Suddenly, she was standing, moving to the door, delicately gesturing that he should stay where he was, undisturbed. She paused briefly in the shadows before leaving, a ghostly filigree of womanhood.

'You must always show consideration to your father,' she said. Then, with a rustle of exquisite skirts, she was gone.

Milking was well over when Ted arrived at Brookfield's gate. He paused there, his breath hanging on the chill morning air, amiably watching Dan roll the last full churn from the cooler across the yard and on to the small collection platform by the gate. At Ted's almost inaudible but sharp command, Grit – the labrador by his side – sat, still and attentive. Dan had barely straightened his back when the sound of Walter Gabriel's horse and float drifted towards them, down the lane. Ted reacted quickly.

'George Nugent sent these, Dan,' he muttered, deftly slipping a brace of pheasant from inside his bulky jacket. 'Best hang un, 'fore Walter gets here.'

Dan nodded his appreciation, wasting no time on words. It was an accepted return for having noted the wild pheasant nests along his hedgerows earlier in the year, and telling the keepers. This gave them the chance to lift the eggs and set them to hatch beneath the estate's own broody hens, rather than leave them to be taken by old foxey or some other, possibly even human, predator. Keeper Nugent was shrewd enough to show appreciation where it was due, but especially if it meant getting more help in the future. With three keepers under him, one for each thousand acres of Lawson-Hope land, he wasn't too proud to trade on the goodwill of farmers such as Dan Archer, or even of labourers, for that matter. Game given freely for the pot was better business than putting the man of the house up to regular poaching, out of need, or getting a farmer's back up out of arrogance. It was no coincidence that he'd sent Ted as errandboy, either; he knew well enough how close the friendship between the two men rested, especially over Ted's sister, Doris.

'Tell George thank ye for me, will ye, Ted?' requested Dan, emerging from the dairy where he'd put the birds to hang. He was just in time to see Walter draw the float to a halt by the waiting churns, and moving forward, he returned his neighbour's cheery wave.

'I shall, Dan, ah . . .' agreed Ted, as he strolled with him down to the open five-barred gate.

'Morning, me old mateys!' exclaimed Walter, already in the process of shifting the first churn on to the float. He paused, and beamed wickedly at Ted. 'That dog o'yourn behaving hisself today, is he, Ted . . . ?'

'Weren't his fault,' retorted the young keeper, defensively. He'd already suffered Keeper Nugent's tongue yesterday after the shoot, and his father had followed up by using this morning's breakfast to ram the lesson home. The worst sting of the incident was over now, and only the inevitable leg-pulling remained to be endured. The dog had learned as well, he was sure of that.

'If it weren't the dog, it must've been you, then,' grinned Walter, clanging churn against churn energetically. 'Ears still burning, are they?' He chuckled. 'Yours and Master Anthony's both, I'll bet . . . !'

'Too cheeky by half, you are,' growled Ted.

'Young Master Anthony?' queried Dan, with interest. 'John said nothing about him . . .'

'Made a fool of hisself, didn't he,' stated Walter, humping the last of the churns aboard. 'Lucky for you and him the guns topped a tidy few birds, eh, Ted?'

'I still got tongue pie for breakfast,' came the glum reply. 'The old man wun't let me off that easy.'

'What about the lad, though,' persisted Dan. 'What did he do that was so bad?'

Ted told him briefly, then added, ' 'Tisn't everyone that can finish off an okkard bird like that.'

Walter, laboriously making the requisite entry into his tally book, nevertheless heard, and nodded.

'Mr Harry could, any time. But there, that's half the trouble, in't it.' He passed the book for Dan to check and sign. 'All right, Dan, me old pal . . .?'

'Aye, but only just,' said Dan, drily, writing in his initials and passing the book back. 'Y'know about our John, I suppose?'

John and Walter, brightest of village sparks, had few secrets from each other, whether it be their latest wenching score, a new jape to play on their mates at the pub, or where to pick up some easy beer money for a day's work. Walter threw Dan a straight look, and nodded.

'Let's only hope the feller can hold his peace, that's all,' he declared soberly. He took up the worn reins and clicked his tongue to rouse Pippit into action, then called back over his shoulder as the horse pulled away, 'The Squire's not fit to cross these days, that us all knows!'

Ted said nothing to this exchange, but Dan answered his unasked question with a wry smile. 'John's off up to the Hall about Armistice Day,' he said, then turned and led the way back to the dairy, where he took up a part-filled bucket of milk and carried it to the calf pens next door. 'Seems the Squire fancies putting on a show,' he added, non-committally.

'Got good reason, an't he,' responded Ted. 'And not the only one in Ambridge, neither . . .'

Dan made no comment, but called the first lurch-legged Shorthorn calf to him, gently. Dipping his finger into the

21

warm milk kept specially back from the cooler, he presented it to the moist pink muzzle of the calf. Its tongue slid out, slurping the milk from Dan's stubby forefinger as though it was the cow's teat that it craved after. Now the milky coating was replenished, again and again, each time bringing the calf's eager muzzle closer and closer to the milk in the bucket itself, until finally the proffered finger was actually submerged in the creamy-bubbled fluid, still being suckled by the contented animal. Nose deep in the bucket, almost without realising it, the calf continued to feed happily even after Dan had gently drawn his hand away.

'There's some things that're best kept private, Ted,' he said. 'And that doesn't mean any disrespect, neither . . .'

Ted shrugged. Like Dan, his family was one of the few untouched by the war and its distant finger of death. Not for want of trying, though; like Dan's youngest brother Frank, Ted had tried to enlist by giving a false age, as soon as he thought he could pass muster as eighteen years old. But fresh-faced Ted had been quickly set aside as being under age, and the laugh had been on Frank as well, for he never saw proper service before the war was over and done and peace declared. Even so, it had left him with a restlessness in his bones that homecoming couldn't pacify; the last ungainly letter Dan had shown to Ted was postmarked Sydney, Australia.

'Life goes on just the same,' Ted commented knowingly, sounding the living echo of his father, then added, 'Playing footer this Sat'dy. Coming to watch, are ye . . .?'

Dan removed the empty bucket from the still-questing calf's tongue. 'Who against?'

'Penny Hassett,' declared Ted belligerently. 'They could do with a good hiding . . .'

'No shoot this weekend, then,' said Dan thoughtfully.

Ted played left wing, running keen as a whippet, but only when his keeping work allowed. George Nugent was a fair man, but the job had to come first, always.

'No guests at the Hall, neither,' insinuated Ted, with a knowing wink. 'The Squire and his lady's away visiting, and some o' the girls've got the afternoon off to watch us win.' He paused, then continued airily, 'Come and help 'em give us a cheer, why don't ye?'

Dan collected a second bucket, thoughtfully, and singled out another calf, before nodding agreeably but with a shrewd glance at his pal. 'Mebbe I will, Ted – ' he said, ' – seeing as it's you that's playing!'

And they both laughed, knowing the truth of the matter, that Doris would be there.

Approaching the tradesman's entrance to Arkwright Hall meant going through the stable courtyard that formed the North Wing, and round the back past the kitchens; five minutes early, noted John, checking his turnip watch against the November-dulled gold hands of the stable clock. All about him, there was a constant but quiet hustle of dignified activity. Outside the grand front porch, the Squire's brand-new Humber limousine stood parked and gleaming, while the wooden-faced chauffeur, Alfred Tetsall, supervised the loading of the departing guests' luggage by Sam, the hall boy. The chatter of bright farewells erupting from inside the house faded out of earshot as John removed himself from view and entered the courtyard, pausing there to watch admiringly as Jennings the head man conferred with Joe Lees, the groom, as to the condition of the magnificent chestnut gelding that stood like a statue between them. The holding rein tightened in Joe's gnarled hand as Trumper tossed his autocratic head and blew, scornfully. Jack Jennings bent and ran his wise palm over the animal's front fetlocks, looking up squintingly as John greeted him and passed by .

'Morning, Mister Jennings!'

'Morning, John . . .' was the offhand reply. There was no more to their greeting than this, with only an added, curt nod from Joe; for they inhabited a different world to John even though they acknowledged him as a mark of special respect, on their own patch. Moving on, John left the yard, the crunch of clean gravel under his boots countering the slower, more complex rhythm of the horse as it was walked about behind him; now he was at the rear of the Hall, and stopped. Past the weathered, mellow-red brick wall of the kitchen yard, he looked out over the landscaped gardens stretching away in a casual perfection of immaculate turf, hunched shrubbery, and regal trees. According to Arthur Parkes, the head gardener, there was a Californian pine out there well over 150 years old, and a magic tree — or so Arthur was wont to claim with a nudge and a wink — called the gingko, or maidenhair tree, supposed never to have altered since the days of the Bible. A tight smile crossed John's face as he mentally compared this seemingly evergreen oasis of peace with the muddy, well-worked acres of Brookfield. His expression darkened slightly, as a grimmer, more cruel image intruded on even that homely memory — a brown and black wilderness of pock-marked mud broken only by the shattered skeletons of fire-blasted trees and the funereal grooves of deserted trenches. . . .

Abruptly, as though to blot out what he saw, he turned to the door behind him and pressed the white centre of the gleaming brass orb there. Somewhere inside the kitchens a bell jangled, irritably. Crisp footsteps, and the door opened to reveal the scrawny, underdeveloped person of Betty Collins, her fifteen years made dignified by the scullerymaid's formal uniform of stiff grey cotton. Her dull eyes brightened and blinked, as she took in the soberly resplendent figure that John presented; dark blue demob suit perfectly creased and set upon his taut, arrogant frame as neatly as on a tailor's dummy; the stiff white celluloid collar holding the wind-tanned, bold-eyed head erect, framed by the tight kinks of dark hair still trimmed in that army cut that it pleased John to maintain so proudly; the grey flat cap held slightly too tensely in deft, broad-fingered hands; and the culminating glory of those brilliant boots. Betty looked into John's face wide-eyed, unable to hide her open admiration. He smiled, and melting, she blushed as she questioned him.

'Yes?'

'Appointment with the Squire, love.' Still gazing at him

24

breathlessly, she didn't move. 'If you don't let me in, I'll be late, won't I . . .'

He reached out, casually, as though to touch the hand with which she held the door; in an instant she had withdrawn the admiration from her face and stepped back to allow him to enter, her attitude as stiff and formal as the starched cap on her mousy hair.

'You wait here,' she muttered, closing the door yet managing to avoid any proximity to John. 'I'll go and tell Mister Merrick . . .' And with this, she scurried quickly away into the shadowed recesses of the hall corridor and beyond.

John stood and waited. He had some idea of the form; Mary Ann Hudson had told him enough tales about that. Merrick the footman would tell old Stokes, who'd tell the Squire; eventually, John would be summoned, marched in by Merrick, who was no RSM, heaven knows. But there'd be minutes to wait yet. John eased his Adam's apple clear of the straitjacket of the collar, and his ear caught the cheeky trill of a familiar voice; it came from behind the door opposite, leading into the kitchens. This was Mary Ann's territory, and the temptation to play the gentleman caller here and now brought a cocky smile to John's handsome face. Who was there with her though, he wondered. If it was Doris, that'd really make the morning worth the candle – but if it was Mrs Prentiss the cook, he thought shrewdly, that'd be something different altogether. There was a battle-axe and no mistake, but John didn't pride himself on his honeyed tongue for no reason, even when faced with the one woman in Ambridge who could put the fear of God into Walter Gabriel. Briskly, he knocked on the kitchen door and opening it, stood there smart but apologetic.

His first glance fell on Mary Ann herself, the smudges of baking flour only half hiding the rosiness of her cheeks, her buxom figure quivering as she abruptly paused in rolling out crust pastry. But her look of delighted surprise was immediately guarded as she flicked a warning glance towards the massive cooking range, where stood Mrs Prentiss, scrutinising the intruder as though he was a dead fly caught with his feet up in her best orange syllabub. The stern, beefy face opened to squawk out a strident condemnation, but John spoke first, the perfect gentleman.

'Morning, Mrs Prentiss. Could I bother you for a glass of water, mum?' He adjusted his perfectly knotted tie in a minute gesture of nervous desperation, and croaked, 'Got to see the Squire, y'see . . . so I'm a bit froggy.'

Mrs Prentiss softened and, smiling benignly, nodded her approval of John's spotless appearance. She knows, he thought bitterly; she's heard about me being the glory-boy, the Squire's bloody hero!

'No need for you to be nervous, John Archer,' she crowed at him reassuringly. 'We're all of us proud of what you've been through, my lad!' She turned to Mary Ann, who was struggling desperately to smother the laughter that threatened to flood her flushed and excited face. 'Get this young man his drink of water, Mary Ann, and quick about it,' commanded the burly cook, ' – he's got an important appointment with the Master.'

'Thanks very much, Mrs Prentiss, mum,' John said with a sweet politeness that made Mary Ann spill more water than she was pouring into the glass. 'You give a feller the fortitude to do great things, you really do.'

He turned to face Mary Ann who, with her back to Mrs Prentiss as she handed John the cool, filled tumbler, barely managed to stiffle the bubbling giggles that John's wicked eyes commanded from her. He spoke, straightfaced, but with that lilt of double-meaning that she knew all too well.

'And so do you as well, Miss Hudson.' He raised his glass to drink, but with the merest pause suggested a toast, the meaning of which Mary Ann knew full well referred to the turmoil of their last meeting, and she blushed. 'Great fortitude,' John said, and sipped his water gratefully.

'Drink up,' prompted Mrs Prentiss kindly, 'drink your fill, boy.' She turned away to open her oven and closely inspect its contents. Mary Ann took her chance, her eager eyes alight with a devilment to match John's own.

'You wait!' she whispered. 'I'll give you fortitude!'

'When − ?' murmured John almost silently, while his bold glance shouted his expectations to the wind.

'We'll see, shan't we,' she retorted pertly, then as he frowned, added quickly, 'This Sat'dy mebbe then . . .'

'Saturd'y?' questioned John aloud, then retreated behind his glass of water as Mrs Prentiss raised her head into the line of conversation, inquisitively.

'What was that you said?' she demanded ominously, her steely button-eyes sharp to suspect any hanky-panky or goings-on such as a furtive rendezvous, or worse.

It was Mary Ann who answered, piping brightly, 'Saturday, Mrs Prentiss, don't you remember? The football match −'

Mrs Prentiss's expression showed that she did remember, but it was a close thing; there was no chance of further explanations, however, as Merrick had returned and was standing in the open doorway. At first, John was out of the footman's line of vision; flexing his perpetually quizzical eyebrows, Merrick enunciated carefully, 'Mister John Archer here, is he?'

'Present and correct, Mister Merrick,' answered John, stepping forward smartly.

'What're you hanging about here for then,' grumbled the lean-shanked footman, giving a cursory yet piercing appraisal of John's presentability. 'You'll do,' he decided. 'Come on, soldier, let's see a bit of swagger, eh.'

Almost silently, he led the way out. John, following closely, timed his knowing wink to perfection as he passed Mary Ann, switching it deftly to a winning smile at Mrs Prentiss as he closed the door after him. The cook watched pleasantly as Mary Ann contentedly set to work once more at the pastry table.

'A bright lad, that . . . very smart,' remarked Mrs Prentiss. 'I'd be a bit careful about him, if I was you, my girl.'

Trudging behind Merrick's padding footsteps, John quickly lost all sense of direction; the passageways seemed endless, the doors without number. It seemed that in every corner, on

27

every wall, there were either fine paintings or prettily-painted crocks, suits of armour even, that John had only ever seen before in battered history books at the village school. But the very smell of the place made John uncomfortable; it was all dead stuff, scraped up or left over from the past. Grand, perhaps, and fit for grand people, certainly – but there were more simple pleasures in life, and Mary Ann Hudson was one of them. And there was Doris, of course, a pleasure yet untasted, a cut above Mary Ann – maid to Lady Hester's personal maid Miss Summers, in fact. Mary Ann's place was firmly below stairs, but Doris'd know up-stairs, downstairs and in my lady's chamber. She'd've turned down a bed or two in her time, he chuckled silently to himself, seeing the mental picture of her wasp-waisted figure dipping and bending gracefully, turning at a voice. . . .

'Wait here,' said Merrick abruptly, and went ahead into Squire's study. Through the open door, John could hear himself announced, and almost sniggered with a tight embarrassment. This was worth all the swagger that the regiment could give a lad! He scowled, as a barrage of long-forgotten faces raged through his mind – then Merrick was standing by him once more, indicating the room with a curt nod of his head, and quietly putting this other-ranks visitor to rights.

'In you go,' he said bluntly, 'and mind your *p*s and *q*s, lad!'

John automatically straightened himself, tucked his flat hat under one arm in military fashion, pushed all thoughts of Mary Ann and Doris from his mind, and went in.

The immediate effect of the room was oppressive; rich mahogany panelling, deep-lustred green leather upholstery, and centrally, a massive, cylinder-fronted desk that looked as though it could hold a rollcall of the dead. Eyes still un-accustomed to a gloom only partly softened by the cool November light, John sensed rather than saw clearly the silhouette that was Squire Lawson-Hope.

'Good morning, John.'

'Morning, sir.' John found himself instinctively standing to attention, legs braced, shoulders straining, eye-line set six inches above his superior's head.

'Sit down, there's a good chap . . .'

The gruff words brought him back to the civilian reality of here and now. He wasn't being offered the option of accepting the C.O.'s punishment, and he wasn't on the mat for a petty charge slapped on him by a stiff-necked gate sergeant for rolling in late without a pass. The man before him might be the Squire and landlord of Brookfield and the twenty or so other farms dotted over his three thousand acres, and a J.P. as well, but he had no pull over John Archer. If anything, the boot was on the other foot; John had done nothing wrong, and if any favours were to be asked of him, they'd best be asked nicely. He sat down, rigid-backed and attentive, on the cool leather of the club chair set close by the fire. Lawson-Hope casually threw another log on to the ash-dulled embers, and then sat himself in the winged chair opposite. Here, for the first time since he'd entered, John could at last see the Squire's face properly; iron-grey hair brushed tightly down, thinly framing the ruddy, weathered face, the tired, hooded eyes only partly veiling the clear blue gimlet-stare, and the pinched nose shadowing that lean mouth, so bitterly creased at its corners.

'Thank you, sir,' said John with guarded politeness. He was getting the posh treatment now and no mistake; the laugh was, he already knew the reason why, just as the Squire himself did. Trust the gentry to have to go by the book, though; King's Regulations could square anything.

The man was smart, well turned out, Lawson-Hope acknowledged to himself, and what's more, didn't look unintelligent. No campaign ribbons at his lapel, but then this wasn't a completely formal occasion.

'South Borset Rifles, wasn't it?' he asked pleasantly.

'Sir.'

'Lost a lot of good men,' nodded the Squire soberly, 'but a splendid record at the front . . .' His face clouded at his own glib phrase. Of all those to come back, this jaunty farm tenant was the nearest thing to a hero; it would be his privilege to lay the wreath of honour in memory of the dead of Ambridge, and for that one tragic hour, he would epitomise their glory and the stark emptiness that remained, captured so pitiably by the brittle laurel and bay leaves of the wreaths. For one snatched second, Lawson-Hope saw as though by a ridiculous trick of light, not John Archer in the chair beside the fire, but Harry. He had sat there so many times; lip curled in the semblance of good humour, those clear blue eyes staring so keenly at his companion, his whole lithe body at one with the pattern of his father's mind. Not enough years, barely eight seasons, before he had died in France; a death so wasteful as to seem either a deliberate punishment or a senseless joke. Already a captain at twenty-six, mounted and moving along his column of men on their way to the front, Harry had spotted a desperately wounded horse at the side of the shell-pounded track. He was no sentimentalist, but he had ridden over to put the beast out of its misery, when the shell struck, fired from a German howitzer three miles away. That was in 1917; fifteen months later, a bare month before the Armistice was signed, at the full flood of the British advance under Haig, Andrew too was killed. His death had been equally anonymous – picked off by an unseen sniper as he prepared to lead his men over the top. Like Harry, Andrew had grown into the image of his father – physically hard, mentally needle-sharp, and totally devoted to country and to home. Had it been only Andrew's lot to be the needful sacrifice, his father could have borne it; but with Harry taken, all ambition died with him. The Squire had experienced an almost physical contraction, as though his soul had been gutted from him leaving only an articulated shell. Life went on, though there was little pleasure in its seasons now; but the remembrance must be kept.

'And a lot of my mates, sir. Copped it like I did – only worse,' gritted John, coldly impassive on the surface, even though his mind raged at the balance sheet so casually presented – death for glory was a bloody poor bargain by any-body's count!

'Gas, wasn't it?' queried Lawson-Hope, brought back to the logistics of the present as the ex-soldier's brusque response disintegrated the futile recollection.

'Yes, sir,' came the flat response. 'From our own side.' A slightly too quick, razor-edged denial followed. 'No hard feel-ings of course, sir. The wind changed to the wrong direction, d'y'see . . .'

Suddenly, Lawson-Hope's mind cleared as the sour impli-cation etched its way home; the man was playing bolshie, he wasn't going to co-operate!

'It's what you fought for that's important,' he said curtly. 'Whatever happened, it doesn't make you any the less a hero to the people of this village.'

'No, sir?' queried John politely. Never let the bastards do you down, he thought; it's *his* shoulder-pipped sons who'll be at the top of that bloody metal plaque shoved up in the church – I'm only the stand-in!

'There'll be a roll of honour, but of course, your name won't be on it,' the Squire explained. 'In fact, you'll be the living representative for all those . . . lost comrades. It'll be quite an occasion – ' He gave a perfunctory and condescend-ing smile that totally assumed John's agreement.

'Sorry, sir. Shan't be there, shall I.'

The silence that clamped the room tight after John's bludgeoning words seemed to suspend even the crackle of the fire. Both men were standing now; Lawson-Hope's face was a mask, but the rage behind it threatened to choke his words into incoherence.

'You will kindly . . . explain,' he finally demanded, ice-cold eyes blazing in a parchment skin.

'Regimental parade, sir,' responded John, with that blank-faced air of calm invulnerability that the army would un-erringly class as silent insolence. 'In Borchester,' he added, 'at the cathedral, nine thirty ack emma, sharp.'

'A word to the commanding officer will soon clear that

duty,' crowed Lawson-Hope, triumphantly.

John was unmoved. 'Not a duty, sir. It's a matter of personal choice. A tribute to my mates who died.'

The Squire, almost choking on the surge of grief and anger, knotted his hands knuckle-white, rigid by his sides. 'Two sons!' he eventually gritted out. 'What do they deserve . . . ?'

'I never knew them, sir, did I?' John stared at him, unmoved by the man's furious agony. Kitchener had been his god; even after three years of mud, frustration, and the passing finger of death, John swore they had been the happiest years of his life, a desperately longed-for escape from the millwheel of working the land. Let Dan do that; stepping into the old man's shoes had been his choice, and welcome. But then that pride of arms toppled and fell; lung-scarred and tainted with the gas, John had been invalided home, a surly and reluctant hero. The regimental bugles, the parade, banners and old comrades – these were the only pride left now. Let the rest, Squire included, bury their own; they had no claim on his.

'They'll be playing Last Post over my old mates,' he explained inscrutably. 'And it's my right to be there . . .' He added, almost as an afterthought, ' . . . sir.'

Lawson-Hope stared at him as though he were a buck to be culled, ruthlessly and dispassionately.

'Very well, Archer,' he replied at last, and moving to the fireplace, activated the bell handle that would summon Merrick.

'Permission to leave, sir,' requested John quickly, sardonically formal.

The Squire said nothing, but kept his eyes fixed on John, still standing to attention as he waited for dismissal. Neither had moved when Merrick knocked and entered, questioningly. Still no word was spoken; Lawson-Hope simply turned his back on John as though he had never existed, and casually kicked the smouldering logs into a flickering spark of life. Behind him, Merrick swiftly steered the unwelcome intruder from the room, closing the heavy door behind him with a near-silent click of the lock. Now only Lawson-Hope's lean mouth showed movement, imperceptibly communicating with the faces he could see so clearly in the sluggish flames. He was not alone; the whole room was peopled with shadows.

CHAPTER THREE

'DOH – I tell ye, it's a grand day for a footer match!' Walter protested to the tap room of The Bull. It was the lunchtime before the game with Penny Hassett was due to be played. 'It'll clear up a treat, you just see if it don't!'

'It'll rain,' said Old Herbert. Sitting in his accustomed chair by the fireplace, his tankard set between his boots, he gazed with thoughtful eyes through the haze of blue smoke spilling upwards from his pipe, to peer knowingly at the grey sky outside the windows, then shook his head. 'Them clouds blew up on us too quick this morning,' he muttered, adding with a spiteful relish, 'Wet and windy it'll be, says I!'

The declaration was in the nature of a challenge, but Walter didn't answer straight away; his eyes were fixed upon the fully charged pint of ale being set down before him on the bar by Seth Tibbs, the landlord. Wiping his mouth with the back of his hand in a quick ritual of anticipation, Walter at last took up the glass. 'The sun shines on the righteous, lads,' he chuckled. 'Good health!' And he drank deep. Seth deftly flicked Walter's coins from off the counter into his waiting palm, before raising his own nip-sized, 'friendly' glass of bitter in acknowledgement.

'Ernie Ashford's playing, remember,' he said with a dry smile, and took a token sip.

'If Walter was playing, it'd make a blessed thunderstorm, in that case!' cackled Old Herbert. 'But seeing as it's only Ernie Ashford, it'll rain.'

Ernie was Willie Ashford's only son, a wiry, shifty-grinning lad of unknown years, with no fixed occupation other than to help his father follow his chosen calling of full-time poaching. As an inside forward, he could turn on a sixpenny piece and run in a shimmying scutter that usually sent his footballing opponents lunging every-which way — a skill that he had used more than once, successfully, as a poacher. Even so, he and his crinkle-eyed father had shared over eighty convictions between them, including a three-month spell, as a result of Constable Gregory's long arm of the law.

'He'll catch a cold today, then,' chuckled Walter. 'What with Jim Gregory playing centre half behind him, and Ted Forrest outside him on the wing, he won't get away with much!'

'Aghh! That little blighter could get away with anything inside those bloomers he wears for footer,' observed Old Herbert testily. 'If there's as much as a rabbit show its head on that patch o' grass, why Ernie'll have it!'

Ernie's football knickers were the laughing stock of every visiting team — until they came to tackle him. Flapping and billowing well below his knees, they more resembled a clipper in full sail or a clown in the circus, than a lad dressed to play a game of football. It was even said he'd once smuggled the ball inside them, half the length of the pitch before anybody had realised, including the referee. Nobody denied it, he was a lad to be watched.

'Think we stand a chance then?' asked landlord Tibbs. His own boy, Roddy, would be playing in an Ambridge shirt for the first time, at left half; he'd be well and truly blooded today, playing in such a derby match against hated rivals Penny Hassett.

'Course we do,' declared Walter. 'Thrash 'em holler, we will!'

'They got that feller Curly Cobb playing for 'em again this year, as I'm told,' commented Old Herbert with a wicked despair, knowing full well that the very name of the player spelt gloom and despondency for Ambridge supporters. Hadn't the *Borchester Echo* compared Cobb's scoring skill with his head as the equal of the great Dixie Dean himself? Certainly no player in the Ambridge side was known to be able

35

to beat him in the air, and that's where the Penny Hassett wingers would float it, every time.

'Mebbe Jim Gregory ought to take his night-stick out to him,' suggested Walter.

'He'll put a few past Barney Machin,' gloated the old codger, puffing lovingly at his clouded pipe. 'Like nails in a coffin – bang, bang, bang!' His glee spluttered into a fit of coughing, considered by the others to be fit justice for such a Job's comforter.

'That's as mebbe,' retorted Walter, 'but don't you forget our Sidney!'

Sidney Platt was the village blacksmith; chunky, strong as an ox, and just about as quick – given the chance to get a bit of speed up.

'Oh ah,' coughed Old Herbert wisely. 'He's a living wonder all right. Just as long as someone gives him the ball on a blessed plate, wi' a knife and fork to tackle it with!' He paused and puffed a quick burst of aromatic smoke, before delivering the *coup de grâce*. 'And he an't got but one good foot to kick with, and that's a toe-ender!'

The truth was, Sidney could only score from the penalty spot; a moving ball presented altogether too difficult a target for him, though his eye for wrought iron work, rivets or horse-shoes was dead true. Nevertheless, his burly frame could inspire a genuine respect, and the force with which he could strike the ball never left the memory. In last year's game against Churcham, he'd burst both the match ball and the spare; upon which the referee declared the game abandoned and both sides retired to a challenge match of darts and dominoes, ale and cider, and mutton sandwiches all round.

'True . . .' mused Seth, '. . . but y'never know with Sidney.'

'Give him a chance, that's all,' growled Walter.

'If it rains,' cackled Old Herbert gleefully, 'he'll spend more time on his backside than on his feet – and it'll rain all right. . . ! That's bible truth!'

It was with some surprise that John realised his brother was getting ready to go out.

'The footer match,' was Dan's laconic reply to the question. 'They'll need cheering on, will our lot.'

'Makes a change for you, don't it?'

'Ted's playing wing,' was the only explanation that Dan offered as he carefully threaded and tightened the leather laces of his Sunday boots, a fact that John noted with shrewd interest with a sidelong glance. Until now, he had thought little of the match itself; it was an excuse, a necessary preamble in order to meet Mary Ann Hudson. After due consideration of the world at large, he'd offer to walk the young lady home by way of the lane back of Sixpenny Farm, a seemingly innocent enough rural promenade that normally took little more time to travel than the more usual, direct way past the Lodge. But it so happened that by happy accident the grassy-banked lane contained a gate; a gate leading to an outlying haybarn which for November lovers offered a more secluded refuge from nature's more unruly elements, especially those storms of the flesh that helped keep the chill of the winter months at bay. It wasn't John's only bolt-hole; neither was Mary Ann the only wench who had melted to his burning touch, there. The jolly Borchester landgirls knew him for a randy lad, and Polly Harper was no stranger to him either, though none of them had an inkling that the passion he spent on them so freely was rooted in the night his mother died. There weren't many who'd say no to this sad-eyed hero, for he had the instinct of a buck in rut, seizing only on those who knew and frankly accepted his hot-bodied needs. But it wasn't enough. 'Nothing venture, nothing gained,' as Walter would have it, but nothing satisfied, either. Except the thought of Doris.

Mary Ann was a willing partner in her own happy ruination, easily coaxed into pleasure, while Doris was always out of reach, a family girl, not only good but with a father and a brother as her keeper. Altogether, a challenge that stirred John, all the more for knowing that Dan, too, had his eye

37

on the gentle-faced girl; she was one of the rare things that could get Dan into his best boots and away from Brookfield. Suddenly the football match took on a new importance.

'I'm going, as well,' said John.

Dan straightened up to confront his brother, his face surly with suspicion. 'Since when's that been arranged?' he demanded.

'Since I was at the Hall, t'other day,' retorted John with a confident grin. 'Ask Mary Ann Hudson, if y'like.'

Dan took the implication slowly; he knew his brother's wild-oat wanderings only too well, but for once the realisation gave him comfort. With Mary Ann Hudson on his arm, he'd hardly be likely to make eyes at Ted's sister as well – or even be given half the chance in such a crowd as there'd be today.

'She's your latest, is she?'

'That's my business,' John answered coldly.

'Thought she was sweet on Walter,' Dan persisted stubbornly. John wouldn't be above 'borrowing' Mary Ann, probably with Walter's full permission, just to help set up his chances with Doris on the sly.

'If you're thinking of trying your luck y'self,' said John deliberately, 'ask her.' His eyes laughed tauntingly, as he went on, 'You might just be in for a surprise, old son. . . .'

The craftily ambiguous answer left Dan mithered and confused, just as was intended. Mary Ann Hudson was a merry girl, everyone knew that. But she was no Polly Harper, taking anything in trousers, young or old. Was John in fact warning Dan off, genuinely suspecting he was interested in the obvious talents of the kitchenmaid – or was he having the gall to put the wench up for barter, like taking a cow to market? Dan almost laughed aloud at this; the girl'd hardly swallow that even from John, besides which it wasn't Mary Ann that Dan fancied stirring the cooking pot at Brookfield. The only thing left was to take John at his word.

'We'll be late,' growled Dan, and picked up his trilby. 'Y'want a ride in, I suppose?'

'Fair enough,' responded John cheerfully, and followed his brother outside into the yard, and clambered with him into the waiting wagon.

The field was already crowded with milling spectators by the time the girls from the Hall arrived – Mary Ann, Betty Collins, and Doris. They had walked briskly and full of laughter down the lanes from Arkwright Hall, carrying an ancient umbrella knowingly provided by Mrs Prentiss against the threatening sky.

'I don't want any of you girls on my hands with bronchial pneumonia,' she declared sternly, at the same time surreptitiously passing a paper bag of cough lozenges to Mary Ann, to be shared with the others. She herself would be passing the late afternoon taking tea with Mr Stokes and Mr Merrick, neither of whom were inclined to put their rarified physiques to the test of a damp November afternoon. Far more pleasant to take their ease in the fashion of their masters, whose occasional absences provided some of the more discreetly enjoyed perks of being in service. With the house virtually unoccupied, the three girls had been given the whole afternoon off, on the clear understanding that they should be safely inside by ten o'clock and not a minute later. Reminding them of this, Mrs Prentiss had neither seen nor expected any untoward reaction from Doris or Betty, but in Mary Ann's eyes there was a button-black brightness that suggested something more than girlish high spirits. It was this sparkle and fizz that had infected both of Mary Ann's trim companions on their mile journey into the village, and by the time they'd reached the freshly marked out green, their faces were flushed with a teasing liveliness.

'Let's find Ted – ' insisted Doris eagerly, ' – to wish him luck!' She darted forward through the clusters of waiting spectators, pulling Betty and Mary Ann with her.

'In their changing room?' cried the bouncing kitchenmaid, bubbling with enthusiasm as they rapidly approached the cricket pavilion that also passed as players' dressing room on

39

muddier occasions such as this. 'They'll never let us!'

'He's my brother, isn't he?' Doris demanded gaily, and led the way round to the back entrance of the green and white balconied wooden hut, only to find Ted and Sam Fisher already changed and outside, stamping their boots into the turf with a knowledgeable concern. It was Sam, with his sallow, pimply face and vacant smile, who saw the girls first. He nudged Ted, who put on an expression of noble resolve and manly dedication, all the while flexing his uncovered right knee. While Doris ran up and gave Ted a hearty, sisterly peck on the cheek, Mary Ann and Betty drew back in a wind-blown huddle, and giggled at the revelation of Sam the hall-boy's naked legs prancing bonily before their girlish eyes.

'Don't I get a kiss for luck then?' demanded Sam, un-abashed at the direction of Betty's coy glances; Mary Ann's response was a smacking kiss on the palm of her hand, blown to Sam with teasing gusto. Betty pretended to look the other way, just as though she wasn't blushing in the least.

'Dan's got his light wagon over there,' pointed Ted, his other arm about his sister's wasp-tight waist. 'He says as ye can sit in it with him and watch, if y'like – all three of ye,' he added hastily, as Doris gave him a quick, straight glance. He grinned sheepishly in answer to her implied accusation, blow-ing with relief as she nodded and smiled, calling gaily to the others, 'Come on – we've all got seats!' Then, with a quick wave to Ted, she swept the others to her, arm-in-arm, and jogged them over to the Brookfield wagon.

This was how Dan saw her – nimbly running over the grass towards him as he stood tense but patient-faced by Dot, the mare he kept for taking the wagon to market. Betty and Mary Ann came gaily to him at her shoulder, but Dan saw only Doris and his mouth was suddenly dry. He could still recall the sunlit memory of a prettily ringletted eleven-year-old presenting a posy to Lady Hester Lawson-Hope at the village Coronation party, and catching her heel in the hem of her smock with an overquick curtsey. Three years later, Doris had entered service at the Hall, to discover a new world of spotless daily linen, silent service, and an elegant but rigorous discipline the like of which she'd never met before even at home or in school. It was in service that she'd grown into a young woman; her oval, well-boned face and soft, warm eyes had quickly learned when not to be seen laughing. But her sweetly chiselled mouth dimpled all too easily into a radiant smile when so permitted, and soon she was favourably noticed by Lady Hester herself. Now, at nineteen, she was third housemaid; maid in fact to Lily Summers, the lady's maid, and earning a full thirteen pounds per annum, a credit to her father, the pride of her brothers, and in Ted's words, 'a proper beauty, well worth being wed to'. Words to which Dan had so many times added a silent, dourly shy 'Amen'.

Doris, her arms still linked through the arms of her two friends, halted, slightly breathless, in front of Dan.

'Ted says you've got room for us to sit in your wagon,' he stated pleasantly, looking for at least a welcoming smile in return. But Dan seemed almost disinterested as he muttered his low-voiced, offhand reply.

'I reckon that'll be all right . . .' With that, he turned to Miss Dot, leaving the girls to clamber aboard by way of the wagon-wheel spokes. 'I'll hold her steady,' he said, 'while ye get up there. Can y'manage?'

Doris had half a suspicion that Dot would stand statue-still till kingdom come, without Dan's help; most lads would have jumped at the chance to hold Doris's hand to help her up, and most she would have refused, being of a bright and independent nature. She had often wondered lately, seeing him in company of brother Ted, whether the young farmer's manner was the result of living and working alone for so long, or shyness, or just plain indifference. But common politeness cost little enough; if he couldn't be bothered to notice her, why then, she'd do without. He was probably more interested in the shapely charms of Mary Ann, anyway; a girl who wasn't slow in coming forward and who could tease even the dourest woman-haters, Old Herbert, into cackling life. Mary Ann Hudson had often spoken warmly of Dan's prospects as a

41

marriage catch. Perhaps this had been the reason for the kitchenmaid's bubbling excitement all the day, knowing that she'd meet this shrewd-eyed, solemn landsman, and that after the football match, she'd be given a ride home with Dan Archer, alone. If that's what he wanted, then let him get on with it.

'It's no trouble,' she replied with a lift of her pretty chin and moving to the wheel, raised her skirt hem so as to set her foot upon the wheelhub. The firm grip of strong hands about her neat waist surprised her – but before she could even object she'd been lifted up and on to the wagon in a brisk flurry of skirts.

'Anything to oblige a lady,' smiled John, as Doris stared down at him, disturbed by the easy strength of those lean hands and the bold disregard for formality in his laughing eyes. In a second, he had turned away and performed the same service for Betty, who gasped audibly, then blushing sheltered at Doris's side away from John's attentions; next he turned to Mary Ann.

'You as well, my lovely,' chuckled the wiry hero, as she prepared herself happily for the grasp of his hands about her; she didn't make it easy for him, but what was in fact a shy delight in the physical contact, appeared as only a fumbling awkwardness in raising the buxom girl up alongside her primping friends.

'All set then?' Without waiting for a reply, John nimbly raised himself on to the wagon, and ranged himself close by the girls. Mary Ann edged along tight against Doris, who not without some relief realised that John couldn't sit himself between them; her confusion quickly returned when he chose to stand behind Mary Ann, but with one hand lightly set on Doris's shoulder. It was this casual gesture that Dan noticed and he raged inwardly as he clambered up upon the wagon shafts, and then to the driving seat. He found himself close to Betty Collins's shy smile, and set himself to be pleasant to the pallid girl. A ragged surge of cheering started up, and pointed across the pitch towards the pavilion.

42

'Here they come,' he said, and led the shouts of 'Ambridge boys, come on!' and 'Good old Ted, let's have a couple, lad!' John cheered with the rest, but his thoughts were in his hands. Doris, however, took the chance to lean forward out of reach; Mary Ann glimpsed backwards over her shoulder at John with a sparkle in her eyes, and let her plump shoulders rest against him, meaningfully, not noticing the momentary glance of secretive curiosity from Betty. In another moment they were all caught up in the naming of their friends and favourites, and laughing, as did so many of the crowd, at Ernie Ashford's starch-stiff football knickers.

But young Tom Forrest had eyes only for his brother Ted. Looking down at the boy at his side, Tom's father smiled at the blazing excitement there and shared his pride; so many years' difference between the two lads, yet they were alike in so many little ways. At eight, Tom was already useful with a football. His keenness to follow Ted's footsteps into keepering was sharper and altogether more long-lasting than any of his young pals' desires to become the driver of a steam train, or a soldier-boy. Ted had been the same at his age, forever trailing his father, watching, asking, listening; as for Tom, he continually and innocently put his father to the test by blurting out fragments of knowledge gleaned from Ted, as though they were new-found pearls of wisdom far beyond challenge.

'Tufted ducks are divers, Dad,' he'd say, bright-eyed and hoping to be contradicted, 'and they can stay underwater for n minutes . . .!'

'Can they now,' his father would reply, drily. 'And how y'know that then, son?'

'Ted says so. He's seen 'em!' scored the boy triumphantly, then went on with innocent condescension, 'Have you . . .?'

'Not for that long, no,' Bill would confess with a smile, then pass the baton back. 'But when you sees 'em for y'self, lad . . . time 'em, why don't ye, eh? Then y'd have someat to tell Ted about!'

Tom would look thoughtful, and nod in agreement; the flatting image gave his father a constant and secret pleasure,

43

with its echo of Ted's ways, something that Liza found, too. It was good to see Doris treat the youngster with an affectionate kindness that she had rarely shown to Ted, and it seemed that it was only through Tom that she could let her reluctant admiration for Ted's physical achievements show; and bicker though sister and elder brother might, neither tried to score against each other through Tom. Their fairness was returned in the rumbustious affection the youngest showed for both of them. Today, however, was Ted's day of glory, and Tom was desperate for some sign of triumph, a solid trophy that he'd be able to parade in front of his schoolmates.

'He'll score at least one, Dad,' Tom piped, ' – or even two, won't he!'

'He'll more'n likely have a foot in scoring, aye . . .' countered his father shrewdly.

'A hat-trick!' glowed Tom, jigging about with excitement desperate for the game to begin.

The coin to decide ends was tossed, under the benevolent guidance of the diminutive referee, a normally waspish mannered schoolteacher from Borchester; the teams, waved into their positions by their respective captains, indulged themselves in the small personalised rituals that always precede the kick-off whistle, a performance in itself. Barney Machin settled and resettled his goalkeeper's cap over his eyes, even though there wasn't a glimpse of sunshine; Ted Forrest doubled on the spot, legs pumping furiously; Jim Gregory turned up the stiff collar of his shirt for the umpteenth time and rolled up his sleeves; while Sidney Platt crouched like a sprinter on his marks, hunched over the dubbined ball, waiting to kick off and run. The referee held the fortunes of conflict trembling in the balance as he meticulously waited for the precise minute of three o'clock; it came, he blew, and the game started.

At first, all was shouting and furious encouragement, though that first heavy pass from Sidney out to his wingman might develop into a cavalry-like, goalscoring charge upon the enemy defence; but soon the cheers and the brute purpose became more spasmodic, and the ball bobbed gustily about, struck alternatively by mighty kicks from each side's burly fullbacks, and respondingly forceful headed returns.

Gradually, a dour pattern of thrust and bludgeon began to assert itself on the game; Sidney pounded through to miss a pass he had no hope of reaching, and was cheered valiantly; Ernie Ashford lost the ball in the flapping of his own knickers, and watched with a gap-toothed grin as his opponent booted the ball mightily up the field to the stern figure of Curly Cobb. He seemed almost to climb on air, as his dull-sheened bald head flicked at the dropping ball and sent it, bullet-hard, towards the Ambridge goal, and in this instance, the safe hands of Barney Machin. But Jim Gregory, straining to match Cobb's effortless jump to the ball, succeeded only in colliding clumsily with the opposing centre-forward's iron head. While the mighty pillar of the local law stumbled to the ground half-stunned, Cobb shook his head briskly and trotted to one side, seemingly unharmed. The game stopped at the referee's stern whistle, and amid the concern of the Ambridge crowd, big Jim was patched up, though the deep cut on his eyebrow still trickled blood.

The game was resumed with a bounce-up won by Roddy Tibbs; catching the Penny Hassett defenders off guard, he sent a smoothly skimming pass fizzing over the turf to Ted Forrest, whose swerving run left the Penny Hassett fullback standing, and brought the crowd to their feet in a roar of delight. On the wagon, the three girls were standing and shouting wildly, urging Ted on. As the wagon quivered, John deftly put a steadying arm about the waists of Mary Ann and Doris, whose excitement drowned all sensation of the familiarity, leaving John freely enjoying his position of privilege. Running almost to the by-line, hotly pursued by the fullback and the handkerchief-waving linesman, Ted paused in his stride and struck the ball across the face of the Penny Hassett goal. The goalkeeper lunged, the ball skidded from his fists, and falling at the feet of the grateful Ernie Ashford, was nodded home with the same quiet flair that had landed many a shot-stunned salmon in the past. The crowd erupted in a mighty cry of 'Goal!' before enjoying the rare moment of seeing the poacher's hand shaken by constable Jim Gregory, a gesture never to be seen away from the football pitch. As the laughter and the excitement died, the girls turned to each other in flushed delight; while Mary Ann gave John a pneumatic hug, Doris came down to earth to find her waist still encircled by John's hot hand. The protest on her lips died as he squeezed her warmly and cried out, 'Three cheers for Ambridge!'

Disarmed by this calculated cry of loyalty, and aware that the pressure of John's touch wasn't at all unpleasant, Doris decided to act as though ignorant of what was happening, and secretly enjoy the innocent excitement of the situation. Elation quickly changed to gloom, however, as Ambridge's moment of triumph was ended by the deadly skills of Curly Cobb. Not once, but twice before half-time, his head struck home and scored, once from a corner kick, and yet again from a finely floated centre from his right winger, with big Jim Gregory left dizzy-headed and floundering. Small wonder that Walter looked so glum as he came across to the Brookfield wagon and was hauled up to join the others.

'Blessed if Old Herbert in't going to be right,' he grumbled, 'Two goals b'that feller Cobb, and it *is* going to rain!'

The rain came in gusts and squalls, but the greater part of the spectators stood firm, determined to watch until the end. While the players changed ends and huddled together to suck and chew great chunks of orange sections, Dan handed over clean sacking for his guests on the wagon to wear over their heads and shoulders. The girls, bunched tight together beneath Mrs Prentiss's umbrella, glowed and blossomed beneath the attentions of their escorts, albeit dourly silent from Dan himself; but there was a subtle shift of contact now that Walter had arrived. With the umbrella acting as Hindenburg Line behind the girls, and Walter sheltering to one flank, John was reduced to either crowding against Betty, or to standing apart. At the same time, Mary Ann had begun to realise that she wasn't the only honeysuckle that John was slyly paying court to; as if by secret treaty, both she and Doris now virtually ignored the strutting hero, throwing their attentions both to Dan and Walter freely. Walter, no stranger to Mary Ann's winning smile already, took particular delight in spiting John; Dan observed with a certain dry satisfaction that his brother's gaiety was slowly drowning in the November rain, and he no longer looked the dandy beneath that leveller of all classes, a jute sack.

The second half was ruled totally by the whim of the weather. With the wet ball a greasy, uncontrollable blob, it was barely possible to raise its trajectory to head height any more, and Penny Hassett's most dynamic weapon – Curly Cobb's head – was now rendered useless. The rain-soaked, muddy turf equally turned Ernie Ashford's nimble skills into clownish nonsense, and the game slowly and bitterly slid deeper and deeper into soggy gloom. Desperately, the visitors clung to their slender lead; knowing they had little hope of increasing it, they defended with a rain-streaked grimness that eventually infected the spectators, standing and sitting in a sodden silence.

Then, with barely ten minutes left to play, justice prevailed. The heavens opened, and in the cloudburst that followed, few of the spectators saw what happened, for they were stampeding frantically for shelter, all thought of the match forgotten. The heavy ball, miskicked by Sam on the right, skidded wildly across the field to Tom, who, half-blinded by the sudden downpour, lashed out first-time and sent it volleying into the penalty area. Like a bull let into a field of eager cows, Sidney Platt lumbered forward, head down and arms flailing to preserve his uneasy balance, even though the ball was desperately out of his reach. But with the rain came panic; the Penny Hassett centrehalf, for so long the rock upon which Ambridge's attacks had foundered, found the ball looming at him at chest height, impossible to control, and instinctively used his hand to bring it down. Even in the same second that the Ambridge players screamed 'Hand-ball!' he lashed out a mighty kick to clear the golden leather; it flashed away at waist height just as Sidney

Platt took his inevitable fall, and struck his massive chest with the force of a cannon's shot blasting at a castle wall. The rebound, travelling close to the speed of an express train, hurtled past the clay-footed, gaping goalkeeper — and the score was even.

Five minutes later the game was over. While his team mates hared for the shelter and privacy of the pavilion, Ted ran instead to Dan's wagon. The rain, as though to point its heaven-sent influence on the game, had eased to a gentle drizzle, and the Ambridge spirits were high once more. The centre of congratulations, Ted was suitably modest, until a voice from behind him made him turn, beaming.

'Well done, lad. Ye made a lot of running.' It was his father, nodding at him with that shrewd half-smile that spoke volumes. Kid brother Tom, prancing at his father's side, punched Ted excitedly on the arm again and again.

'Deserved a medal, didn't he Dad!' he yelped happily, eyes shining proudly up at Ted who, though patiently suffering, decided it was time to retreat and get changed.

'Here, I'd best get meself out of this gear,' he mumbled, and ran off — but not before shouting up to Dan, 'Give us a rid back, Dan, and you can have some tea at home, eh?'

Bill Forrest took up the invitation himself, more forcefully, 'Liza told our Ted to invite ye before the game started, Danie She wun't take no.'

Dan nodded. 'Be glad to, Mr Forrest.'

'And the girls,' indicated the keeper, pleasantly.

'Very kind of you, Mr Forrest,' murmured Mary Ann, the gave a wicked look at her new escort. 'But y'see, Walter her has offered for to see me safe back home . . .'

Doris saw the quick tightening of John's face, and eve knowing the tricks that he'd been up to, felt sorry for him 'You'll come though, Betty?' she asked, and Betty nodde eagerly. 'And you, John?' She turned to her father, knowin how he felt about Dan's brother, but he didn't seem put ou 'Is that all right, Dad?' she begged.

'If John'd like to, ah,' was his reply.

48

But John's mettle was up; he'd been made to look a fool by Mary Ann and Walter, and the last thing he wanted now was Liza Forrest's home comforts. Doris alone, yes; but he'd not spend that evening seething with frustration, while Polly Harper slept alone and unloved.

'Thanks, but I've plans already made,' he said, throwing a dark glance at Mary Ann; she pouted, and moved away on Walter's arm, calling her goodbyes.

'As ye like, boy,' murmured Bill Forrest placidly, and raising his walnut stick, moved away. 'See you at the house then, daughter,' he said, and was lost in the rapidly thinning crowd.

Dan knew only too well that sullen fire burning in his brother's face; it begged and yet rejected help.

'Will I expect ye later then, John?' he asked flatly, half-expecting the sour reply.

'Don't trouble,' growled John, flinging off the wet, protective sack. Without another word or glance at either girl, he slouched away into the grey evening.

Chapter Four

Mrs Forrest's idea of Saturday supper was a feast, whether or not there'd be visitors sitting with the family. To have not only Doris home, but her young friend Betty, and Dan Archer too, made the simple feast into a grand occasion and a pleasure to see. The scrubbed wood of the kitchen table was almost totally hidden under the profusion of good food; home-made breads, one gleaming loaf speckled with carroway seeds; cheeses and stone jars of Mrs Forrest's home-made pickles and chutneys, sweet and mustard-hot; cold game pie, brawn fresh from the mould, and chitterlings; and to quench any amount of thirst, cider and mulled ale for the chill November night. With the bright fire glowing in the Triplex grate and the mellow gleam of the green glass oil lamps, the kitchen of Riverbank farmhouse offered a welcome that no sane person could resist. Young Tom, home early with his father from the football match, helped by laying out the cutlery and slyly picking at titbits, knowing his mother was turning a blind eye, seeing as it was a Saturday. Clinking and clattering about the table, he gleefully told her all the thrilling details of the game and Ted's brave part in it, while she smiled fondly at the bright sparkle in his hero-struck eyes.

'It was Ted's doing, Mam – both our goals!' he declared. 'It was him that made the both on 'em!'

'That was one in the eye for Penny Hassett, then,' replied his mother, cheerful in her total ignorance of a game that in all honesty only meant extra washing for the tub on Monday.

'We'll beat 'em next year,' declared Tom confidently. 'They've only got that big bloke Curly Cobb, and he's old . . . !'

Liza Forrest laughed out loud. 'Just wait till you'm playing for Ambridge yourself, my little man,' she said, rumpling his tousled hair. 'Then you can talk . . .'

Tom was already halfway out of the room; he had heard the grind and clatter of Dan Archer's wagon in the yard outside, and within seconds he was at the door letting in the visitors and hero Ted.

'No grub for you, Ted – ' he yelped mischievously, ' 'cos you didn't score any goals!' Growling with laughter, he and his brother tumbled into the house, grappling and romping like puppies, while the others drifted thankfully into the cheerful room, its warm glow bringing a softness even to Betty Collins's pinched cheeks.

'Sit y'selves down, m'dears,' fussed Doris's plump, hen-cheerful mother. 'Ye must be shrammed with the cold!' She gave an especially gentle smile to the scrawny girl from Cannock, who couldn't help but smile in return. 'It's ale for the men, I know – how about someat warming for y'self, Betty, my pet . . .?'

Betty nodded, pleased to be so noticed. 'Yes, please, Mum Forrest. What can I do?'

'You'll do nothing while you're under my roof, girl. You're visiting. Now sit down and drink up . . .' Whenever she saw the thin-armed scullerymaid, Mrs Forrest took on a motherly concern; at fifteen years, Doris had been twice the girl that Betty was. It was her upbringing, Doris's mother would say, meaning no offence; it was a well known fact that leaving home for service was the only salvation for the daughter of a miner's family, short of quick marriage to a local lad. Beneath the countrywoman's cossetting touch, Betty blossomed – but only briefly. Work at the Hall was hard and constant, with few concessions for a home-sick Black Country girl; it was part of her station in life to be put upon and used, her crake-voiced mother had so often drilled into her. 'Be good, or they'll send ye back home, and for that I'll skin ye alive!' The shrill warning still echoed in Betty's sullen dreams, but these visits to the farmhouse now used as gamekeeper's cottage were like a candle to her constant nightmares.

51

Doris had slipped into the role of helping her mother as though she was at home each and every day, instead of living in at the Hall. Cheerfully she mulled and served the ale to Dan and Ted, meeting the grateful smile from each with a dimpled radiance. 'There,' she said pertly as she handed Dan his pewter mug, 'that'll warm you up a bit, Daniel Archer . . .'

Dan wanted to tell her that it was her laughing eyes that made him flush so readily, but the only words that emerged from his slow-smiling mouth were 'It'll do me a treat, ah . . .', then adding, 'Your good health, Mr Forrest,' as the under-keeper came into the kitchen from the sitting room.

'Thank ye, Daniel,' was the pleasant response, then more firmly, 'Excuse me, mother – we'd like Ted in with us.'

His mother nodded, as Ted looked surprised. 'You go on in with your father and Mr Nugent, my son. I'll bring ye a platter o' grub in there in just a minute.'

Ted followed his father out, leaving the others wondering, until Liza Forrest explained. 'Mr Nugent's here on business, y'see.' Her eyes crinkled in a slow, secret amusement. 'Seems that while my Billie and young Ted were at the footer game, Willie Ashford's been making hisself busy . . . the wicked old devil!' And she laughed with the others in reluctant admiration for the poacher's craftiness and gall.

In the sitting room, George Nugent wasn't so charitable.

'Set snares for pheasant, he has, damn his eyes!' the head keeper exclaimed forcefully. 'Henry found three – theym Ashford's handiwork all right.'

'On my patch?' Ted asked blankly.

'Where better, lad,' murmured his father. 'With you playing footer . . .'

'But Ernie was playing as well,' protested Ted lamely. It was standard practice with Willie that he always used a net for taking birds and rabbit, with Ernie as his necessary helper. The job just couldn't be managed properly by one man alone. It was for this very reason – Ernie being in the team – that Ted had been let off to play. Willie had properly turned the tables, and no mistake!

'Banking on us thinking that, weren't he,' Nugent growled. 'Then while we're off guard, in he slips and tries his luck!' He bit on his short-stemmed pipe, and grinned savagely. 'But he's done hisself a mischief this time . . .'

Ted took the point, shrewdly. 'He'll be back to clear the snares,' he nodded. 'We could nab him, then.'

'He's no fool,' commented Bill Forrest. 'And we don't know yet where the rest of his wires are, do us . . .'

'If we can just catch him with the birds on him,' Nugent emphasised, jabbing the air with the stem of his pipe, 'then I'd be well satisfied! But it'll mean a full night's work for all of us. He could come back any time.'

'How shall we take him, George?' asked Ted's father quietly. 'It'll take some doing, knowing him . . .'

'You and Ted know that patch the best,' mused Nugent, 'so you'll likely know where he'll come in and go out. We got three snares – now then, when he comes for them, it'll be you there, Ted, hidden and watching, right?'

'Right, Mr Nugent.'

'But y'do nothing about it. You just stalk him, slow and careful, while he picks up the rest of his bag. Only signal with your stick. I'll have my glasses on ye.'

Bill Forrest saw the skill and simplicity of the plan, and it pleased him. 'So when his bag's full . . .' he smiled.

'Why,' said Keeper Nugent past teeth clenched tightly on his pipe, 'we stamp on him, that's what!'

By the time that Mary Ann Hudson and Walter had reached the back lane at Sixpenny Farm, the rain had stopped. To the casual glance the narrow, grassy-bordered lane was apparently deserted, but keen eyes might have seen the shift of darker figures locked in an upright, breathlessly rigid embrace within the pool of shadow cast by a massive oak.

'Doh . . . Mary Ann Hudson, you'm a poppet . . . !' growled Walter, reluctantly drawing his mouth from hers. 'Fair got me a-tremble, you have . . .'

'I know,' she responded with a soft giggle, and pressed a

salvo of small kisses on his lips. 'I do wish it hadn't've rained,' she said.

His thoughts full only of the press of her body against his, Walter savoured the sweet softness of her mouth and, letting his hands wander slowly downwards from the small of her pliant back, wondered at her preoccupation with the weather. 'Got a brolly, an't ye?' he murmured, when her kisses gave him breath to utter.

'Oh, you dunce . . . !' she laughed in a low whisper, setting her hands lightly on his shoulders and looking up into his puzzled face with a sparkle that even the shadows couldn't hide. 'I want someat more comfy than that!'

He chuckled now, as he took her meaning, squeezing her plump body tight against him and murmuring wordlessly as she kissed him long and hard. At last, breaking the tongue-tipped embrace, she brushed her hot face against his ear and murmured, 'I know of a place, love. . . .' Then, laughing, she broke free and ran, drawing him gaily after her down the night-dark lane.

With Betty innocently choosing to sit on the outside of the wagon's driving bench, each jog and shudder of the wheels moved Doris against Dan's burly left shoulder in spite of herself. Over a particularly rough piece of track, just where the lane from Riverbank Farm joined the main road out of the village towards Sixpenny Farm crossroads, she found herself forced to cling to his forearm for fear of being bounced off the seat altogether; her hands felt the taut muscles tighten as he guided Dot round a half-seen pothole, then relax, but the brief moment of gentle strength strangely warmed her. Surprised, she found that she hadn't drawn her hands away; a sudden movement of his head brought her looking up at the broad face, shadowed by the trilby hat's brim. He was staring at her, but as she questioned his dark glance, he looked just as suddenly away again. She flushed in the chill darkness, and thinking that he'd shown a flicker of disapproval at her instinctive gesture, made as if to remove her hand from his sleeve –

only to find that her right hand was firmly tucked beneath his elbow, and he wouldn't let it go. She looked at him again, and smiled to herself in the darkness; his grip was gentle, but no accident. It wasn't bold, full of dangerous implications, as John's touch had been; it was like the man himself, quiet and reassuring, strong without force.

Betty, her pale features lit faintly by the wagon lamp beside her, settled herself against Doris's left arm, and raising it, Doris held the tired girl comfortingly against her. Betty's weight forced Doris in turn to lean lightly against Dan, and her face was now pressed against the coarse tweed of his sturdy jacket. The slow clop of Dot's hooves lulled her mind, taking it back to the early evening when she and Betty and Dan had sat, eating and joking together, telling her mother of the exciting game and the brave part that Ted had played in it.

Perhaps it had been the ale in him, or the drawing warmth of Mrs Forrest, or even – dare she hope it – the gaiety of Doris herself, that had brought words to Dan. He had suited the homeliness of the place, she decided; John would have been restless there, his mind a burning glass preoccupied with . . . what? Secretly, she knew; though telling no tales, Mary Ann Hudson had dropped enough hints about Walter Gabriel, and John, and even Sam Fisher. Those bright-eyed lads – and more that Mary Ann wouldn't even name – had wicked intentions that were all the more dangerous for being enjoyable, if you'd that kind of nature. It was these same lads who as schoolboys in their final year had indulged in the traditional corner playground sport of snatching up the girls' smocks 'to see their colour' – that is if any there was to be seen. Rumour had it that the greater part of their informal education had been conducted in the enthusiastic company of Polly Harper, a simple, happy girl whose history was a warning in itself.

Three years after leaving school, and pregnant, Polly had been forced to leave her father's cottage under the threat of his eviction by the Squire. After a brief establishing spell in a Borchester factory, Polly had quickly earned herself the reputation as being a generous friend to lonely soldiers; even after the war it was said about her that she still had a special regard for those men of Ambridge who had known her in childhood. But to the village girls, Polly Harper represented the world of sin; to be shocked by, wondered at, and by some even envied for the life she led. Whatever people said about her, though, her greatest crime seemed to be that she was never unhappy, however wicked her ways. This puzzled Doris, and innocent as she was, she vaguely knew that in this curiosity lay the greatest danger. She also sensed, as if her father didn't say so often enough, that John was the key to that curiosity. 'A wild boy,' said her mother. 'Full of easy promises,' sulked Mary Ann; but all agreed that swanky John Archer was a hero of the war and could charm a trout from the brook, if he so chose. She'd taken his eye, Doris knew that, but protected by the twin disciplines of work and fond parents, she had felt no response to his distant interest. But today had been different. Today she had felt the danger in him, and been excited by it. And she suddenly knew she was afraid.

As if searching for a haven, she nuzzled against the broad, comfortable shoulder at her side. She felt, rather than heard clearly, Dan's warm voice.

'Nearly there. Won't be long now . . .'

'Betty's asleep,' murmured Doris. 'We could be alone for all she knows we're here . . .' she added, and her heart jumped at her own audacity. She caught her breath as his head turned and hovered for a split second over her upturned face; then, just as he seemed to dip nearer, the pitch of the wagon which had thus far brought them so innocently close, jerked them apart. Dan cursed, silently; Doris's hand on his arm pressed tight, seeming to pull him back to her, and she gave a tiny, breathless laugh. But it was too late. The jolt had half-woken Betty; she sat up, peering about her nervously, and the moment was past. The tone of the wheels changed to a thin rumble as the wagon arrived on the fine gravel fronting the Hall.

'Are we here then, Mr Archer . . .?' asked Betty wearily.

'Yes, we are, you ninny,' retorted Doris, leaving Betty wondering what she had done to irritate her friend so.

Dan had drawn the wagon to a stop beside the ghostly cliff of masonry that was the North Wing, and clambered down. He stood for a moment looking up at Doris, who was about to bundle Betty off the other side of the wagon, but changed her mind. Turning towards Dan, she leaned over him and rested her hands on his sturdy shoulders; taking her by her trim waist, he lifted her down into the shadow of the wagon, out of sight of Betty and the looming windows of the Hall. And then, gently and firmly, he kissed Doris full on the mouth. Almost instinctively, she stiffened in protest, but his strong hands wouldn't let her go and her token resistance was snuffed out like a candle in the wind. As her mouth softened to his, her hands gripped his shoulders tightly, eager to make the stolen moment last. It was Betty's plaintive moan that broke the spell.

'In't anybody going to help me down? I'm caught!'

With a quick, guilty movement, Doris pulled her face away from Dan's, matching his own involuntary gasp; for a tiny second, her hands still rested against his chest, not pushing him away but acknowledging the intimacy that had gone before.

'You're a strange one, Dan Archer,' she whispered, then with a laugh, ran around the back of the wagon towards Betty, calling, 'I'm coming, Betty – wait a bit!'

Walter opened his eyes to see, dim in the gloom of the sweet-smelling haybarn, Mary Ann kneeling by him prim and proper, her hands raised to the back of her hair, pinning up loose strands. With a contented, teasing growl, he reached out for her with fondling hands; laughingly, she brushed his hands aside, and pinning him down with straight uncompromising arms, showed him the night games were over.

'Leave my bubbies alone, wickedness,' she ordered fondly. 'Time for you to get me home, it is.' Then giving him a quick kiss, she got to her feet, finished buttoning up her blouse to the neck, and began brushing the hay strands from her full skirt.

57

She paused for a moment, watching Walter grovel in the shadows about her feet.

'What're you up to now, daftie,' she commented drily.

'Lost me blessed collar, an't I,' grumbled Walter, innocently caressing her left ankle in his search, and getting his fingers trodden on for his cheekiness. 'Ghow . . . !'

'Serves you right,' giggled Mary Ann, pinning on her hat slightly askew, lacking a mirror to see herself. 'Are y'ready then?'

Walter lurched to his feet, half-buttoned and crumpled in his haste. 'What's the blessed hurry, me love,' he demanded, finally giving up the effort of fixing the stiff collar to the back of his shirt. Stuffing the offending article into his trouser pocket, he took up his jacket and shrugged it on. 'You in't going to change into a pumpkin come midnight, are ye . . .?'

'Ten o'clock's my time,' was Mary Ann's pert reply, and she led the way out into the grey November night. 'And I in't chancing losing my position for you nor any man,' she continued, confronting him boldly. 'Now then, is my hat on straight?'

Walter took her hands and held her at arm's length, taking in her fulsome charms with an appreciative chuckle. 'You'm a grand wench, Mary Ann,' he complimented, then added as she drew herself up warningly, ' – and your hat looks a treat, it do!'

Her frown eased into her usual merry glance, and fondly she slipped her arm through his as they walked towards the gate and the lane beyond. Walter strolled with a rolling swagger, thinking with a rare contentment how John's bad luck had been his good fortune, and wondering if his chance with their shared lady love would hold beyond tonight. There'd be no hard feelings, Walter was sure of that, for John had no special regard for any wench, further than what he could make of her, and Mary Ann was fizzgig enough to take her own revenge for John's wandering attentions, for which Walter was truly thankful. Opening the gate, he gave her a firm hug, but said nothing.

She paused before stepping out into the misty lane, and looked Walter full in the face; for once, she wasn't smiling though her eyes still sparkled from their lovemaking.

'I didn't take you there *just* to spite John,' she said, and perched up to kiss him lightly on the cheek. 'What time does your watch say, lover?'

Walter produced his father's gold fob-stopper and peered at it keenly. '' 'Nother ten minutes,' he grunted.

'Never!' cried Mary Ann, then holding her skirts with one hand and her hat with the other, she dashed ahead of him down the tree-shadowed lane, calling back gaily, 'Run with me, Walter! Come on . . . !'

It wasn't until she was safely inside the servants' door, leaning against it to catch her breath back, that Mary Ann remembered Mrs Prentiss's umbrella and where she'd left it – lost in the tumbled fragrance of the haybarn. Somehow she'd have to get it back, she thought as she climbed the wooden hill up to her attic bedroom; perhaps Walter would be pleased to play the gentleman and help her. And she went to sleep laughing at the promise in the thought.

It was almost dawn before Ted heard the near-silent approach of Willie Ashford and, unseen by the shadowy figure of the poacher, raised his stick above his head in a warning sema-phore to Nugent, watching from the distance. In the ride before him lay the feathery corpses of the pheasants caught in the deliberately high-set wire loops; a nasty but efficient trick, one of many known by the keepers to be used by Ashford. Peering intently past the screen of woodland rhododendrons that hid him from sight, Ted admired the old man's deft movements with the critical eye of a fellow-professional. Hardly a twig stirred beneath the poacher's feet as he removed the limp corpses and slipped them into the sack he carried; then like a ghost he moved away unhurriedly, heading to-wards the remainder of his as yet unseen traps. Again Ted raised his stick in silent signal, before taking a parallel course in order to stalk the unknowing poacher in his tracks.

Willie had picked his time well, acknowledged Ted, as the furtive figure ahead became lost from time to time in patches of mist rising through the undergrowth; if he made a break for it now, he might easily dodge the waiting keepers ready to pounce on the funnel of his escape route. Step by step, Ted matched the poacher's crafty stealth, but the long wait had stiffened his legs and the sudden cracking of his joints sounded in his ears like a gunshot, both barrels. He froze, eyes fixed on the hunched figure just ahead putting more feathered loot into its bulging sack, but it seemed not to have heard and finishing swiftly, moved on to be lost like a wild animal in yet another patch of mist. Ted moved forward too, taking care even as he glided forward at more speed not to make a sound; but suddenly a swirl of thickened air was all about him, and coming out of it he knew he'd lost his prey. He paused, taking in his bearings, then raised his stick to give the prearranged signal that would send Nugent and Henry Adsall to the point where Willie Ashford would have to leave the wood. They'd known full well that he'd the ears of a buck deer, and that stalking him was a game that Ted could easily lose; but Nugent was as cunning as any poacher, and had set his plans accordingly. If Ashford chose to slip his tracker, he'd run straight into Nugent's trap.

Ted went to go forward, but checked his pace and listened, puzzled. From not so far ahead, muffled by the trees and bushes and November mist, a totally unexpected noise drifted towards Ted – a quietly insistent clanking of tin cans. Fixing the source, Ted advanced more quickly; it came from the edge of the wood close by the road that turned toward Grange Farm and the river, the route that Wilile Ashford was almost certain to take for his escape. Then, as he stepped from the wood into the clearing just beyond, he saw the girl.

She was a gypsy, likely a few years younger than Ted, but with a dusky assurance that gave her a graceful dignity, a lithe poise like an animal. Her knowing eyes were full of bright amusement as she confronted him, not ten steps from the painted gypsy wagon standing behind her. Her skirts were caught up to the knee, revealing even in that chill morning light nut-brown, dew-dappled skin that walked barefooted in the roadside grass. She carried a brightly painted wooden pail, obviously to carry water from the nearby stream, and her bare forearms, though tanned and slender, were sturdy and well-formed. Her rich black hair fell untied well past her slender shoulders, but it was her face that captured Ted's surprised stare the most; broad at the cheekbones, tapering in a taut curve to an almost pointed chin; the mouth well-shaped and wide, offering a constant glimpse of perfect teeth; a small, straight nose, and dark, daring pools of brilliance, almond-formed, shrewd and slanting, that were her eyes. One hand on her hip, she challenged Ted, silently; he walked slowly to her, but stopped on the far side of the ditch between them.

'I heard cans,' he said, lamely.

'No tinkers here,' came the curt, not unfriendly reply; a strong voice, low, almost that of a lad. Travelling folk weren't unwelcome, provided that they stuck to the rules, and it was estate practice to greet them, tell them where they stood, and wish them well. They rarely stayed for long, and if they poached the odd rabbit only for the pot, then small harm was done and no enemies were made. But tinkers were bad business, and liked neither by Romany nor keeper.

'I'll look elsewhere then,' nodded Ted. 'Good day.'

He'd barely turned away when that low, boyish accent called to him again. 'Where the water runs . . .' it said, with the barest hint of mockery.

He looked at her, uncertain whether she was joking or not; she said no more, but indicated with a graceful gesture of her head that part of the ditch that ran out of sight beneath the track turning from the road into the woods. Something in her face told him not to take her lightly; he stepped down and straddled his legs across the ditch, leaning to peer beneath the watery, shadowed arch. Something was there, kept clear of the trickling water by a concealed bridging plank – something that looked like a bulky sack. By the time he'd groped for and retrieved it, the girl had vanished, without another word. One glance inside the sack told him he had no time to spare offering polite thank-yous to whoever was inside the gypsy wagon; that would have to wait. Slinging the find upon his shoulder, he turned and hurried down the road.

When George Nugent saw Willie Ashford stepping jauntily along the road towards him making not the slightest attempt to conceal either himself or the load he was carrying, he knew that something was up. When he heard the crabby-faced poacher actually whistling as he came, the keeper was sure of it; unless he was very careful, he was going to be made a fool of. Nevertheless, he stood his ground, squarely set in Willie's path and glared silently at the wiry old man before barking, 'You're early about, Willie. A bit too early, mebbe!'

'It's a fine day for some,' croaked Willie, crinkling his eyes, cheerfully, and shouting first to one side of the lane and then to the other, 'Morning, Bill! Morning, Henry!' Then with an apologetic cough, he added, 'And not forgetting yourself, Mr Nugent sir.'

In fact of course, Henry Adsall and Bill Forrest had been placed well out of sight; but now the game was up, out they came at Nugent's nod of command. Slightly sheepish, they crowded in on Willie, looking with dark suspicion at the sack he was carrying and, like the wary-eyed head keeper, wondering just what his game was.

'You haven't been to market, have ye, Willie?' suggested Henry Adsall drily, walking round to the back of Willie and studying the sack.

'And he's not on his way to church, either,' growled Bill Forrest. 'What's your game, Willie?'

'Game?' asked the poacher, innocently.

'What's inside that sack, lad!' boomed keeper Nugent, and seeing his massive fist clench fearsomely, Willie suddenly came alert to what was expected of him.

'Ah, you'm wanting to see what I'm carrying!' he croaked, and with a shrug of his shoulder he dumped the sack on to the ground with a muffled clatter of old tin cans.

The sound alone was enough to confirm Nugent's worst

suspicions, but he looked into the open neck that Willie presented to him, all the same. Then Bill looked, too, and so did Henry; and all three keepers looked at Willie with eyes that cried bloody murder, and he smiled.

'Not what y'wanted, then?' he chuckled, his slow mirth building into such a hearty cackle that he didn't hear young Ted come up and drop his sack until the flushed lad spoke, a rasp of triumph in his voice.

'Forget someat, didn't ye, Willie?' So saying, Ted let the neck of the sack fall open; from it, he produced a single tin can, then motioned that George Nugent should look inside and see what there was to be seen. Nugent did so; so did Henry, and Bill Forrest too. This time they turned faces beaming with dark joviality upon Willie, who hadn't bothered himself to look. Instead, he shrugged, and gave the sack of tins a mighty and frustrated kick, before turning and staring hard at Ted.

'Careful, Willie,' crowed Henry Adsall, 'those tins are King's Evidence!'

Willie ignored him, and questioned Ted with some respect. 'How did y'know where to look, young'un?' he demanded without rancour. 'I left you yards behind in that copse. You couldn't've seen . . .'

'Used my eyes,' retorted Ted drily, aware that George Nugent was studying him with unconcealed approval. Willie shook his head as though not satisfied with the curt explanation, but Nugent had no more time to waste.

'Let's get ye to Jim Gregory,' he said brusquely. 'It'll be three months for this one, I reckon.'

Willie nodded, soberly, then looked back along the lane, the way he'd come, his face suddenly flushed with anger. 'It were them bloody gyppos, I bet!' he croaked bitterly, then let himself be urged away towards the village by Henry Adsall. While Ted's father took up the sack of cans and moved off after the others, Ted made to heave the bulky sack of game on to his back. Nugent waited until the lad had got himself balanced, before murmuring to him quietly, hand on his sleeve, 'There's a brace of hares hung in my pantry up at the Lodge, Ted.'

Ted took his meaning, and was pleased; Nugent's gesture showed that nailing Willie Ashford was something special, deserving a mark of appreciation to all concerned.

'It's only right those gyppos should share in our good fortune, eh, lad?' suggested the head keeper. 'See to it, then. Tomorrow morning.'

'Fair enough, Mr. Nugent,' responded Ted with a broad grin. The prospect was enough to make him whistle all the way to Sunday breakfast.

CHAPTER FIVE

IT WASN'T until Monday morning that John returned to Brookfield. Dan had just finished putting down fresh straw for the calves; turning to leave, the pitchfork in his hand, he found his brother looming in the doorway watching him.

'You're back then,' was Dan's only comment, moving out into the yard. John had only reluctantly stepped aside, his sullen face brooding with sarcasm.

'It's a wonder you noticed,' he sniped acidly.

Once out in the daylight, Dan could see more clearly the state his brother was in; the usually trim suit crumpled, the shirt soiled, the neat tie marked with food, or liquor. His special pride, the boots, were scarred and muddy, and he hadn't shaved. Even so he held himself erect, every inch a soldier for all his seedy bitterness.

He saw Dan's glance and swaggered across after him.

'Rough weekend,' he smirked. 'Bloody marvellous.' Dan didn't answer, but paused at the barn long enough to thrust the pitchfork into the kerves of hay there, ready for feeding the cattle later. He walked past John, and paused by the door to the scullery.

'Kettle's on the hob,' he stated flatly. 'I'm making tea. Want some?'

'Gnat's!' sneered his brother, pushing his way inside. '. . but better than nothing. I'll have a mugful, ah.'

Putting the cracked china teapot to warm by the steaming kettle, Dan watched as John dragged a chair to the table, and sat down wearily. He'd probably walked at least from Bornchester, perhaps from even farther afield; whatever else he'd been doing this past weekend, it had drained him. Slowly spooning the tea into the now-warmed pot, Dan let his mind drift back to the night their mother had been buried. Restless as a wild animal, John had finally stormed from the house after hours of brooding silence. Coming down to that lonely farm kitchen in the dawn, Dan had found his brother hunched just as he was now, haggard and unkempt, at the bare table. In his fingers was a creased photo; a pretty, sephia-tinted face staring blankly back at his dark and bitter eyes. The image was almost the spitting image of their mother, as she'd been thirty years before. John had turned his head to see Dan standing there, staring at the photo, wondering.

'Keepsake,' he'd boasted tensely, ' – for services rendered.' His eyes burned into Dan's unmoving face, challenging him to react, to protest, to show disgust. 'Married, she is,' he went on, voice grating insistently, '. . . a proper comforter in times of need . . .!' He glared at the photograph, and viciously tore it into four, his features creased and distorted, close to tears. 'Lover-boy she called me, the crabby whore . . .!'

Dan had said nothing as John put the shreds of paper into the slow-burning fire, to smoulder, then to burn in a small puff of brilliant flame. Only when it was ashes, did John speak, looming over the miniature pyre, his eyes fixed darkly trance-like on the last glowing curled shred.

'I'd've sooner the old man had died twice over,' came his choked whisper, 'than Mother go. . . .'

At last he had touched Dan to the quick. Dan had lunged towards his brother, fist clenched, mouth ugly with pain; but the blow was never given. John had made no gesture of defence but stood his ground, eyes fixed unrepentantly on Dan's desperate face.

'And I'll celebrate her going how I like. . . .'

The clink of spoon on pot brought Dan back to the present, and he found that he had automatically poured on the boiling water.

'It's stewed enough, for God's sake, isn't it?' blurted John angrily, raising his rumpled head from his arms, folded on the table-top as a pillow.

Dan poured out the steaming tea into mugs, and set them

down at opposite ends of the table. Next he produced the canister of milk and its loop-handled ladle, followed by the familiar bowl of sugar. John made no move, and Dan helped himself stolidly to both, then sat holding the hot mug cupped between his calloused hands, watching the steam cloud the enamelled sheen, before sipping the sweet brew.

'They caught Willie Ashford, Sunday morning,' he muttered. 'Snaring Ted's patch.'

'They were lucky, then,' said John, barely sweetening his tea, then adding a splash of milk. He pulled a face at the pallid colour, but drank deep, regardless.

'Could mean three months, they reckon. . . .'

'Spoil a few Christmas dinners, won't it,' John said with a short, forced laugh. 'Ernie'll never manage on his own.'

Practised though Ernie was, Willie was the brains behind the business of poaching; and business it was, with fifteen or so birds sold a week at around five shillings a brace to discreet customers as far afield as Loxley Barratt. It was said that the Ashfords could number two doctors, at least one vicar, and three or four local butchers among their regular clientele; there was no denying Willie would be sadly missed.

'He's had to before now,' said Dan, and supped more tea. John drank too, and there was a thoughtful silence as they both regarded the lowered depths within their mugs.

'How did it go with you, after the match . . .?' hesitantly questioned John, not looking at his brother.

'All right,' allowed Dan.

'Take Doris back to the Hall, did ye?'

'Aye. Betty Collins, as well.'

'Not much chance of fun, then,' commiserated John slyly. 'Or did y'take 'em both on . . .?' His mouth grinned, but his eyes were flint-hard and resentful. Unabashed, Dan met his stare and was indifferent. Like most of the young men of the village he was no innocent at twenty-three; but sowing wild oats had taken second place to running the farm at Brookfield almost single-handed since the day his father had taken to his bed and slowly, desperately, coughed his life away. That had been in 1914, after buying himself out of an early enlistment on compassionate grounds; since then, work and the mill-wheel of the seasons had brought a slow but sure success and the growing determination to bring a wife to Brookfield. Let John and Walter have their rut; Dan was after something better. He could afford to shrug aside John's suggestive need-ling, and normally would do; but for once, clumsily, he decided to retaliate.

'Didn't come off so well y'self, did ye, lad,' Dan said bluntly. 'Too sure of y'self, mebbe.'

It was a mistake. He saw the anger rise behind John's eyes and knew the nerve he'd touched was pride, raw and smarting still. John's only answer, inevitably, was to attack.

'Tumbling Mary Ann Hudson's nothing new – she's a push-over, mate!' John snapped, eyes blazing. 'And I could have Ted's sister just like *that*!' He slapped his fingers hard down on to the edge of the table; the sharp sound seemed not only brutally emphatic, but sensual and coarse. Dan put down his mug, fists clenched.

'Just try it, that's all . . .' he gritted out.

Suddenly, John knew he had the whiphand, and he smiled.

'Worry you, wouldn't it,' he taunted. 'Especially if she *wanted* to . . . with me.' The tiredness seemed to slip away from him and the sheer delight of torturing his brother brought a new liveliness to his face. 'She half fancies me already, you know that. . .'

He was right of course; the fear was already planted in Dan's mind. If the choice was put to her, the balance was cruelly one-sided; where Dan was an eligible farmer, John was a hero. Where Dan was careful with words, John could talk birds from the tree; what Dan knew about the land and the seasons, John could easily cap with tales about the great cities of the world that Dan had never visited – London, Paris, Birmingham and Dover. John moved even now with the swank of a soldier; Dan's movements, even during the Harvest Home dancing, were the considered reactions of a man with one eye always on the weather. What's more, Dan knew from that last stolen kiss when he took her and Betty Collins home the other night, that Doris could be melted . . . but for God's sake, not by John! He'd kill him first!

'She's got more sense,' muttered the taut-faced farmer defensively. He knew John; he was playing for a challenge. He mustn't be given the chance.

Then John laughed, bright-eyed, and Dan had lost the game.

'So you don't reckon I could roger her then . . .?' demanded John, his voice edged with triumph. To deny him must invite the challenge, the inevitable lewd wager that Dan feared; to agree was to admit defeat and concede Doris as John's rightful trophy. Harshly, the chair scraped back as Dan stood abruptly, knuckles braced on the table, his voice thick with anger.

'You lay one finger on that girl,' he blurted out, 'and God help me, but I'll break your back. . .'

The wagon was still there. Ted paused for a moment in his approach, looking from its bright and intricate patterning, its prettily curtained windows and its half-shut, half-open stable type door, all about the small clearing in which it stood. A sturdy horse, head lowered and grazing, was tethered nearby. Smoke drifted upward from the still-burning open fire, and a small, sharp-nosed mongrel peered out warily from beneath the shadows of the wagon's wheels. He took a stride across the ditch separating him from the tiny encampment, and immediately the dog sprang up, rapping out a shrill warning, but there was nobody there to respond, it seemed.

'Easy there, Jukey,' murmured Ted, and moved forward to the short rise of wooden steps that led up to the wagon door-way. One foot on the lowest tread, he turned at the sound of the small, hard voice behind him.

'Keep away, gorgio!' It was the girl, no smile on her dark face now; in her hand was a broad-bladed kitchen knife. The dog moved to her ankle and stood there facing Ted, hackles raised and head slightly down, growling.

'No trouble meant,' said Ted, and held out the brace of

hares for the girl to see. Her sharp gaze flicked from Ted's frank face to the furred offering in his hand, and back again; then she jeered, suspiciously.

'To hang on the vardo, are they?' Her head indicated the richly painted wagon. 'So's the gavver can find 'em and run us in!'

'They'm a gift,' insisted Ted gently. 'And I got no reason to have the law on ye, my lass – just the opposite.'

She paused, a shadow of puzzlement crossing her features, before responding curtly. 'What for? I've given you nothing. . .'

'Helped me catch a thief, you did,' said Ted, then felt himself tremble as her dark glance turned to laughter. 'Take 'em,' he insisted, thrusting the offering towards her again, 'though it's small return for the favour. . . .'

A muttered word, and the mongrel sat still, silent now but watchful, where she had stood. Lithely, eyes set on Ted with a secret amusement, the girl came forward and took the hares from him; then, hanging them on a hook conveniently out of reach of the dog, she whirled about in a flurry of gay, untidy skirts, hands set provocatively on hips, and stared at Ted, bold-eyed.

'That all y'came for?' The slight, swaying movement of her hips kept her skirts in teasing motion, and Ted felt a tightness in the pit of his stomach that wasn't fear. 'Or are they – ' she indicated the hung hares, with a pert flick of the head, ' – in place of lovel to buy a quick tumble with a Romany wench . . . ?' And seeing the young keeper's obvious confusion at her brazenness, she laughed gaily, tossing her dark frizzy hair back from that bewitching face.

'They'm a gift . . .' repeated Ted lamely.

'It wasn't me y'fancied then?' she demanded, her eyes daring him to deny the fact.

'Don't even know your name, do I,' mumbled Ted, caught at sixes and sevens by her bold directness.

'Emma,' she said more softly. She folded her arms, gathering her bright shawl about her, its gap only helping to emphasise the swell of her young breasts beneath the patterned blouse. 'I knew you'd come back,' she smiled, tilting her head, now sweetly innocent. 'I read it, y'see. In the cards.'

Now he could see her little game, Ted told himself; she was out to make a fool of him, to work the old tricks of the fairground on him, tell his fortune for a silver tanner. Well he'd show her that he knew something of the words and ways of the travelling folk!

'Mebbe some mumpers go with gorgios,' he said, 'but not a proper rachli . . . they keeps to their own kind, I knows that. . . .'

For a moment there was a silence between them; then, arms still folded, she stepped towards him like a dancer; a yard away she turned in a lithe, fluid movement that took her circling round him, toe pointed, back arched, head tilted to the side. He tried to follow her with his eyes, but she was like quicksilver; suddenly she was standing before him, quite still now, her face solemn.

'I'm Romany, all right,' she said, chin tilted proudly, 'but married gorgio, didn't I. Now I'm neither.'

Ted's heart lurched, miserably. 'You'm wed, though.'

'Was,' she retorted brightly. 'My man died, six month back. Now there's only me and him. . . .' Her head nodded towards the wagon; Ted followed her glance, then faced her again, questioning. 'My Daddo,' she answered. 'He's sick, dying, mebbe. . . .'

'Doctor Meadows,' suggested Ted, 'from the village. He's a good man —'

'It's me that tends my Daddo, our way,' the girl stated firmly. Her eyes softened, teasing him again. 'Thought you knew all about our kind . . . ?'

'Can I help?' asked Ted gruffly, knowing himself to be lost to her. He hardly cared what sort of a fool she made of him, only that this meeting didn't end. Her eyes welcomed him, but still she kept her distance.

'This atchintan,' she looked all about the little clearing, serious-eyed, '. . . there's herbs here. It's a kushti place. . . .'

Ted nodded. 'Ye don't have to move on. Not yet.'

71

A wracking cough tore its way out of unseen lungs inside the wagon, and Ted saw the gleam of gratitude in Emma's face turn to concern.

'Emm . . .!' a cracked, aged voice called, between bouts of coughing 'Emm . . . ?'

Before the voice had faded, the girl was already up the steps, opening the lower door-piece, looking back at Ted through a veil of dark hair.

'Come to me again,' she said, and then was gone.

'The truth of the matter is,' declared Mary Ann Hudson as she grated a fine drift of nutmeg on to the gleaming surface of a perfect junket, 'he's a townie, and he doesn't know what's what!'

'Then he'll have to learn, won't he,' Mrs Prentiss ordained grimly. 'He'll eat in here with the rest of us, or do without. It's as simple as that!'

Betty Collins darted to and fro, taking used dishes and implements to be cleaned, out to the scullery; she tried to time her re-emergence so as to chip in discreetly with her own plaintive comments about the subject in question: Alfred Tetsall, the recently appointed chauffeur.

'Walks about like he's got a smell under his nose,' Betty complained, bringing back a large mixing bowl that had been cleaned and dried, for Mrs Prentiss's eagle-eyed inspection. With a nod, it was permitted to be stored.

'Just because he knows all about motor-car engines,' retorted Mary Ann, 'doesn't make him a cut above the rest of us!'

'Them Brummies're all the same . . .' added Betty on her way out, keeping an eager ear pricked, listening for any more scandalous titbits of information normally kept from her youthful innocence.

'Twenty shillings, they paid for his leather gloves,' Mrs Prentiss revealed bitterly.

'That's never a fact . . .?' wondered Mary Ann, shocked at the thought that this sum represented a whole month of her year's wages.

'And *six pounds* for a coat!' came the cook's sour rejoinder.

Alfred's skills as a mechanic were only matched by the nasal superciliousness of his airs and graces and the perfection with which he maintained the Squire's brand-new Humber limousine. The fact that he had been employed to avoid repeating the automobile crash that had cost the Squire over £100 in repairs to the previous machine, was ignored by those below stairs. He was a usurper, too well paid, and stuck-up into the bargain. And now he wanted his meals taken separately. All the house staff ate in Mrs Prentiss's kitchen, including Mr Stokes the butler. Alfred's bluntly expressed request had not only caused a flutter of acid agitation, it had produced a feeling of 'whatever's going to happen next?' amongst the older staff particularly. A straw in the wind, maybe – but it smelled uncomfortably of change. Mr Merrick had gloomily announced that this was how the Bolshevik revolution had started, and Mrs Prentiss had a nasty feeling that Alfred was at the very least a Republican, set on bringing down the monarchy.

'When the working class gets too big for its boots,' proclaimed the dreadnought-proportioned cook, 'it's pride going before a fall, mark my words . . . !'

'The way he sits!' giggled Mary Ann, mimicking the straight back and tucked-in chin of Alfred in the driving seat. 'Like a tailor's dummy, he is!'

'Perhaps he wears a corset,' wondered Betty with genuine curiosity, then blushed slightly as the others chuckled openly at the thought. 'I don't mean stays,' she tried to explain, only to be checked by Mrs Prentiss.

'It isn't proper for us to think about what he wears . . . underneath,' she said firmly, fixing a reproving eye on the embarrassed scullerymaid. But no sooner had Betty scurried from the room, than Mrs Prentiss burst into muffled laughter, joined by Mary Ann, as she carried the set junket out to the cold slab in the pantry.

'Have to tickle his ribs and see, won't we,' she called back gaily, and Mrs Prentiss gave a little whoop of delighted mirth. Certainly a cocky sort of man, thought Mary Ann to herself, carefully setting the junket down. 'I'll bet his hands're cold, though,' she giggled, as she returned to the cooking-scented warmth of the kitchen.

'According to Mr Merrick,' murmured Mrs Prentiss looking cautiously about to see that Betty wasn't within earshot, 'there's been certain lady guests at Chester Square who could tell you a thing or two about that. . . .' And she looked very knowingly at Mary Ann, whose eyes grew quite round at the wickedness implied in this choice rumour. But Betty had bustled back into the room, and Mary Ann had to bite back the eager questions rising to her lips. It'd certainly go a long way to explain the coolness Alfred had always shown towards both Doris and herself; and why he only seemed friendly with Miss Summers, Lady Hester's maid, who always accompanied her to the town house. Perhaps there really was a man beneath that smooth, almost creaseless blue-grey coat; in fact, with its buttoned lapels, and the addition of matching peaked cap and black leather gloves, he did have a certain military appeal when you came to think of it. She even fancied that she'd seen an arrogantly romantic look about him as he'd stood holding open the limousine door for Lady Hester to enter; his polished black gaiters setting off strong legs, his peaked cap tucked under one arm, his cold, clean-cut features, chiselled mouth, and sleekly brilliantined hair had given him an almost foreign, aristocratic air. His eyes, though; narrow and glittering like a snake. He'd no time for kitchenmaids, that Mary Ann was sure; and if a cold fish was what the ladies wanted, why then they were welcome to him.

'I don't think he's a patch on our Sam,' she announced, pleased to see Mrs Prentiss nod in agreement. 'Sam's nice – and he can make you laugh.'

Sam made even less money than the girls, and it became increasingly obvious year after year that he would find it impossible to reach the standing of footman. Full of good intentions, he had the grace of a day-old bull calf; he had neither reading nor writing to speak of, which meant that if a card was presented at the door, Sam generally had to take it to Mr Merrick or Mr Stokes to be deciphered, a fault not always found tolerable by visiting gentry. Sam had his own ambition, though. He made no secret of his delight that a regimental bugler was to attend for the coming Armistice Day ceremony. Now he was eighteen at last, a soldier's uniform was a glory no longer out of reach. It seemed that the only thing that kept him tied to Ambridge was a carping, widowed mother; before long the inevitable choice would have to be made between home and flag, and patriotism, in the shape of infantryman's dress blues, was certain to win.

'He'll find his feet as a soldier, will Sam,' decreed Mrs Prentiss. She didn't notice, as Mary Ann did, Betty's desperate escape to the scullery at this thoughtless remark. But before the older girl had the chance to wonder at Betty's brimming eyes, Doris had entered with Lady Hester's breakfast tray and set its delicate debris on the nearest table with a dangerous clatter.

'Well, miss,' exclaimed the cook, rather put out by the abruptness of Doris's arrival, 'we're a bit heavy-handed this morning, aren't we . . . ?'

Mary Ann was more sympathetic, seeing Doris's excitement. 'Whatever's the matter, chuck?' she asked gently.

'Sorry, Mrs Prentiss,' Doris apologised, then turned her flushed face towards her friend. 'I've had such a surprise, Mary Ann – you'll never guess!'

'No need to keep us in suspense though, surely to goodness,' grumbled Mrs Prentiss good-humouredly. 'What's it all about then?'

Now Betty, eyes wiped red and dry but overcome with curiosity to hear Doris's news, came back into the room, and as Doris glanced from one questioning face to the other, they all crowded closer, eager to share her exciting secret.

'Her ladyship's going to Chester Square straight after the service, with Master Anthony – ' the words bubbled out in breathless gushes, – 'and she says I must go with them!' Her eyes were alight with expectation. 'To London, Mary Ann – to London!'

Chapter Six

THE DRUMS and bugles of the South Borset Rifles, gaudy and
gleaming in their crimson and gold dress uniforms, white pith
helmets and burnished instruments, cascaded into the old
market square with a flourish of brave music, regimental
colours, and dead glory. John watched them pass, his features
set like stone. The clamour of the bugles ended; marching
now only to the sound of side and bass drum, the band and
following platoons wheeled into position alongside the ancient
market cross, marked time, and at last halted, with a practised,
coarse precision. N.C.O.s shouted orders; markers stepped
crisply forward. Arms extended, rank upon rank swept their
eyes to the right, and with a brisk clatter of steel-tipped heels,
reformed their lines to perfection. Another sharp, incoherent
bark of command and all eyes snapped to the front as one,
arms brought slapping down to sides. The wire-taut figure of
the R.S.M. rocked almost imperceptibly on polished heels,
gimlet eyes glaring from beneath the mask-like visor of his jet-
black cap peak, before turning about and presenting himself
like a crimson exclamation mark to the more languid figure of
the Adjutant. Satisfied, the officer nodded, and muttered the
formal instruction to relax the assembled men. Pace stick
exactly levelled under his left arm, the R.S.M. pivoted fiercely,
glared once again at the precisely poised regiment, then
bawled the long-drawn-out pre-command warning, pausing
only fractionally before the final explosive shriek.

'Regiment . . . stand at . . . HAIE !'

From the side street leading on to the square, John took a
last critically admiring glance at the regulars on parade, then
turned back to join the other blue-suited civilians officially

76

classed as Old Comrades. At close range, their semi-uniformed anonymity took on the details of the damned; for every ribbon at their lapel buttonhole, they seemed to bear a physical scar. The comfortably brisk ex-C.S.M. in charge had his left sleeve tucked, empty, into his jacket pocket; the leading marker stood proudly waiting for the others to fall in on his left flank, though on that side he could see nothing for the black patch that covered an empty socket; the man in front of John carried a great weal-like scar across his neck and up under the hat he wore; to John's left, the puckered and livid flare of a healed burn made his companion's face cruelly inhuman, while on his right a rigidly formed black glove completed the arm of the young man standing there. Arriving early, there had been few there that John had known; a few close pals of the past refought their last skirmish, or told of the emptiness of being a helpless hero. Amongst that grim, proud company, John felt almost an intruder. The scars he bore were buried, out of sight; when asked, he could answer no more than 'Gas, mate . . . gas.' To describe that pain-fogged moment of distant terror, or recall the faces frozen in choking panic all about him in the fume-filled trench, was beyond him. All he had to show was the strip of bright ribbon at his lapel, and suddenly it meant nothing. Only the faces that weren't there, silent voices mouthing in his memory, brave ghostly faces smiling . . . all this would mean damn-all to them! John's rush of anger was cut short by a quiet command from the calm-eyed C.S.M.

'Are we ready, lads?' he called, the light, crisp voice carrying surprisingly well. 'Lots of swank, now.' He paused, and swallowed; now when he spoke, there was the merest hint of a break in his voice, the choke of elation. 'Remember who we're marching for, eh. . . .'

There was a slow ripple of movement along each line of men, a straightening of backs, setting of brave shoulders, chins were lifted proudly. A glance to his right for John to check that he was in line, showed him that the handless boy was weeping, silently. Jerking his stare to the front, John clenched his balled fists and silently begged the parade to begin. As if in answer, the drumbeats filtering into the narrow side street from the square momentarily checked their slurred echo, then on the wordless command of the bass drum took on a new, relentless beat; slow time, a pace for dead heroes, a call for old comrades. Bowler-hatted officers in front, the march began.

For John, that short journey to the square and then beyond, following the drums and proud bugles to the massed gathering outside Borchester cathedral, was a jangling confusion of drumbeat, bugle-call, marching boots and blurred, impassive faces. A few excited children ran alongside the tramping column until diverted by constables on duty; overhead, blowing gracefully in the damp breeze, flags at half-mast from both permanent and makeshift flagpoles set over shops and houses. The cathedral was reached at last, the town's silver band already placed to one side of the swagged dais on which the mayor and other civic dignitaries stood in solemn, decorated pomp. The drummers and the buglers halted, then marched briskly to take their set place opposite the silver band, while the uniformed troops, Old Comrades, and the several small contingents of Red Cross and similarly represented parties formed tight ranks before the dais. The figures there jerked upright as the wind-blown bishop stepped forward to speak, his elegant voice losing whole words and phrases to the bluster of the mounting wind.

'. . . we are gathered here . . . this solemn occasion . . . eleventh hour of the eleventh . . . the eleventh month . . . to pay tribute . . . tribute . . . tribute . . . to those glorious dead. . . .'

John had stopped listening. Words, he thought bitterly, nothing but bloody words! What did they know, what did those po-faced bloody big-wigs know . . . ! His mind, and the surging gusts of wind, blotted out the speeches; the silver band struck up 'Abide With Me', and the paraded ranks did their bit, thickening the ragged voices of the mournful crowd, but this wasn't what John so desperately wanted. Blank-faced, he mouthed the words, but his eyes peered upward to the great church tower and the clockface there, willing the hands to

78

reach the appointed time. Someone on the official dais proclaimed a volley of meaningless, incomprehensible slogans; a pigeon fluttered idly on to the ledge of the clockface; a motorcycle's brutal roar faded, streets away . . . and then, as the massive minute hand pointed itself to heaven, the eleventh hour rang out.

At each reverberating stroke, it seemed as if the air quivered more and more with the command to silence. As the last bell-boom shuddered on the wind, every head bowed in muted acceptance, but still John waited. His hair rumpled curtly by the fitful wind, his mind and memory were blind to everything but what he knew must follow; the next two minutes were simply an aching void, a limbo to be patiently endured. Suddenly, the wind dropped. A crimson-coated, solitary figure stepped crisply forward – and at last the majestic, lonely bugle spoke.

The sorrow and the pride of that sweet, inhuman voice was both salute and farewell to all those lost souls death-rooted in the mud of war; its dying fall seemed to caress even the wind into stillness, carrying the only message that the living could offer to the dead beyond the grave : we shall not forget. Tight-throated, John turned his face upward to the crumpled sky as the last poignant note throbbed and echoed from the gaunt cathedral stones. A brief pause, barest of a token respect for grief, then the combined bands launched rousingly into the national anthem. The salute to the fallen had ended. God save the king !

Doris almost jumped with alarm as, with a warning shriek of steam, the mighty locomotive snatched its train of carriages into the soot-black depths of the cutting tunnel, muffling the sharp clatter of the wheels into an ear-splitting roar. In the dim light of the compartment emergency light, Lily Summers, travelling third class with Doris and not liking it, sprang to her feet and struggled to close the ventilator, coughing delicately as she did so. Doris pulled a face in the half-darkness as the acrid tang of coarse smoke reached her, and she stood

79

and tried to help. Lily, a strong young woman for all her fastidious ways, had already managed to shut the smuts and the sound out, but gestured angrily to show her soiled white cotton gloves.

'Look at that!' she cried peevishly, 'Filthy!' As though to emphasise the unclean quality of life travelling third class, she took out her anger on the empty seat cushion by her side; it gave out several puffs of dust, dirtying her precious gloves even more. 'Third class simply *isn't* good enough,' she despaired, then salved her indignity by pointedly remarking, 'Next time you'll just have to travel by yourself, child. I'm used to better things, you know . . . !'

'I don't think I'd've managed by myself,' said Doris pleasantly. 'It's all so strange – and I've never travelled so fast in all my born days . . . !'

'The Humber's cleaner *and* more comfortable,' stated Lily airily, then added knowledgeably, 'Mind you, it'd take a month of Sundays to drive to London by road. . . .'

Doris didn't know much about cars or their speed, but she'd heard Sam the hallboy tell Mr Merrick that Alfred often broke the limit of twenty miles an hour if he could get away with it. It was difficult to imagine being able to race along the open road at the pace of a galloping horse, when all she was used to in Ambridge was a farm wagon or, at the very best, Lady Hester's horse and trap.

'A train seems safer . . .' suggested Doris, looking out of the window at the grimy reflection of the carriage, empty apart from the two girls. With a shrill wail, and a sudden burst of thin November light, the tunnel was behind them, and they could hear clearly the strained chuffing of the distant engine as it took the incline ahead with shuddering dignity.

'I'll be happier when we've arrived,' frumped Lily, and settled back to gaze with sulky, pouting face at the passing countryside.

Ambridge and Hollerton Junction even, where they'd had to change on to the train for Paddington, was already over an hour behind them; London seemed to be just as far away as it had ever seemed to Doris – the edge of the world, for all she knew, never having been further than Hollerton in her life before. And it wasn't simply the hundred miles or so that they were travelling that gave her tummy the collywobbles; the thought of seeing not only the house in Chester Square but London itself was enough to give her grey hairs before her time.

She glanced across at Lily, Lady Hester's maid for the past five years; her pretty, violet-coloured eyes were closed, and she was dozing, the gentle but erratic rocking of the train nudging her flowered, black straw hat decidedly skewiff. She usually travelled with the Squire's lady, first class, but today Lady Hester had Master Anthony as her travelling companion, and Lily had been casually relegated by her mistress to guide and reassure Doris. Doris was made of better stuff than that, and if put to it, could've managed quite well enough; but she'd been glad of Lily's company, however patronising her ways. Doris leaned back, regarding but not seeing the countryside lumbering past the window. Her mind was back in Ambridge, only hours ago that morning; attending the dedication of the bronze War Memorial plaque at the Armistice service in St Stephen's would have been more than enough excitement for one day, normally. Moving and significant though the simple ceremony had been, she wasn't sorry to be able to put it behind her; it was a proud but sad day for the Lawson-Hopes, and few folk could bear to look into the Squire's stony-eyed, impassive face for long without coming close to tears themselves. He hadn't faltered once; the grief had become like iron in his soul.

All the staff from the Hall had been present, many of the men uncomfortably formal in stiff collars that they would never otherwise wear, except perhaps at weddings and funerals. In fact the whole village had been caught up in the event, if not for their own sakes, for the loss of old friends or neighbours. The Reverend Mr Dudley had greeted them all, grave and unsmiling, by name, reserving an especially sympathetic clasp of hands for the Squire and Lady Hester. Stranger to the normal congregation had been the uniformed bugler, standing throughout alongside the church organ; not everyone had known his purpose at first. It wasn't until the Reverend Dudley had given his plain but graceful prayer of dedication, and the Squire had revealed the bronze tablet set into the wall, that the bugler had stepped forward. Doris had never heard the Last Post played before; it was Sam who had nudged her, his eyes bright with expectation, as the trim soldier placed the gleaming mouthpiece to his lips.

'It's for when they lower the flag,' he whispered, ignoring the stern glance of reproach from Mr Stokes, '. . . at sunset . . . !'

After the mellow, reedy tones of the hand-pumped church organ, the ring of the bugle had resounded through the echoing columns of stone, harsh and uncomfortable, more like a summons to judgement than a salute to the dead. It had been the final bars that had caught at the throat, sad as a distant call to hounds. For a full minute after that final note had throbbed its way upward to the vaulted wooden beams, nobody moved. Then, until the precise moment of eleven, a single bell tolled; suddenly, the remembrance of those names set in dark metal on the stone took on a reality that touched everyone present. That same bell had marked the coming to burial of every villager for the past two hundred years. It was as though that handful of lost souls had been summoned to home ground, to final rest. In the silence that followed, there were few who didn't weep.

'The Old Hundredth . . .' it was the Vicar's clear, unimpassioned voice that broke the spell. A mighty chord from the organ, a shuffling of feet and hymnbooks, and bravely, the summons to praise rang out, fullthroated and stern, led by Ted's sturdy, true baritone.

'All creatures that on earth . . . do . . . dwell. . . .'

It was in that moment of release that Doris, raising her eyes from the printed word to gaze with bright curiosity around the crowded church, saw Dan – and then realised who, most of all, was bitterly absent: John. For no known reason she felt anxious and disturbed; losing all track of the words, she let her soft eyes search frantically amongst the faces all about her. He wasn't there! And in the same split second, a more alarming truth dawned on Doris. She had to know the reason why: it mattered.

With careful precision, Anthony added more of the pale gold wine that his mother liked so much, to her glass; she smiled graciously, but her thoughts were obviously elsewhere. The spotless, plushy upholstered seclusion of their compartment was hardly the ideal place to have an afternoon picnic, but the hamper that Mrs Prentiss had prepared for Lady Hester was full of tempting things, and they had eaten well. Now, as Anthony languidly repacked the diminished container, he glanced across at his mother's graceful form swaying almost imperceptibly with the motion of the train. She had faced and accepted the distant deaths of Harry and Andrew once already; today, what had been a ritual of glory, performed to purge his father's grief, had swept her into a smiling mist of pre-war recollections, more fluid and more painful than any she kept hidden inside the padded leather covers of the family photograph album. Anthony had his memories too, but they were put aside for private moments.

Father had at last buried his dead; the small monument now placed inside the church proclaimed names, dates and places, but in due course of time only those cold barren facts would remain, an intriguing historical statistic without flesh. The act of recognition completed, Father had abdicated from all further acts of love. Leaving the empty, echoing church, he had given one last look back at the gleaming metal plaque, and nodded in grim salute. Then, leaving his wife and son to make their own return to the Hall, he had turned away, ignoring the forelock-tipped greetings of his wary tenants as he walked briskly and with set face, away from the village. Beneath the veil of dark netting draped from her elegantly funereal hat, Mother had watched him go, her face set and pale, eyes brimming with a vague sadness. Inside the car,

Anthony had taken her hand in his, comfortingly; with a small squeeze of apology, she had withdrawn her gloved fingers from his, and sitting up quite straight, was herself again.

'We mustn't think only of ourselves, Anthony . . .' she said, and with a brief, sad smile, turned her face away into the shadows of the past. Now she had re-entered that same soft-focussed dreamworld once again; it was a rejection that Anthony couldn't bear for long, and he determined to draw her out of it.

'Who'll be coming to the house tomorrow night, Mother?' he asked brightly. It was to be a small soirée, one of Lady Hester's special weaknesses, the perfection of which she was justly proud. As his baited question registered, she turned towards him; her eyes were clouded and she gestured vaguely with a disinterested hand. Then her face brightenend.

'The Fitzgeralds, my dear. Perhaps you remember their girl, Ursula?' She laughed, gaily. 'It'll be her first season . . . the poor girl!'

Anthony smiled. Mrs Fitzgerald's constant ambition was to achieve the impossible and turn her tomboyish daughter into a society beauty. Unfortunately, Ursula's co-operation wasn't exactly whole-hearted; she made no bones about the fact that she much preferred horses to many of the young men that her mama indefatigably introduced to her. Anthony was one of the few male acquaintances that she could endure, probably because they shared an enjoyment of country life that their parents couldn't fully understand.

'That'll be fun. Will she be there? I quite like her . . .' remarked Anthony lightly, implying that his mother was a romantic schemer to be proud of.

'I thought you might,' she cooed, eyes sparkling, her mind completely taken up with the social merry-go-round that would fill the remainder of the week. 'The Harfords will be there as well, with Mildred and Ronald . . .' she paused, aware of the frown behind Anthony's eyes at the mention of the last two names; for some reason he didn't get on very well with them, for all the fuss they made of him, especially Mildred. 'They're so looking forward to seeing you again, you know.'

Mildred Feckenham was over thirty, elegant and witty, and to Anthony a disturbing enigma. She seemed to enjoy his company, yet teased him unmercifully about his admitted pleasure in the rural life. The hints that university would educate him in the more sophisticated paths to adulthood, left him confused, just as did the exquisite scent that always drifted from her bare arms, so innocently and yet so provocatively on display. Ronald was brusquely companionable, fond of a wager, and for ever leaving Anthony to act as escort to his wife; there was a game here, Anthony suspected, but as yet he had no idea of the rules.

'Do they know why I can't go up until Hilary?' he asked politely. He had been forced to miss the first term at Oxford through an attack of jaundice; he didn't enjoy having to explain why, least of all to Mildred.

'They were quite concerned, my dear, but I've told them that you're fully recovered now.' His mother smiled at him fondly. 'A few days in town will be just the thing for you,' she murmured.

'What about Father . . .?' Anthony suggested carefully.

They both knew that Father had a positive distaste for towns, London in particular. But Anthony was looking for information, and his mother unwittingly obliged.

'Oh, London won't do at all,' Lady Hester insisted pleasantly. 'Not for your father – he enjoys his sport too much.' She passed the now-empty glass in her hand to her son to pack away in the hamper. 'He's only got one visit planned away from home, in fact. To Lanark, for the New Year shoot, with Sir Gordon.'

It was almost exactly as Anthony had hoped, and he tried to hide the feeling of elation that surged through him at the news. The annual sporting pilgrimage to honour the giant capercaillie usually took his father to Scotland for up to a month, and this year, with Anthony due to commence at Oxford in late January, there could be no questions asked at his exclusion from the shoot – which would suit Father well, but Anthony even better. He almost laughed aloud at the pleasing prospect. For three whole weeks, Arkwright Hall and the estate would be his free domain — alone. It almost made town bearable.

'You won't be able to go with him, my dear,' murmured his mother, explaining apologetically, 'University — '

'It's what Father would want,' stated Anthony, bowing nobly to fate. 'I'll just have to make the best of it, Mother, shan't I ?'

The sight of the giant Great Western locomotive arriving at Hollerton Junction and sweeping past the waiting passengers on the platform there in a rowdy clamour of clanking piston rods, grinding brakes and hissing blasts of steam, was nothing to the majesty that greeted Doris's amazed eyes as she stood with Lily on the platform at Paddington station. While Lily fussily summonded a porter to fetch out their luggage from the train, Doris could only stand and stare, open-mouthed, all about her. Row upon row of platforms stretched almost out of sight, with even more hidden from view. Travellers, porters, cleaners, the whole world, it seemed, walked, ran, and bustled to and fro with an intensity of purpose that brooked no obstacle — but to step aside from one meant certain collision with another. Desperately, Doris shifted with Lily's every move, no more than two steps from the precious security of the luggage. A grinding surge of steam-driven machinery filled the great cavern of wrought iron, as a huge locomotive drew slowly into the furthest platform; with a shattering scream, another engine flexed its pistons and moved slowly and inexorably out along the gleaming curve of track. Startled, Doris jumped, almost knocking the dusty porter into Lily; a burst of released steam from their own mighty engine drowned what she was saying. A pigeon, disturbed briefly by the cascade of urgent feet, flew upwards, taking Doris's eye to the immense glass and iron canopy far above her head. Head back, eyes wide with wonderment, she gaped comically. Suddenly, Lily's hand was gripping Doris's arm, urging her to follow the porter guiding their luggage on his trolley nimbly through the shambling crowds of people, to where Lady Hester and Master Anthony waited at the ticket barrier. Doris managed to glimpse Lily's amused face staring at her and mouthing words, but the maelstrom of noise and people blotted out what she said. But then Lily's mouth was close by Doris's ear, smiling, and at last her words carried home. 'Don't look so mithered, child – it's only London!'

CHAPTER SEVEN

FOR THE most part, Grannie Gabriel kept herself to herself and most of the village were thankfully in favour of such an arrangement. Three hundred years earlier, she would have been named as a witch; her touch with animals and her skills with herbal remedies commanded a grudging respect akin to awe, though tempered with fear for her ever caustic tongue. Not that she said very much, but what she did say was always close to the knuckle, and usually hurt. Meg Machin found the old woman scrabbling about in the tangle of weeds she called her herb garden, and approached warily.

'Morning, Mum Gabriel,' she called out sweetly, then paused, waiting to see how the land lay. The bent figure swathed in layer upon layer of fabric and shawls, carefully straightened up but with a suppleness surprising when one saw the weather-worn face; the skin, though plump, had the crinkled bloom of a foxglove leaf and the deepset eyes were shadowed by wild, bushy brows. Iron-grey wispy hair loosely framed Grannie Gabriel's normally stern features, but she had been known to laugh, revealing something of the beauty that at sixteen years had made her the prettiest girl in the village. But that had been sixty years ago at least, for nobody knew her age for certain – nor dared to ask.

'On the cadge, are ye,' came her sourly withering reply.

It was a good sign. The more usual answer was a fierce volley of pungent abuse, followed by an unanswerable silence. Meg moved closer, her several dimpled chins quivering into a tentative smile.

'It's for Lizzie Roberts,' she said.

'Another bun in her oven, has her!' proclaimed the old

woman, and gave a brief cackle of mirth at her little joke. Charley Roberts was the miller and baker, with a firm belief in raising sons to comfort his old age and save on labour costs once the lads were strong enough to hump and carry. Few people had known Lizzie without a child in her arms, since she got married; but each babe had brought greater problems each time of carrying, and each one had been a girl. There were five girls so far, and Charley hadn't given up trying.

Meg wasn't surprised at Old Mum Gabriel's acute observation, even though Lizzie had only just told Meg, as her closest friend, of the inevitable news. Some people said that if the old woman was ever to tell all the secrets that she knew, there'd be more than a few red faces behind latched doors. Meg herself, as keeper of the village shop, knew most of the local gossip and indeed was often the primary source; but Grannie Gabriel, when so moved, knew everything without seemingly ever being told. Meg's visit, however, wasn't to exchange notes or even pry for further information; it was purely medicinal in intent.

'Liz couldn't come herself,' apologised the comfortably-formed shopkeeper. 'It's the usual trouble . . .' For Lizzie Roberts, morning sickness was almost the greatest burden of early pregnancy, made all the worse by the hot-oven smells of Charley's early batches of bread, and his need for a hearty breakfast in good time for the shop to open. Doctor Meadows had offered remedies that had been tried and found sadly wanting, and although Charley would've disapproved if he'd known, Lizzie's only sure recourse, like so many other women of the village in their time, had been the more down-to-earth wiles of Grannie Gabriel.

'It's Charley that should be tekkin stuff, not her,' shrewdly commented the old woman. 'Don't worry. Her'll have some . . .'

'Shall I fetch it to her now . . .?' offered Mrs Machin, her face all innocence. The truth was, she wanted the chance to look into Grannie Gabriel's herb store, said to contain concoctions fit to cure a king. But this was a place kept so secure that no one would ever discover its mysteries, let alone be able to offer it at a suitable profit to the world at large. Many a time before had Meg suggested that she should stock a regular supply of the old woman's medicines and even cordials, but the crone would have none of it. Money was a poor thing, when gratitude could be better shown by payment in kind. The one medicine Charley Roberts had accepted from this furtive source, a syrup for his hacking cough, had worked well enough for him to make the old woman a present of a sack of flour; this had seemed to be less of a commercial loss to the burly baker, though the truth of the matter was that Grannie Gabriel didn't fancy his manner of baking anyway. Her own bread, subtly aromatic from the mixture of wood with which she made her oven fire, was rarely seen but said to stay fresh for months after it was baked. From Dan Archer, even though she had done little to ease the old man's final agonies, she had received a flitch of bacon; from Henry Adsall, rabbits in exchange for chilblain ointment; from Godfrey Pound, who home-killed his own livestock, fresh meat; and even, from Willie Ashford years ago, a season's supply of brown trout for taking the soreness from Ernie's left eye. Even Walter's honeyed tongue had failed to move the old woman from free trade into commercial enterprise. She knew her worth and did favours only where she chose; she was also wise to Meg's sly blandishments and had no intention of letting those twinkling, piglet eyes see her secrets and broadcast them round the village, even at second hand.

'None o' your craftiness,' she retorted. 'It's between me and Mrs Roberts. It'll be there, *I'll* see to that!'

'It'll be much appreciated, I'm sure,' murmured Meg, not in the least put out, but intrigued by the old woman's earlier remark. 'Is it a fact then,' she asked, wide-eyed, '*is* there someat as she could give to Charley?'

The old woman grinned, showing a brief sparkle of bright teeth. 'Wouldn't *you* like to know!' she chuckled, then turning way, added, 'Or mebbe it's the other sort you'm after ...!' Hunched over her precious weeds, she cackled cheerfully to herself, apparently oblivious to Meg's continued presence.

'You wasn't at the dedication then,' said Meg pleasantly, arms folded and not yet ready to leave. 'Squire had a lovely panel put up he did. Real bronze, cost a fortune folks reckon. . . .'

This time, the old woman didn't stand, but peered almost balefully over her shawled shoulder. 'Trust you to put a price on the dead, Meg Machin!' she croaked.

'There's some as can't even bring themselves to show even a mark of respect,' replied Meg pertly. 'Present company excepted, o'course. It was John Archer not being there, I meant . . .'

'At Borchester, wasn't he . . .' The old woman no longer looked towards Meg, but busied herself searching among the tangled plants. 'He'd his own to bury, not the Squire's.'

'Squire lost two sons,' Meg retorted sharply. 'There was ten names put up, all told. What did John Archer lose that was more important than them, folk from his own village, eh – I ask you!' One of the names had been a cousin to Meg, though never close; one way or another, all twelve names had been related to nearly everyone in the village, however slightly. John Archer had chosen not to be there, and for that, he wouldn't easily be forgiven, certainly not by the Machins.

'Mebbe he lost more'n you . . .' mumbled the old woman, and having apparently found what she was after, turned and walked with quick, bird-like movements, back to her tiny cottage. Mrs Machin watched her go, soothing her irritation with the thought that she'd made the old hag beat a retreat, at least. Blandly, she made her way to the moss-greened gate and out into the lane that would take her back into the village.

Inside the tiny scullery, Grannie Gabriel peered out from behind the curtain screening the pokey window, and watched Meg Machin out of sight. Then, satisfied, she moved into her warmly cluttered parlour and sat down firmly in the chair opposite her primly nervous visitor.

'Now then, Miss Betty Collins,' demanded the old woman, not unkindly, 'what's it you wants of me . . . ?'

Ted had made his way steadily down the flank of Heydon Berrow, carefully skirting the edge of the woods and keeping a sharp eye open for any traces of the fox he knew hunted there, when he first caught the smell of the cooking pot. The thin patches of evening fog hanging amongst the trees about the clearing hid the vardo at first, but drawn by the scent of the food, he soon saw the glimmer of a window and beyond it outside, the open fire itself. He paused, as the dog there gave its brisk warning; then her voice came, low and welcoming.

'Come close,' she said, 'the dog won't bite you!' And she laughed, a sound that welcomed and yet commanded Ted to come to her. A few paces more and he was by the fire; the cooking pot hung from its tripod set alongside the smokey flames, and in its simmer he glimpsed steamy portions of meat, jointed and gleaming richly. Emma crouched beyond the fire-glow, her eyes glittering with reflected embers, her shoulders wrapped for warmth but even then hinting at a nut-brown litheness that turned Ted's knees to water. Forcing himself to sound casual, he nodded towards the wagon, its door closed, but the glimmer of a lamp just visible through the net curtain at the windows.

'The old feller all right, is he?'

'Sleeping, now. He's ate already,' stated the soft-eyed girl. She indicated the box set close by the fire at her side. 'Been waiting for you to come, haven't I . . .'

Ted didn't sit at once, though he moved round so as to see her more clearly. His mind burned and flickered, like the fire-glow on her face; he should go on, checking his coverts, making sure Ernie Ashford wasn't out picking up enough game to pay for the fine he'd hope his Dad'd get away with . . .

'I only come by to see –' he started to explain, but her firm gesture checked him. Again she pointed to the makeshift seat.

'There's time enough to spare for Emma,' she ordered, then chuckled into his face as he sat sheepishly by her. 'Does a rachli frighten you . . .?'

'I shouldn't be here, by rights,' Ted evaded her question. 'I can't stay –'

For answer, she took up a sharpened hazel twig, deftly speared a portion of meat in the pot, and handed it to him with smiling eyes.

'I ask you to stay,' she said. 'Eat with me.' The look in her eyes held him, and would take no argument. Breaking their glance only long enough to take up her own piece of cooked flesh, she smiled upon his shyness but without spite or malice; almost in the same motion, her pretty teeth bit into the steaming meat, and murmured appreciatively that he should do likewise. As his strong jaws bit into the succulent flesh, he grunted with surprise; it was delicious with flavours he hadn't tasted before, but largely with a peppery strength that made him catch his breath. Emma laughed and chewed at the same time, reaching across to hand him a large stone jar.

'Ale,' she said. 'You'll need it.'

Swallowing, he nodded, and couldn't hold back a smile; then, thrusting the heel of the hazel skewer into the earth and thus suspending the piece of meat safely, he took up the jar and drank. Now he returned to the stewed hare, devouring it eagerly, savouring every last shred of flesh before throwing the bone, as Emma did, to the patiently waiting dog.

'Can I cook, gorgio man?'

'I never tasted anything so good in all my born days,' confessed Ted, amazed at his frankness. 'Beats even my Mam, that does – and she's the best there is.'

'There are no mothers here,' she teased. 'Take more.'

He needed asking only the once. Whether it was the ale, the spiced ardour of the food, the crackling warmth of the fire or simply Emma's embracing eyes, Ted felt a languor in his bones that he had never known before. Ted knew well enough about nature's ways, but his worldly experience went little further than fondling the shadowy form of some half-willing, giggling girl at the Harvest Home dance; an only partly achieved coupling that left him with a confused and furtively guilty memory, nothing more. But there was more knowledge in Emma's eyes than he would ever understand; instinctively he sensed that she would lead him, where he didn't care. There could be barely two years between them, if that, but she held all the secrets that would bring him into manhood and her arms, golden and glowing in the firelight. Her every movement told him that he had only to wait, and he would achieve paradise.

'What do they call ye, pretty lad,' Emma smiled, handing him her hazel twig to bring food to her gleaming lips.

'Ted,' he answered, eyes shining as her hands clasped about his, guiding the food to her luscious mouth. Still eating, she kept her hands on his, and he didn't pull away; as she ate the rich flesh, so her eyes ate up his soul, and he burned, helplessly.

At last she'd fed enough. Wiping her bare arm across her mouth, she then wiped her greasy fingers on the rough material of her skirt, showing a blood-racing glimpse of bare leg as she did so. Then gently, she took his hand, and laying it face upwards on her knees, fondled it with subtly exploring fingertips.

'How many years behind ye, Ted?' she murmured, for once not holding his eye with hers.

'Eighteen,' replied Ted quickly. 'Near enough.'

She looked at him through the sheeny veil of her long dark hair. 'A man, then.' His throat tightened, and involuntarily, his young but strong fingers clasped at her hand. She smiled, softly, but smoothed his palm open again with firm fingers, holding it so that the firelight threw the ingrained marking into stark relief. 'Shall I tell you what sort of a man you are, my dordi . . . ?'

The strange-tongued endearment melted him, and he slipped forward on to his knees, the better for her to study his hand, all the while groping for a coin from his trouser pocket. She realised, and laughing, shook her head, pushing the proffered coin aside.

'No, my Teddy-lad, no . . .'

'But . . . it's the custom, in't it?' he said weakly.

'Not between us, it in't. Now be still . . .'

At first he watched her worn but supple fingers as they slipped so gently upon his palm flesh; then his glance rose to study her face, and his heart lurched with dismay. Her face was bitter, almost close to tears, and for a second she closed those darkly glittering eyes, as though confronted with something unbearable. But then, in the moment that she turned to him and shook her hair back, her face was serene again, sweet as ever it was before, without even a shadow of sorrow.

'What's there?' asked Ted, hesitantly, wondering if what he had just glimpsed was simply a trick of firelight.

She looked down at the hand again, but he sensed she was no longer intent on seeing what was there as hiding what was in her mind. 'You have good health,' she continued, 'but no great wealth. There are young faces there, too . . .' A pause, and he could swear her voice darkened as her face had done, but she went on, 'You'll have good masters . . . and a happy home. It's a lucky hand, my Teddy . . .'

Her fingers were still now, neither holding nor rejecting his hand in hers. Gently, he took both her hands in his, and looked into her face, serious-eyed.

'It can't all be good,' he insisted, carefully.

She lowered her eyes, fractionally, then met his gaze boldly. 'There are two crossroads,' she replied. 'On one, you'll meet with violence, mebbe even death . . .' She squeezed his fingers reassuringly, as he tensed. 'Beware the ring of silver and you'll be safe,' she said.

'And the other crossroads –' demanded Ted. 'What's waiting for me there, Emma . . .?'

She gave no reply at first but let her eyes roam over the face before her with a deep, almost sensuous questioning. Flushed with wanting her, fire-glinted eyes brightly begging her, he had no way of knowing the bitter truth that promised to leave its scar on them both, whether or not she told of its eventual end. Then she let what-might-have-been well up and drown the darkness that threatened them, and smiled, slowly.

'Why, dordi,' she murmured softly, 'I am . . . me . . . your Emma . . .' And drawing him to her, she kissed him hungrily. . . .

'And how did the Squire enjoy his bloody service, then,' demanded John, setting the food down briskly on the table, and drawing his chair up, waited impatiently for Dan to finish drying his hands. Slogger Dan looked fed up, thought John wryly; how any man could stick the daily grind at Brookfield in this miserable weather, he didn't know.

'Looked like he was made of stone,' commented Dan, coming to table, trying to hide his surprise that John had done the laying of the table and the serving, for a rare change. 'There was a bugler,' he added as he took his first mouthful.

John shrugged. 'If he'd had his way, it'd been a state funeral, Brigade of Guards, the bloody lot!'

'The two boys meant that much to him, aye,' agreed Dan, calmly. 'He's a different man without them.'

'Well the bloody war's over now,' growled John, perkily. 'Everyone's buried the dead, twice over. It's just a memory.'

'It's not as easy as that, for some, John . . .'

'It is for me, mate,' John spoke between bites, ' – finished and done with. For good.'

'What're ye going to do now, then?' queried Dan, suspicious of this new, forceful John. When he got all of a bustle, John was usually up to something, and usually no good.

'Look for the silver lining, old son . . .' John's wicked glint brought Dan closer to the boil, but he was too tired to be drawn, tonight, John could see that. 'It's going to be a bitter cold winter, and that's a fact – so mebbe I'll find someat to warm me up a bit, eh?'

Dan finished eating before he answered, deliberately flat-voiced.

'She's gone to London,' he said.

John looked at him, blankly, then mumbled, 'Y'what?'

'Doris,' patiently explained his brother with a certain dour satisfaction. He'd only learned of it from Ted, coming away from the service, and it'd given him a jolt. Now John could have a taste, as well! 'Her ladyship's taken her up to London, to the town house. Ted didn't say how long for,' he added as an afterthought.

'London?' demanded John, unbelieving still.

'How many more times do I have to tell ye!' snapped Dan, irritated by his brother's thickness. 'London!'

John leaned back in his chair and laughed, a bold harsh guffaw that wasn't all amusement. Through half-closed eyes he saw Dan staring at him in amazement, and laughed all the harder before spluttering out the reason.

'One in the eye for you then, isn't it, old son!' His laugh died into a chuckle; Dan still didn't understand, so John went on to explain, sharp-eyed, 'Once she's been there, mate – d'y'reckon as she'll ever fancy a codged up place like this? Do ye?'

But Dan was not to be baited. He'd had his own bitter thoughts, a quiet despair at Doris leaving without so much as a blind word, not in writing nor as a message passed on through Ted. 'Who says she's coming back?' he growled, into his food. This took the smile from John's face, and Dan pushed home the point. 'It's the both of us she's put behind her, remember that.'

'She's never going to stay up there for good – ' John frowned, needled by Dan's counter, ' – is she?'

'Why not,' deliberated Dan. 'It's her ladyship that's took her to Chester Square. If she chooses to stay on up there, it's Doris's place to stay there with her, like that other one, Lily Summers. They got no option.'

John could see the situation clearly enough, but refused to see only the worst side of it. 'The Squire won't have it,' he insisted. 'His lady's place is down here, at the Hall. They'll be back,' he added confidently, 'well before Christmas if not sooner!'

'You know, do ye,' jibed Dan, darkly.

'It only stands to reason, mate,' John smiled, thinly. 'And anyway, it'll be an education for her, won't it . . .'

Dan stood, restless. 'She don't need it,' he grunted, but with the growing realisation that maybe John was right. A village girl in service at the Hall still kept her home ties with friend and family alike, and had no chance to give herself airs and graces above her station, certainly not in Ambridge. But Lily Summers had brought back tales, eagerly passed on by an envious Mary Ann Hudson, of how living below stairs in the big houses of London was more than a cut above the world of their country cousins. As things were, Doris was right for Brookfield, better than Dan deserved perhaps, but there was much that he could offer her; hard work and good harvests had made the farm into a holding to be proud of, and there were better days to come, Dan was sure of it. But London could make things very different; a girl with London ways could hardly be expected to look twice at a horny-handed farmer with mud on his boots.

'Mebbe not,' insisted John, leaning back comfortably to watch his brother suffer. 'But I still say it'll put the kibosh on you, Daniel my lad . . .'

'I don't see why,' Dan lied, pigheadedly.

'Society life,' explained John gleefully. 'It'll change her all right. She in't going to look twice at this place, for a start!'

'It's one of the best farms on Squire's land,' retorted Dan fiercely, ' – and it'll get better still!'

'It's muck,' stated John bluntly. 'If it was three hundred acres of your own, and if you were a gentleman – which you're not – she might let you hang your hat in her parlour then . . .' He laughed, cruelly. 'Might as well give up, old son . . .'

'Just 'cos you say so, d'y'reckon?' glared Dan, turning hard-faced to confront his sprawling brother.

'It's how you're made, Daniel. You're a feller that knows his place, a tenant for the rest of his life.' Slyly, John offered a straw of consolation. 'There's others who wouldn't say no to taking you on, y'know. Nora Machin for one . . . and Mary Ann Hudson, if you'd but look at her twice . . .' Nora Machin was nearly thirty, plain as an old broom and, as first house-maid, dedicated to serving the Lawson-Hopes if necessary for the rest of her born days, as a spinster. Mary Ann was a strong, jolly lass – but not for Brookfield. Dan saw his chance to strike back, and took it, astutely.

'Mary Ann's got her own ideas,' he said. 'About Walter, mostly. Or hadn't you noticed . . .'

'Y'don't fancy one that's been broken in then?' John sneered, but he had been stung; sitting bolt upright, he was rigid and tight-faced with anger.

'Not by you, tup,' grunted Dan insolently, and turned to poke the dying fire. John leaned forward, his savage smile aimed like a stab in the back.

'Not even if it was Doris . . . ?'

In the split second that Dan wheeled round on John, there was naked fury in his eyes. His grip on the poker was knuckle-white with tension, and John shifted his feet, ready to spring up and grapple for his life; but then Dan's jaw clamped tight, determined not to let John get the upper hand. 'You got no more chance with her than I have, boy!' he gritted fiercely, then added, even though saying it hurt him as much as he knew it would John, 'And if it's a man she wants, she in't going to take him from Borchester stews!'

John grinned, but his eyes were icy-cold.

'Y'reckon . . . ?' he asked lightly, his arrogantly thrusting head intended to taunt Dan as much as the sting in the words. But Dan had said his piece, and had bent back to the grate, rattling a small shower of glowing ash down into the pan below.

'We'll see about that,' muttered John. 'When she comes back, we'll see . . .'

'If she ever does,' was Dan's dour-faced reply. And gazing into the fire, both brothers fell silent.

Chapter Eight

THE HOUSE in Chester Square was altogether different, Dori[s]
decided. Not only was it tall and narrow and packed into [a]
whole terrace of similarly gracious dwellings, but the colou[r]
and style of its elegant interior were, to put it in a nutshel[l]
the spitting image of Lady Hester herself. Although the hous[e]
was narrow it was deep, but managed nevertheless to see[m]
clearly but softly lit even by day. By night, it glittered an[d]
glowed from candelabra, gaslight, and chandeliers, giving a[n]
even richer sense of well-being to the house. Each lofty, wel[l]
proportioned room had its pastel walls picked out with a con[-]
trasting colour for the elaborate mouldings and decorativ[e]
plasterwork, the fireplaces, burnished black, had graceful su[r]
rounds of cool white marble, fluted columns, intricately carve[d]
centre-pieces showing little naked cherubs mounted on ornate[ly]
frolicking sea-monsters – totally unlike the gaunt stone cano[-]
pies guarding the massive log fires of the Hall. There were n[o]
grim suits of armour here to clutter dark corners, no massivel[y]
framed portraits of unnamed ancestors hiding these delicatel[y]
tinted walls. The floors here were of parquet wood, richl[y]
polished, the carpets, like the furniture, graceful, and – accor[d]
ing to Lily, who knew it all – foreign. The bedrooms, an[d]
Lady Hester's especially, charmed the eye; the oyster and pin[k]
setting that was the master bedroom showed no sign at all [of]
the influence of the Squire; its draped bed, frilled pillowsli[ps]
and gilded wooden furniture echoed only Lady Hester's ex[-]
quisite taste, and its influence affected the whole brittle hous[e]
hold.

For this was the other great change that Doris found; th[e]
people. Though fewer in number than the staff at the Hall [it]

Ambridge, these faces were less kind, their voices less welcoming, their gestures more urgent; in all her brief stay, Doris was only to know one name to fit to a face other than Lily's, and that was Ethel, the first maid. With Lily more and more involved with tending the needs of Lady Hester, it was left to Ethel to show this handsome newcomer the ropes; she for one didn't laugh out loud at Doris's soft burr, having been born herself near Durham, and not afraid to use her native tongue below stairs. The butler-footman was virtually unapproachable; above stairs, among the gentry, he was the picture of polite dignity and a tyrant to the staff. Off-duty and below stairs, he was in complete subjection to the cook – who also happened to be his wife – a hawk-faced harridan whose tempers had drawn blood many a time before. Doris's chores largely kept her from the kitchen, and for this she was silently thankful. Almost the whole of the first day she had arrived was spent, apart from her work, in alternately losing and finding herself among the convoluted maze of rooms set about the graceful ascending spiral of the house's central staircase. Doris herself, of course, only had access by way of the cramped wooden corkscrew that passed as servants' stairs at the rear of the house; but moving along each landing, she couldn't help but let her eyes be drawn down to the hall below, or upward to the graceful oval skylight that topped the uppermost floor of all, with the slowly uncoiling wrought iron balustrade linking top to bottom. The sense of simple grandeur held her enthralled for moments on end; caught out by Ethel, she had blushed and laughed artlessly at her own sense of wonder.

'It's so grand, Ethel,' she said brightly, 'but I have to laugh when I think of my Dad's cottage ceilings!'

'Just the same with me, pet,' came the pert reply. 'Y'could put my old man and a hundred miners like him on that staircase, y'know?'

'Not if I have to clean up after them you won't!' laughed Doris, and went about her chores.

Ethel, a sturdy girl with thoughtful eyes and a brisk way of walking even short distances, had quite happily taken Doris under her wing; seeing so many echoes of herself when she had been first brought face to face with the great city, she quickly determined that Doris shouldn't be left to fend for herself, as she had been, five years previously.

'Haway, lass,' she giggled as they ate their evening meal with the silently gobbling scullerymaid as their sullen companion, 'ah'd never seen such a place . . .!' Ethel gestured around the vast kitchen, dominated on the one side by the great cast iron cooking range, and on the other by the wide arched sash window that separated the kitchen from the scullery; in comparison, the kitchen at the Hall was more like a farmhouse, with its natural stone walls, brick salt chamber, and smooth flagged floors. In the town house, the kitchen floor was oak parquet, scrubbed and spotless. 'All this was like a palace to me, y'know that?'

Doris nodded. Compact though the house was, tightly held in place by its elegant neighbours on either side, it nevertheless seemed to contain as many work rooms below stairs as the Hall in Ambridge; crossing the narrow basement area that acted as a dry moat separating the house from the pavement outside, Doris had been shown the spacious, brick-arched coal cellars, extending not merely under the pavement but several feet beneath the road itself. To her amazed eyes, they had seemed big enough to live in. Another wonder had been the dumb waiter, with its simple contraption design to raise food from the serving kitchen in the basement up to the discreet cupboard from which it was served to the magnificent dining room overlooking the square, with its tiny, immaculately kept gardens.

The scullerymaid, her meal finished, left the table with the barest of explanations. 'Going out,' she said, and left.

Ethel dropped her voice, watching the girl go up to her room at the top of the house by way of the servants' twisted stair. 'Courting night tonight,' she murmured with bright eyes, testing Doris's reaction to the thought of male involvement. 'A gunner in the artillery, comes all the way from Woolwich barracks!'

'Is that far from here?' asked Doris innocently.

'Miles, it is!' Ethel giggled wickedly. 'She has to make it worth his while, to keep the lad interested, I reckon!' She gave Doris a shrewd, twinkling stare. 'You've a lad or two back home, an't ye, I'll bet.'

Doris nodded, and blushed prettily. Ethel saw, and smiled broadly. 'Real courtin'?' she demanded, hopeful for details. She saw the moment of hesitation and she laid a hand on Doris's arm in a brisk, complimentary gesture. 'Tha's a clever one then. Good for you, lass.' She indicated upstairs with a nod of her head. 'Not like that Miss Summers, mind.'

Doris looked at her, wide-eyed. She had always thought of Lily Summers as one who kept herself to herself, a perfect lady without as yet a gentleman friend – to the knowledge of Ambridge, that is.

'Didn't ye know that, pet?' queried Ethel. 'It's Alfred – that new chauffeur laddie sleeps over the mews stable round the back, don't he.'

'They never have anything to do with each other back home,' said Doris, wonderingly. 'She'd hardly so much as pass the time of day . . .'

'They do better than that here, pet,' laughed Ethel. 'But they've a need to be careful, mind. The mistress'd be rid of both of 'em if she ever knew. Not like some, though.' And here she nodded, with the air of the worldly-wise. Then seeing the country girl's look of bewilderment, she patiently explained.

'The fast set,' she said, eyes gleaming brightly. 'Them that has their country weekends at Brighton – *they* don't care *what* goes on under their roof!'

Old Herbert accepted the jar of ale set down by him with a curt nod of thanks and an appreciative signal of smoke from his pipe.

'I thank ye, Daniel lad,' he said gruffly, and taking up the ale, supped it as a token. 'Your good health.'

'Yours too, Herbert,' acknowledged Dan, then with a nod across to the bar, 'Seth . . .'

There was a brief silence as each man paid his personal respects to the ale, before Seth Tibbs spoke up from behind the bar counter.

'Twenty horses under your bonnet,' he said thoughtfully. 'How would ye fancy that, Dan, eh?'

'It'll never happen,' growled Old Herbert. 'Never in a month o' Sundays!'

'It already has,' Seth countered with a rueful shake of his head. 'Saw it in the *Echo*, didn't I. Y'can't argue with that old feller ...'

The subject under discussion was motor tractors. Seth claimed that the Yanks were making them as strong as twenty horses, a fact that Old Herbert wouldn't tolerate.

'Twenty horses!' he said scornfully. 'You'm never going to get twenty blessed horses inside one o'them contraptions!'

'Don't be so blessed okkard, Herbert,' chuckled Dan. 'Jus cos you're not in favour don't mean it can't happen.'

'When was the best harvest we just had?' demanded the old man. 'Nineteen eighteen! Did motor tractors make that happen? No! It were God's good weather, men and real horses not they daft machines!'

'Aye,' agreed Dan. 'It was a fair old year, that. This las crop didn't turn over too bad either ...'

'Planting more acres for next year then, Dan?' suggested Seth. Many of the local farmers could see a grand future fo grain harvest. The demand was there, they said.

'No more'n last year, Seth,' Dan answered carefully. He ha a feeling in his bones that good things didn't always come i threes, good harvest weather least of all. 'Hay for wintering m stock's what I want,' he said, and drank.

'Sensible, that is,' croaked Old Herbert. 'Now young Walter he ain't bothered, the daft grummit. Seeded blessed near ever acre he got, and nothing down to pasture at all!'

'Can't feed stock on fresh air,' observed Seth wisely, wit the knowing look of a bar-room farmer.

'If he don't grow it, he'll have to buy it, won't he,' sug gested Dan.

'He'll come a purler if he ain't careful,' growled Old Herbert in a voice of doom. 'He don't deserve to keep stock if he don't intend to feed un!'

'He'll be all right with a good harvest, mind,' admitted Dan. 'A corn crop like last year, and he'll be able to buy feed *and* the steers to eat it.'

Walter was one for the easy life; beef cattle, no milking, and play the market as it came. Somehow, however, he never seemed to make the fortune he had planned. When that blazing summer of 1918 brought forth golden bushels of wheat, Walter had gone a burton on peas and beet. This year it had been potatoes and wheat, but the weather had rotted one and laid the other flat for being left too late.

'Tries to be too clever,' warned the old man through his haze of clinging smoke. 'Too clever by half . . .!'

'He manages, though,' admitted Seth.

'More be luck than judgement then,' came the tobacco-reeked reply. 'It's no wonder he can't keep help!'

'It's getting it, old feller, not just keeping it,' said Dan. 'A pound a week for the right man, but it ain't that easy . . .'

'What you wants, Dan,' said Seth knowingly, 'is some o' them pupils, living in.'

'Got to be as family, Seth,' Dan pointed out curtly. 'They an't be expected to fend for themselves, not on top of working. Wouldn't be right.'

'Ahrr,' nodded Old Herbert. 'That sort o'thing works fine if there's a wife or mother about.' He glanced at Dan shrewdly. 'Time you was thinking about getting wed, my young cocker, an't it.'

'Time enough for next year's harvest first,' murmured Dan into his ale as he supped up.

'A good wife *makes* a good harvest,' proclaimed the old man, who'd been a bachelor and a roadman most of his life. 'Have ye thought o'that?'

Dan looked at Old Herbert, and chuckled. 'Tell that to Grannie Gabriel, old feller!' he declared, and they all three laughed.

Walter's grandma had married a smallholder who ploughed a more fertile furrow on her than on his land; she borne sixteen babes, twelve of whom had lived into the teens, though only nine of them beyond that. Now, his parents passed on, only Walter and his grandmother remained in Ambridge; the rest had scattered on the wind, rootless and restless. Most folk agreed that it was in the blood; a few even went to far as to claim that Grannie Gabriel was diddikai half gyppo – which would explain a lot.

'Wife or no, a man needs help,' Seth announced. 'John shows no signs, do he?'

'Not a lot,' accepted Dan, without rancour.

Old Herbert nodded. 'Like a lot of lads come back from the war,' he said. 'It's a different world.'

'It in't good,' muttered the landlord, finishing off his nip of bitter, 'seeing too much of what's outside. Takes away a satisfaction, I reckon.'

'It's them bloody machines,' growled the old man. He had known men who couldn't afford a horse even, plough up the smallholding acre pulling the blade themselves, wife following after. But the horse was the one; faithful was the only word for it. Machines could never challenge that, but they could break men's hearts. 'Factories,' he went on bitterly. 'Monsters they are, taking good men off the soil that's bred and fed 'em for generations!'

'Trouble is, old feller,' commented Dan, 'they pays good money, and no lay-offs out of season. They sweat a man blind, though,' he added with a sad shake of the head.

'There's soldiering, mind,' suggested Seth. 'Bit of glory and a smart uniform for not much pay, but young Sam Fisher took it.'

'So would brother John again, if they'd have him,' Dan said confidently. It was all John wanted, Dan knew that; if he could re-enlist tomorrow, all the bitterness would be wiped away. But it was all lost to him now – the swank of uniform, the comradeship, the self-respect – what was left was second-hand hero's charity, and John deserved better than that.

'He knows damn well they won't,' commented Old Herbert drily. 'Ought to do what your Frank done, if he can't settle yere . . .'

'Where's Frank now, Dan?' queried Seth.

' 'Stralia,' grunted the burly farmer. 'Won't be staying there though, he don't reckon. Says it's too blessed hot.'

'Not thinking of signing on as an Anzac, is he?'

'Sheep's the thing out there, he says.' Dan looked thoughtful, remembering his father's rambling flock, not a quarter as big now. 'He always got on right with sheep, did our Frank . . .'

'Needs more'n sheep, these parts, lad,' croaked Old Herbert. 'You knows that, you'm wise to put your eggs in more'n one basket.' He rapped his pipe bowl on his heel. 'Keep clear o'they bloody machines, though!'

'Y'can't say as a steam thrasher don't do a good job, old feller. Quicker, an' all,' insisted Seth, hiding the smile that revealed he was baiting the old man, gently.

'Steam engines!' snorted Old Herbert. 'Gurt mucky things! Nothing to beat a sail driven binder, my lad, there weren't! And they'm still being used by fellers with brains!'

'When the wind blows, aye,' agreed Dan with a chuckle that Seth had succeeded in rousing a flush to the old man's cheek. 'But that's a machine, whatever drives it, in't it . . .'

'If Charley Roberts's mill and that sail binder can be drove b'the good grace o'heaven, why then good luck on 'em, says I,' the old man crowed. 'But they stinkin' petrol machines is someat different again! Gurt mangling noisy things . . . !'

The rest of his complaint was buried beneath an avalanche of rattling coughs, silenced only by a hearty swig of ale, and soothed by further aromatic puffs of smoke.

'Like it or not, old feller, they'll come, I reckon . . .' remarked Dan with a quiet resignation. 'That's progress for ye . . . for lack o' men, mebbe it'll needs must be machines.'

'Don't have to come any sooner'n us wanting it though,' decided Seth, clearing Dan's glass.

'Not for my part, no,' agreed Dan. 'It'll be a long day before I does without Jacko and Badger, or shires like 'em.'

'That's the ticket, Daniel lad!' boomed Old Herbert, raising his near empty jar in a fond toast to old times. 'Horses is God's own creatures, honest and true – and what man can say that about bloody engines! Eh?'

It was Ethel who insisted that they should take a ride on a motorbus.

'We've only got the afternoon, pet,' she protested, 'If you want to see Piccadilly *and* Buckingham Palace, we're going to have to shift!'

They had already walked past Eaton Place to the porticoed mansions of Belgrave Square; except for the occasional clatter of tradesmen's horsedrawn vans, a couple of stylish broughams, and one dignified taxicab, they had seen no traffic and barely any people.

'Where the nobs live,' grinned Ethel, perkily indicating the grand houses on right and left. 'The real nobs, I mean – aristocracy, lords and ladies.' Black-painted railings with gilded leafy points held riff-raff and casual passers-by at bay; at one entrance as they passed, the door was standing partly open, with a grave-faced footman receiving a fashionably-dressed lady visitor.

'Don't stare!' whispered Ethel, sweeping Doris quickly past, head slightly down, in a suitably modest scurry. 'They'll have a bobby on us, soon as look at us!'

But Doris couldn't help but cast her wondering eyes about her; the haughty grandeur of the fine houses became almost oppressive in its repetition, each one seemingly identical, only made different by the boldly scribed number on the portico pillar. The pavements and the roadways were immaculate here; it was as though all unseemly interference, including noise, had been banned by royal decree.

'They can't all be lords and ladies . . .?' Doris asked her sprightly friend.

'They're all of 'em posh, whatever!' exclaimed Ethel, adding

108

teasingly, 'Mind you, they let barons live here as well . . .'
Doris was too wide-eyed to even smile.

Suddenly, coming out of Grosvenor Crescent, they were
within sight and sound of Hyde Park Corner, and in a new
world of rush and bustle, noise and confusion. Left behind
were the tranquil pavements of Belgravia; for a shrinking
moment, Doris felt she was back on that shrieking platform at
Paddington, and she stopped in her tracks. Ethel looked at her
face and laughed, then catching her arm, pulled her into a run.

'We've got to cross over, just up here,' she cried. 'That's
where we catch the bus.'

Clutching her hat, Doris ran, trying not to see the welter of
people and vehicles all around. At the edge of the pavement,
Ethel checked, looking for the chance to scamper bravely to
the other distant side of the road.

'Now, pet,' she stated firmly, gripping Doris's limp hand,
'When I pull, you run, right?' She gave Doris a cheeky, reassuring grin. 'Close your eyes, pet, if y'like. Y're safe enough
wi' me holding on to ye !'

Doris didn't answer, but nodded in mute, petrified agreement. Like Ethel, she gawked her head to scan the oncoming
traffic, tensely biting her underlip; the flood of horsedrawn
wagons, motorvans, cars and buses raced at and past them
without pause, there seemed no end to the deluge. Suddenly
the curt pull came, catching Doris off guard and yanking her
forward half off-balance, only to pull her to an abrupt and
breath-taking stop in the middle of the roadway. The peril
was twice as terrifying now, with hooves, wheels and engines
crowding at them from both directions, a crushing waterfall of
constant sound. A taxi blared its horn, not at the girls but at
a handcart of fresh fruit being wheeled suicidally across without pause for safety; the casual daredevil at its handles shouted
back a cheerful rhetoric the exact wording of which was for-
tunately submerged from Doris's ears by the almost physical
shudder of traffic sound.

'Now !' shouted Ethel, and pulled hard again, timing her
breathless rush to perfection. 'There !' she exclaimed, confront-

ing Doris with excited eyes, 'I said we'd be safe, didn't I!'

Doris had no time to draw breath, let alone discuss the affair for, with a small whoop of alarm, Ethel drew her hurriedly to where a motorbus was coming to a halt. Almost unaware of the details of what was happening, Doris found herself cheerfully bullied into clambering aboard the harshly vibrating vehicle, with Ethel's firm hand on her arm, guiding her into sitting on the postured curve of the wooden slatted seats, close by a grimy window. With a roar and a judder, the motorbus went on its way, transporting Doris through a sea of vehicles filling the mighty thoroughfare ahead; Ethel, gay with vicarious delight at pleasing her country cousin, wriggled cheerfully with nudging elbows.

'Piccadilly!' she cried, indicating the street along which they were driving. 'What d'y'reckon on that, eh?'

Doris looked from Ethel's bright face to the dingy yet brutal river of life roaring and threatening outside; she had never seen so many in a crowd before, hustling and shoving yet with hardly a flicker of feeling on their haunted, pallid faces. The 'ping' of the conductor's ticket punch drew her face inward as Ethel paid their fare; now she was aware of the stuffiness of the air, the heavy smell of damp-coated, herded animals, the coughs and snuffles of November sickness, all about her. A small wave of nausea come over her, and hand to mouth, she held her breath. Recovering slightly, she touched Ethel's arm with a silent, gentle plea; but her guide was carried away with the sights she was describing so pungently to her innocent, wide-eyed companion.

'That's the Royal Academy, pet!' she squealed, and the words were followed by a merry nudge, 'where the artists go . . .!'

'Ethel,' murmured Doris plaintively, 'I feel sick.'

The quiet, apologetic words were nearly lost in the harsh scrape of the braking motorbus, but the picture that Doris' miserable face presented needed no explanations.

'Oh, pet,' said Ethel, her eyes full of understanding, 'this isn't the place for you, is it . . .' She stood up to pull the sag ging cord above her head, and helped the pallid girl to her feet, swaying with the uneasy motion of the motorbus, as the responding bell rang in the driver's cab. 'Let's get away off of it, come on . . .'

Doris could only nod; words were impossible now. Ethel looked at her soft eyes, and gave a gentle, fond smile that promised safety and protection.

'Haway, but I should've realised,' she said, brightly. 'Home's the best place for you right now, in't it, pet . . .'

It was all that Doris could do not to burst into tears.

Chapter Nine

CROP IN hand, holding Trumper on a tight, almost viciously corrective rein, Squire Lawson-Hope wheeled his nervously treading mount past the dapper figure looking up at him with hat in hand, and gave his decision with an arid finality.

'Do what you think's best, man!' he exclaimed sharply, turning the restless horse towards the stableyard gate. 'Don't bother me with stupid trifles!'

With that, he gave Trumper his head and cantered briskly out across the parkland and his favourite ride over Blossom Hill. Left standing in the small shower of fine gravel thrown up by the horse's hooves, Alexander Wickham held his curl-brimmed derby to his head in formal salute, then tapped it into place more firmly as his master rode out of sight. His lean thinly moustached face gave no indication at all of the thought racing through his mind, but he was far from calm. As the Squire's agent, it was his job to advise his master on the day-to-day management of the estate, and see to its efficient running; it was a task he took great pride in – or had done, until these past two seasons. Now, more and more, he was being expected not so much to give advice as to make the decision which by rights should be made by the Squire alone. He was all too well aware that should his actions result in unfavourable consequences, the responsibility would be lumped on to his Norfolk-suited shoulders, right or wrong, and he was distinctly uncomfortable at the thought.

'No great change from the Squire this morning, Mister Wickham,' growled a familiar voice behind him, and he turned to find the head keeper moving to his shoulder, amiably grinning, his stocky gundog close at heel.

'No change at all, Mr Nugent,' answered Wickham drily. 'Y've spoken with him yourself, have you?'

'Tried to,' was the blunt response.

'With what effect?'

'See to it meself,' said Nugent, making it clear that it hadn't been the answer he had wanted. 'That's all he tells me. Just can't be bothered . . .'

'He has his reasons . . .' the agent said carefully.

'Aye, mebbe,' retorted Nugent, too honest to be polite. 'But life's for living, says I. He can't go wearing a blessed black band on his arm for the rest of his days – it's not natural!'

Wickham shook his head, thoughtfully. 'That side of things is over and done,' he said, crisply. 'There'll be no more grieving.'

'What's he up to then?' growled the burly keeper. 'Why don't he give us some straight answers to honest questions? That's all that's needed . . .'

'Because nothing matters any more,' said Wickham.

Nugent frowned, at first saying nothing; he could understand the desperate sense of loss for he, like most men of his age, had seen many dear ones taken, young and old. His own Martha, wasted and spindle-thin at forty, had seen happy release in death; even now he talked to her tremulous face, smiling at him from the glowing coals he sat by, deep into the night. There was no pain in that quiet communion now, only the fondness of shared memories, a burden no longer. Death was a fact, but life went on, that's all there was to it.

'He's got a grand estate, a fine lady, and a handsome lad,' Nugent commented drily. 'I reckon I could bear the misery, for that.'

'Not if you'd lost the cream of your line,' suggested Wickham with sensitive precision. 'Mr Harry was special. Nothing else like him in the Squire's life, not even Mr Andrew. . . .'

'Master Anthony's all right,' insisted the keeper. 'He knows what's what. He'll do.'

Wickham nodded. It was a fact that, for his years, Anthony had an unusual grasp of the broad pattern of the estate's affairs, though possibly with rather too much consideration for the rights of his tenants. In his own quiet way he was already making contact with his people, much as his father had done in the old days. But charm wasn't authority, and that's what was needed in these troubled times.

'It'll all be his, one day,' agreed the dapper agent, checking his watch against the stable clock, then winding it, unnecessarily. 'But he isn't the master yet. . . .'

'Mebbe not in our time, either,' commented the burly keeper. 'So it's left to us.'

'It's where our duty lies,' declared Wickham with urbane resignation; he was aware of Nugent studying him with shrewd eyes, silently marking him as the Squire's man, come what may.

'It's what we're paid to do, y'mean,' murmured Nugent.

The normally suave agent prickled defensively. 'I hope there's more to it than that,' he said stiffly, making a small adjustment to the set of his derby on his head. 'There's such a thing as loyalty . . . pride. . . .' There was more to it than that, of course, much more than he would ever admit to Nugent who, after all, represented only a part of Wickham's overall charge. Whether it was the physical elegance of the open parkland, the neat and fruitful cropping of the tenant farms, or the more sociably pleasant sporting accomplishments of the estate, each item of activity, even reduced as it eventually must be to an entry in the great leather-bound accounts book that Wickham kept so meticulously, provided a source of deep personal achievement to the otherwise passionless agent. Where some men – even George Nugent – might have allowed themselves to use terms of affection regarding their conditions of service, Alexander Wickham's objective assessment of his own feelings would have used the word *goodwill,* and nothing more. His emotions, however outwardly cold, nevertheless ran deep; Nugent, aware of this, was quick to smooth the hackles of self-justification implied by Wickham's stumbling outburst.

'It takes some folk different ways,' grunted the keeper. 'Like Willie Ashford, now. He's got more'n a fondness for poaching . . .' Nugent grinned, good-humouredly, '. . .but that don't stop him admitting he takes a good living from it!'

Meeting his shrewd, honest eyes, Wickham accepted the shift of ground, and even allowed himself a brief smile.

'The Forrest boy managed to catch the rascal out, I hear . . .' he said with quiet relish.

'He's learning, is Ted,' confirmed the keeper, smug that perhaps his greatest local enemy would shortly be spending valuable hunting days behind bars. 'We'll make a keeper of him yet, I reckon . . .'

'You've informed Mr Lawson-Hope, of course.'

'I did. Took it very offhand, though,' grumbled Nugent. 'Just said as to keep a weather eye open for any tricks young Ernie might get up' to – not even 'Well Done' for young Edward . . .'

'I'll try and mention it to him myself,' suggested Wickham, making a mental note that a golden guinea at Christmas might not be out of place for Ted. It was a gesture, thought the trimly hatted agent with quiet satisfaction, that would have been typical of the Squire himself in better times; tipping his hat good-day to Nugent, he allowed himself one further smile before walking briskly out of the stable yard.

'Now you just look here, John me old pal . . .' protested Walter over the steady trip-trap of Pippit's hooves, 'it were your own blessed fault, admit it!'

'You didn't have to be so bloody sharp, did you?' demanded John, then laughed, much to Walter's relief. 'She was ripe for a tumble, an' all . . .'

'Ah,' agreed Pippit's driver, but wisely refrained from elaborating on the outcome of Mary Ann's desires on the evening after the football match. Besides, there'd been more than one meeting since then that John wouldn't know about.

'Mind you,' boasted his spruce companion, 'I looked up Polly Harper, so you can't say I did so badly for myself, eh mate!' It went without saying that any young man fortunate enough to discover pretty Polly alone in her untidy little room of a Saturday evening wouldn't go short of a welcome, particularly if he was knowingly armed – as John had certainly been – with half a bottle of gin.

'Doh, but her's a comforting sort o'wench!' exclaimed Walter with feeling, and chuckled meaningly; he knew her little room and its many tawdry keepsakes almost as well as John did. Where Polly and her favours were concerned, there were no rivals, only friends, companions of honour, a lusty brotherhood of the bed.

John was on his way to Borchester now, and in cadging a ride with Walter on his daily trip in with the churns of milk from Brookfield, the Pounds, and Robin Farm, he had wordlessly declared a truce to the ill-feeling hovering between himself and Walter over the jolly kitchenmaid. Walter had been glad of this, for he was fond of John as he would be of any comrade in arms; but he asked no more questions for his eyes were keenly set on the road ahead, looking not for obstacles or oncoming traffic so much as a solitary figure standing at the road-side.

'There he is,' said John, who'd been told of what was to happen almost as soon as leaving Brookfield, and was equally on the look-out. 'Ease up, pal . . .'

Out of nowhere, the stocky, shambling figure of Ernie Ashford stepped forward to the verge of the road; in one hand he carried a wicker hamper, its broken catch tied up with binder twine. The float stopped and the hamper was quickly loaded into the space beneath John's legs, as Ernie muttered quick, urgent instructions.

'Two and six the cocks, two bob the hens. There's half dozen of each. Good on ye, Walter . . .' With that, Willie Ashford's hard-working lad melted into the hedgerow from which he'd come, and Walter flicked the reins on to Pippit's sack-covered back to get her on the move again.

'Pity the old feller got nabbed,' said John.

'Three months, they reckon,' nodded Walter. 'Ernie's got to keep hisself though, just like the rest of us, an't he . . .'

John chuckled. Walter's milk float into Borchester would be

the last place Constable Jim Gregory would expect to find
Ernie Ashford's weekly catch of birds. By putting Willie out
of action, George Nugent probably thought he'd put the
kibosh on his trade with the Borchester dealer who was
Willie's market; the word would've gone out to keep an eye
on Ernie, and if he'd dared cart the catch in himself, he'd've
been nabbed, sure as sure. For his good turn, Walter would be
paid in kind, no doubt; it also meant that Ernie wouldn't be
forced into bad company by having to seek honest and regular
employment. It was up to Willie's lad to keep the flag flying
for the old film, for the old man wouldn't be let out now before
the season ended, and if the supply stopped, then regular
customers would surely look elsewhere, particularly with
Christmas coming on.

'Ernie'll manage,' John retorted.

'If he don't get catched hisself first,' observed Walter with a
wry shake of the head. 'He knows the trade right enough, but
it's his Dad what's the real brains. Got the pair on 'em out of
many a scrape, has Willie.'

'It's up to Ernie to watch out then, in't it, mate,' muttered
John realistically, 'or George Nugent'll have him, sure as eggs
is eggs!'

They were past the Lodge and the great iron gates that
stood forever open on the drive leading to Arkwright Hall, and
the mellow brick wall set all about the perimeter of the parkland ran endlessly along their left-hand side; beyond the wall,
woodland and field rose upward to the distant slopes of
Blossom Hill, barely visible through the early morning
November mist.

'Sounds like the Squire, the old devil,' observed John, a
pull of malice at his mouth. He had heard the sound of horse's
hoof-beats through the mist; but as he and Walter looked
across the wall to see, it wasn't Trumper bearing the familiar,
ramrod-backed figure across the turf, but the sturdier dappled
roan that was Master Anthony's own mount, that came briefly
into view. For a moment, horse and rider stood poised above
the milk float, heading the other way along the road; the

young rider, seeing them, gave a curt but friendly wave, then galloped down the slope of the field towards the Lodge and beyond that, the village. Walter noted the rider with a wave of his frayed old whip, then turned to face the road ahead.

'You'm wrong then, John,' he said. 'Master Anthony, that was . . . out early, in't he?'

He turned to glance at John, and was surprised to see him sitting bolt upright, with a sharp, calculating cast to his face. In the same moment, John's hand gripped Walter's forearm, fiercely.

'Stop her, Walter! Pull up – here!'

Almost instinctively, Walter did so; even before the float had grated to a halt, John had leapt off and landed nimbly on his toes on the dew-heavy grass of the roadside verge.

'By golly – what's the matter, John?' cried Walter, more than a little alarmed by the bold, almost fearsome expression on his friend's previously relaxed face.

'I'm going back, old son,' said John.

'Hey . . .?' queried Walter, baffled by this sudden change of plan. 'What for?'

'Young Anthony's back, isn't he,' declared John, eyes gleaming. 'That means so's his old woman . . .'

Walter stared at him, uncomprehending. 'I dunno for the life o'me what you'm on about,' he grumbled. 'What's them being home got to do with you . . .?'

'If they're back in Ambridge,' said John, wicked-eyed, 'then so's Doris – and I've got words to say to her!'

Dan had just finished putting the two shires into plough harness, when first the clack of hooves on the cobbled yard, and then Badger blowing a hoarse whinny brought his head up to see Master Anthony, mounted, walking his roan towards him. Dan straightened, a broad smile of welcome on his face.

'Morning, Master Anthony.'

'Morning, Daniel. Ploughing, then, are you?'

'I shall be, ah.'

'Sticky weather for it.'

'South field's middling light, though. And it's the last,' Dan added, feeling rather pleased. 'It'll be a job well done. . .'

'Good work.' The young rider's gentle eyes looked all about, keenly but not snooping. 'Wickham tells me you've calved down well. . .'

'Not done so badly, no. There's a couple yet to come mind, and one of 'em's Dolly – '

'Usually have trouble with her, don't you,' observed Anthony with a nod. 'Will she be all right?'

The flicker of pleased surprise must have shown clearly on Dan's face, for Anthony laughed. 'You remember her, then?' smiled Dan.

'It was five years ago,' Anthony reminded him, lightly.

The memory came back fresh as ever; Mr Wickham had arrived to look over the condition of the roof of the hay barn, just as Dan had checked Dolly and found she'd come to the 'softening of the bones'. Her time due, she'd have need of all the help that Dan and his father could give, and it'd been left to Dan's aproned mother to walk at Mr Wickham's elbow round the barns. The knickerbockered boy who'd travelled over with the Squire's agent had followed Dan and his father into the byre, there to witness Dolly's strenuous and anguished attempts to drop her calf. The event itself, so simple yet so brutally intimate, had kept the shy young visitor backed into the shadows, tense and wide-eyed. Awkward as ever, Dolly had risen to the occasion by making it twins. Afterwards, it was Dan who'd discovered the half-concealed onlooker and brought him forward to view and admire the latest additions to the Brookfield herd. Since then, each year had promised trouble but somehow Dolly had come through with flying colours and produced a fine youngster each time without fail.

'She's never had twins since,' smiled Dan. 'But it's someat you remembering that . . .'

The lightness in Anthony's face faded into shadow, and his mouth tightened slightly. 'The war hadn't long begun,' he said, deliberately without emotion. There was a pause as both their faces grew serious, fighting back old memories, keeping the past at bay.

'That's a fact,' agreed Dan soberly. He shook his head, wondering at the bright slogans of those far-off days. 'Calves was more important then than anything, weren't they.'

'They still are,' replied Anthony, crisply. 'That much hasn't changed.'

'Nor the land, neither,' affirmed Dan. He met the young master's steady glance with a quiet confidence that gave as well as demanded respect. 'Buildings aren't so fortunate though, as Mr Wickham knows. Time tells, there. . . .'

Dan had no need to point out the handful of missing roof-tiles over the stable block; he'd already noted Anthony's enquiring glance there and seen the fault register. It wasn't a question of asking for special consideration, even; the estate had a duty to its tenants, and outside repairs such as that were a matter of right. But the crux of the matter was the Squire himself as everyone well knew; without his consent, nothing could be done. If nothing was done, the damage could only get worse and in due course of time not only the fabric of the building, but the tenant himself was affected. Nowadays, the complaint had to be constant and the need almost desperate; even then, a patch job by the estate handyman was the most that could be expected. Years back, every property had been kept in fair condition without need of so much as a whisper of asking. It was a different story now and not likely to get better, and though this youngster could do little if anything to help, it was as well that he should know how the matter stood.

'You keep a good farm, Daniel,' responded the young rider, his roan shifting restlessly. 'But there are others whose need is greater. . . .'

'Granted,' said Dan. No need to be reminded of worker tenants on the estate with damp walls caused by crumbling mortar, or untreated woodwork slowly rotting. Here was the nub of John's perpetual jibe; a tenant was at the mercy of his landlord, rent paid or no. To some, like Walter for instance, there was no point in taking pride in making things good themselves, however necessary; there'd be no appreciation, and what was done would never be their own, anyroad. Best leave it, and make do.

'Be patient,' smiled Anthony. 'It won't count against you. . .' His horse skittered edgily, sideways towards the open gate; Dan followed, polite but casual.

'My pleasure to see you here again,' he said.

'When's Dolly due to calve,' queried Anthony, curbing his animal with surprising control for his slight frame, '. . . perhaps I can bring her luck again!'

Dan gave a slow, warm smile. 'She was late to the bull this year. Mebbe not until after Boxing Day before she drops it,' he replied.

'We're at home 'til the New Year at least,' nodded Anthony. 'I'll call by again . . .' He raised his crop in a brief salute, and rode out at a trot. 'Good day to you!'

'And to you . . .' Dan replied. It was only then that he realised the full implication of Master Anthony having visited Brookfield. The Lawson-Hopes were back in Ambridge, and with them, Doris.

Chapter Ten

There was nothing else for it but to wait. When John, standing at the roadside watching Walter drive on towards Borchester, had set his own face back along the road into the village, he'd had no plans in his head, only a smouldering excitement. But the road had taken him past the gates of Arkwright Hall and its lodge, and here he had paused, forced to think what next to do. Somehow, he had to see Doris face to face, and soon; but what he hadn't considered, in that impulsive leap from Walter's milk cart, was just where he would find her. She might be at her parents' home at Riverbank Farm, or, more likely, working at the Hall. He'd be welcome at neither place, he knew that for sure, but it wasn't a hardship; it was Doris alone he wanted to see, not amongst friends, relatives, or even strangers. The solution seemed simple : come upon her making her way to or from the Hall, something she was bound to do, either to visit her home or shop in the village. It didn't enter his mind that even if she did come by, she might have a companion walking with her such as Betty Collins or Mary Ann Hudson; nor that she might not be due for her weekly half-day off until the end of the week. The obsession had lodged itself, burning, in his brain – and there it stayed, like a swarm of bees fixed unchanging on its queen.

He had waited for an hour longer, shivering in the damp November air, coat collar rucked up and his hands stuffed deep into his trouser pockets, before finally deciding to make the bold move; he would walk to the Hall kitchens, find Mary Ann, and sweet-talk her into letting him know what was on. The risks of being met and being run off by Merrick, or one of the grooms, were swept aside by the rage swirling around his brain; even the thought of Mrs Prentiss could not deter him. What he wanted was simple enough; to see his girl, his pal. Anything less, and he'd create bloody murder!

It was only when he'd started on his way up the long, tree-lined carriageway towards the Hall, that the idea struck him that he was making a fool of himself. Up until now he'd only ever taken girls of his fancy, those who could meet the challenge in his eyes with a bold mouth and a willing body. Doris was different; wanting her because she wasn't like the others, wasn't going to make her melt to his touch like they had. She had to be courted, not taken wildly like a mare being covered by the stallion. But she fancied him, he thought to himself cockily, and the thought brought a tight, arrogant smile to his handsome face. You didn't put a bull in with heifers just to eat the grass. She'd know what he wanted, and she'd grant it, given the chance; but there had to be a beginning, if he was to score at all.

His walk became swankier, his stride longer, as he reckoned his chances against Dan's; it'd take Slogger Dan a month of Sundays just to hold a wench's hand, let alone give her a peck goodnight! He chuckled out loud at the sullen anger in his brother's face when John had played the gentleman and lifted Doris nimbly up on to the Brookfield wagon; but the very same thought dispersed the sour amusement with the memory of the firm, trim waist, so lithe and fetching beneath his horny hands. In that brief second, he'd instinctively sensed her animal awareness of his touch; it had gone to his head then, and he had lost his chance with Mary Ann, but even Polly had wondered at his brutal, insistent coupling all that night. It had been a storm in the blood made all the more furious by the fact that Polly's pliant white body wasn't Doris's, that her kisses weren't sincere but all too knowing, that her crooning voice was chanting the same words that any bloke that bought her bed would hear, sodden with fondness and stale gin. Grinning to himself, he tried to picture how it might have been, had it been Doris beneath him and not Polly. Then in the same instant, his manhood crumbled; a cruel hand gripped his guts, and he almost turned and ran. Walking briskly round the bend in the drive towards him, a covered basket on her arm, came Doris . . . and seeing him, she smiled.

'Hello, John,' she said, simply. 'Of all places to see you. . . .'

Quick as a flash, the answer to her unspoken question slipped to his tongue as he tipped his cap in greeting.

'Morning, Doris. Going to see the Squire, an't I . . .' There was no shoot today, he knew that from Walter; the chances were the old devil'd be out pushing his great horse over ditch and fence, just for the hell of it. 'Got to make my peace with him, y'see,' he explained, head tilted nobly, eyes serious.

'I'd wish you luck, but he isn't in, John,' said Doris. 'To be truthful,' she added soberly, 'I don't reckon you'd be very welcome anyway. . . .'

John looked down, his toe grinding into the gravel, his voice subdued. 'Mebbe it's for the best, then.' Then his eyes flooded with welcome, bright teeth gleaming with that winning smile. 'Seen you, though, haven't I. That makes up for it.'

She had to laugh, in spite of herself. Her first reaction on seeing his jaunty figure striding towards her had been to turn and go back. But her sudden breathlessness had been swept aside, first by the selfless daring of John's declared purpose, and then by his typically bold compliment. Brash he might be, but she couldn't bring herself to dislike him just on that score.

'I'm off home,' she said pleasantly, 'but I've to be back at the Hall by luncheon. . . .' It wasn't proper that she should ask him to walk with her, but as he wasn't going to visit the Squire after all, there was only one way for him to travel if he was going to the village. For a moment, she wondered if he was going to make his own lonely way home, past Hollowtree and Midsummer Meadow; then he smiled and put his hand on the handle of her basket.

'I'm going that way,' he smiled. 'I'll carry this, for a start.' She let him take the basket from her; as he caught the quick look of gratitude that gleamed at him from those soft grey eyes, his throat tightened. 'Presents from London?' he asked brightly, walking by her side towards the great gates, the basket carried between them.

'London!' snorted Doris, with a peevish grin.

'You don't mean to say y'didn't like it?' exclaimed John. 'Greatest city in the world, is London!'

'Never!' countered Doris, laughing. 'It's the muckiest, noisiest, wickedest place I've ever been to in all my born days! It's never the place for me, no, never. . . .'

'Sounds like you had a bad time of it,' grinned John. 'Probably 'cos you went there with the wrong people, y'see. . . .'

'There was nobody I knew to talk to,' she admitted, not properly taking the point John wanted to make. 'Miss Summers was too busy with her ladyship, and there was only Ethel – ' Doris smiled at the memory of the Durham girl. 'She was a poppet, really kind to me, she was. . . .'

'Should've gone there with me,' offered John valiantly. 'I'd've shown you the sights.'

'Ethel did,' said Doris, innocently ignoring the light-hearted invitation. 'And I was sick. On the bus . . .' She laughed gaily. 'It weren't much fun for her, neither!'

'Y'saw Buckingham Palace, though?' demanded John.

Doris shook her head. John changed hands to carry the basket; his right arm brushed lightly and innocently against Doris's left, but his face was turned to her in amused indignation, and she was caught up in his eyes.

'Piccadilly – you must've seen Piccadilly Circus!'

'We never got there,' Doris confessed, and then laughed again. 'I was too poorly, I can tell you. . . .'

'Shame,' said John softly, and slipped his arm about Doris's waist.

She had taken several paces, heart pumping, before her mind cleared enough to tell her what to do. She stopped, and turned to him, her face firm and gently reproving. He matched her movement, but his hand was now set boldly in the small of her back. She reached behind her to pull his hand away, but John subtly shifted his feet so that she found herself even closer to him, breathing her protest almost into his face.

'John . . .' she murmured warningly. 'Now don't – '

'I'm glad you come back,' he said, and pulling her close, kissed her long and passionately, full on the mouth. Her hands beat flutteringly against his shoulders, but it was long seconds before she forced herself to pull her face from him, in a breathless gasp.

'John . . . no . . .!' she breathed, almost plaintively; but now when he put his lips to hers, the delicious confusion that flooded through her on the instant threatened to sweep away any resistance that she might have shown. This kiss was brief, broken by his groan of desperation.

'Doris . . . for God's sake, girl . . .!'

She was aware of hooded eyes set devouringly on her mouth, the tender fire of his breath against her own flushed skin, the touch of his hands, and his parted lips on hers – and the sudden muffled smash of wrapped crockery. A surge of furious despair raged through her, and she tore herself free. The basket that John had let fall when he had grabbed at her so hungrily, lay at their feet in the open road. Thrusting him away with surprising strength, she crouched and pulled back the covering cloth; inside the basket were various knick-knacks, some prettily wrapped, but she was searching only for one object. It came out in pieces, a cheap, coarsely painted china figure, elegant in a slip-moulded crinoline. The head was hopelessly fragmented; Doris gazed from it up into John's confounded face, her eyes ablaze, cheeks flushed with anger now, not pleasure. She stood abruptly, and wisely, he retreated.

'Great clumsy lummock!' she shrilled, close to tears. 'Get away from me! Go on!'

'It's only crock, isn't it?' he retorted. 'I'll pay for it – ' He reached out for her, soothingly. 'Don't be upset, chuck . . .' The fond gesture faltered and was lost in mid-air; it was all too obvious that Doris wouldn't be that easily placated, if at all.

'It was for my Mam!' she flared. 'From London!' Her face began to crumple into misery, as she looked at the fragments in her hand. 'Smashed it to bits, you have . . . now what'll I say to her. . . .'

'I can get someat else – from Borchester market,' he said eagerly, moving towards her, arms open to comfort her. 'She won't know the difference, love . . . be honest . . .'

It was too much. With a tight little cry of anger, Doris flung the broken pieces straight into his face; more by luck than judgement, the biggest piece – the clumsily frilled skirt – slashed his cheek bone with its broken edge. He stepped back, stunned by the sheer intensity of her rage, and wiped his wrist against the stinging flesh; seeing blood smeared there, his own anger billowed up, but somehow he said nothing. Standing there, white-faced and glowering, he watched silently as she swiftly gathered up the basket. Without another word or even so much as a sidelong glance at him, she turned away and stalked off down the road towards Ambridge village. Non-plussed, John stood for a moment watching her pert figure disappear round the bend in the road. Then, desperate to release his pent-up anger, he saw a chunk of the smashed crock figure lying on the road's surface close by, and lashed out at it with a vicious kick. Splintering, it broke in all directions; he gave a grunt of bitter satisfaction, as he bent to dust the powdered china clay from his gleaming boot – then cursed pungently. The brittle crock had broken easily enough, but its pointed shards had torn a great welt across the once-perfect, polished surface. He crouched, studying the damaged boot with burning eyes, mind bitter with frustration. It was a scar that wouldn't easily be repaired.

The wizened-faced old man sat huddled close by the open fire seemed not to hear Ted's casual approach at first; then he looked up, his narrow eyes squinting into an even tighter line that nevertheless still showed a beady blackness of distrust. Ted came to an easy halt, some steps away from the softly smoking fire; he carried nothing but his gnarled thumb-stick, and his dog had carefully been left behind this once, for he wasn't a keeper checking his woods but a young man visiting.

'Good day, gaffer,' he said pleasantly. The jukel crouched beneath the wagon gave a small growl, but made no move; it was getting to know that this particular caller wasn't unwelcome, but the old man's reaction kept it partly on its guard. Ted sauntered forward, his keen eye searching for signs of Emma; the vardo was the same, no doubt of that, but where was she?

'You're on your feet at last then,' Ted declared with a cheerful nod.

The old man said nothing; the grimy clay pipe simmered a drift of smoke, its stem clamped tight between his silver-stubbled jaws, and he regarded the sturdy youth impassively, almost as though his silence alone would drive the intruder away. But knowing animals had taught Ted something of the art of waiting, and there were few men of his young years that could match his bright patience.

'Emma about?' His murmured question drifted across the smoke of fire and pipe, and at last the old man stirred. A muffled cough heaved in his choker-wrapped chest, and taking the clay stem from his lips, he spat, curtly, into the smouldering wood of the fire at his feet. He stood, stiffly and slowly, legs slightly bowed, head cocked towards the vardo door, and called out in a high, cracked voice as he crabbed forward to the wagon steps.

'Emm! Gorgio!' As he started to haul himself up the worn wooden steps into the vardo, its door opened from the inside, silent and mysterious, by someone yet unseen. It wasn't until the old man had vanished inside, that Emma came into view; she stood for a moment, framed in the doorway and smiling down at Ted, before shutting the door firmly behind her and skipping down towards him.

'Emma . . .' was all the greeting he could say before she was in his arms, and her mouth on his in tender welcome. But the kiss was greeting only. She had barely touched him before she drew back, laughing; pivoting on bare feet, she swirled her skirts to show a sparkle of crisp petticoats beneath. Ted was suddenly aware that she was dressed up, that something special was in the air; her hair wasn't loose, but caught up tightly, with a brightly-patterned kerchief tied about it; her blouse was fine linen, intricately embroidered, with a low collar of frothy lace; there was rich patterning sewn to the hem of her dark, full skirt, and about her waist she wore yet another gaily-coloured kerchief, loosely tied. She stood, poised and still, happily enjoying the frank admiration in his eyes.

'You'm a queen,' he laughed, 'a rawnie, right enough!'

'Don't be daft,' she retorted, eyes twinkling. 'Emma's no lady. Not even for you!' With that, she sat down on the up-turned box that the old man had so recently vacated, and taking up a flame-scorched stick, poked the dying fire into crackling life. Ted watched her intent movements and again sensed the feeling that something was up; there was a for-mality in the air, not unpleasant, but tense, even exciting. Emma looked at him across the flames and spoke with a deep-throated caress in her voice, but her face was serious now.

'We're moving on,' she said.

Ted's whole body tensed hard, as though warding off a physical blow; for a second, the only sound that he could hear was the pounding of blood deafening his ears, the shudder of his heart, kicking in protest. So this was what the show was for – the gypsy's farewell!

'For God's sake, Emma . . . No!' he gritted, holding back from pleading close against her, his clenched fingers knotted tightly together to hide the tremor of his hand. She smiled gently at him, and did not look away; was she taunting him, did he mean so little?

'It's time,' she murmured calmly. Then looking into the fireglow, she added, 'Us've been here long enough, Daddo and me. . . .'

'But it's a good place here,' protested Ted desperately, ' – you said so yourself!'

'Place in't important, my laddie,' she replied softly.

'It ain't nothing without you,' came the half-choked reply.

'Then travel with us. . . .'

The truth of the matter was out at last, and she knelt by

him in a flurry of skirts, eyes shining up into his startled face, her voice low and urgent.

'I want you for my man,' she said simply. 'Stay with me and you'll need for nothing, that I promise. . . .'

He couldn't answer. The conflict within him was too great. He could only look at her with hopeless eyes, and she laughed, cupping her hand fondly to his smooth chin.

'Is it that you're but eighteen . . .? she murmured, tracing the curve of his lip with teasing finger. 'One more than I am then. . . .' She kissed him lightly, her next words a whisper no louder than a rustle of fallen leaves. 'Didn't I make a man of ye, my dordi . . . ?'

Impulsively, his hands gripped her shoulders, lithe and twisting beneath the fringed shawl, and he put his mouth hard to hers. She answered his passion boldly, then pulled away, eyes flashing, lips parted over bright teeth.

'You'll come, then!' she crowed – but frowned as she saw the despair written in his flushed face.

'I cannot . . .' he whispered.

'For me, you'll come!' she demanded. 'For Emma!'

'Girl, I want you for my wife,' Ted blurted out, hands still tightly holding her. 'But this is where I must be. . . .' Her face grew cold, but he refused to let her pull away. 'Stay here with me, Emma – stay . . .'

'Under a roof . . .' Her voice was strangely flat.

'I've prospects here,' said Ted, '– a good living, and better still to come. You said that yourself,' he added pointedly, 'it was in my hand, you said so!'

She pulled away, and stood, arms folded tight about her, staring down at him with a strangely bitter smile.

'Whatever was written there,' she stated, thin-lipped and withdrawn, 'Emma was not. . . .'

In a sudden flush of memory, he saw her dark despairing face hover over his open hand; then that strange moment was swiftly overlaid by the burning recall of her tender but desperate loving, claiming him for her own, in spite of her people's secret ways. Aching to hold her, he rose to his feet and stepped past the fire towards her; with an easy, gliding movement she evaded him, and he was faced only with the softly growling dog. He turned to her; the fire was between them now, its flickering light making the defiance in her stern face seem like a challenge.

'Our ways don't need a church,' she said. 'But I'll come to that if you want . . .' Her chin tilted proudly. 'But after that, my Teddy, the road's our only home this side of God's heaven . . . so it's up to you, boy.'

It was as though he'd been struck dumb; words wouldn't come, and gestures alone could give no answer. He held out his hands, half-begging; for some reason, his eyes were drawn to them as though searching for what she had once seen. They were trembling, and he pulled them back, clenched, to his sides. Her voice, low and insistent, reached out to him across the flames.

'Only you can break what's there,' came her purring command. 'If your heart speaks, then let it answer.'

She moved to the wagon door, mounting the steps slowly, then turned at the top at Ted's desperate cry.

'Emma . . . love . . . I got to think !'

Her eyes fixed on him, she opened the door and stood there, half in shadow. 'Come now,' she said, and slipping inside, pushed the door to gently, so that it would open at his touch.

There was a silence; then, from the vardo, came that faint, racking cough. The image of that ancient, accusing mask loomed up and shadowed all thought of Emma. Blindly, Ted turned and ran. To decide was torment; only one thought was clear. What she had asked of him must wait.

Chapter Eleven

'When I find that girl – ' squawked Mrs Prentiss, face ruddy with ill-feeling,' – oh, but I'll give her what for!'

Neither Doris nor Mary Ann had any time to agree with the irate cook, for they were too busy laying the early morning fires that should have been Betty Collins's task; nobody had seen the scrawny child since the previous night, and it had been six o'clock in the morning before she'd been missed. That first panic had had nothing to do with the girl's own wellbeing; the finely tuned running of the Hall had been thrown out of gear, and it was all hands to the pumps. Donald, the new hallboy, had been ordered to carry coals for the maids and didn't like it.

'Blessed funny time to go running off,' he grumbled in his thin, whining twang of a voice. 'An't her got no feeling for us'n?'

It was a long time since Doris had had to lay fires other than Lady Hester's and Lily's; now she had three more.

'Don't you go spilling slack!' she snapped irritably at Donald as he set the coal bin in the fireplace. He pulled a long, pimply face, then wiped his nose on a corner of his baize apron.

'What's her want to go off *for*, anyroad?' he demanded sullenly. He had no liking for the skinny scullerymaid, for since he was new, she'd been giving him tongue pie on and off, every day.

'How do I know, silly!' retorted Doris, then as she lit the fire and checked to see that all was as clean as could be expected, she grew thoughtful. 'Can't think where she'd run to, though . . . not home, that's for sure.'

Mary Ann, now having to cope with Betty's kitchen chores as well as her own, agreed, breathlessly, when Doris at last had the chance to put the puzzle to her, downstairs. The cheerful relaxation of a normal day had been replaced by an uncomfortable and constant scurry, and nearly everyone's tongue had an edge to it.

'I dunno, pet,' said Mary Ann, on the move between laying out the various trays. 'All I hope is they can get one of the Jordan girls here, double quick!'

Merrick had already made the hasty journey across to Valley Farm, but he wouldn't be back with help before breakfast. Whatever Betty had done with herself, she'd succeeded in standing the Hall on its ear, that was certain.

'What her ladyship'll say, I don't know . . .' said Mr Stokes, gloomily. Until the matter got out of hand, the girl's absence was his responsibility; he had no intention of starting Lady Hester's morning with this sort of news until she had eaten and was ready to give her orders for the day. If the girl turned up merely late, she would be quietly disciplined below stairs. If it was worse than that, then it was out of Stokes's hands. Either way, it wasn't very pleasant. His only hope was that the girl would put in an appearance quickly; it had been several weeks since Lady Hester had produced one of her sudden tempers, and if that happened, everyone would suffer.

'Her bed wasn't slept in,' Mrs Prentiss observed with grim innuendo. 'What's that girl been up to, that's what I'd like to know. . . .'

'What's she thinking of?' whispered Doris to Mary Ann, genuinely puzzled.

The implication that Betty had slept somewhere else could only have one meaning, but apart from her age, there was the question of who'd ever want such an arrangement.

'She's not like that,' murmured Mary Ann, who knew all too well how easy it was to make Betty blush. 'She'd be frightened to kiss a feller, let alone tumble with him.'

Mrs Prentiss caught this last remark, and gave the for once serious-faced kitchenmaid a savage glower. 'Nobody mentioned fornication,' she thundered, 'so just you keep your wickedness to yourself, Mary Ann Hudson!'

'Yes, Mrs Prentiss,' murmured Mary Ann with a meekly apologetic glance which switched into a cheeky grin when the cook had turned her back. 'I will, I promise. . . .'

Mr Merrick erupted into the back kitchen with two of the sturdy Jordan girls, who though younger than Betty by two years, were willing and well trained by their mother. There was an immediate hurry and scramble as Mary Ann took charge of the two girls and set them to work; Doris took up the first of the breakfast trays – Miss Summers's, who always ate before Lady Hester and for a brief moment, there was a lull in which the three senior members of the domestic establishment could confer, frowning.

'No news, Mr Stokes?' queried Merrick, his eyebrows making anxious signals between the butler and Mrs Prentiss.

Stokes shook his head, and adjusted his spotless white gloves. 'I don't like it, Arthur,' he said dolefully. 'It's going to mean telling her ladyship.'

Mrs Prentiss rolled her eyes at this, knowing like the others that their mistress, though sweet-natured when all was going smoothly, could be a savage martinet when staff displeased her. 'Heaven forbid,' she breathed ominously.

'Didn't say anything to the Jordans, did you, Arthur?' the butler asked thoughtfully.

'Just that we'd been took short-handed, suddenly,' responded Merrick, blandly. 'No trouble there. . . .'

'Good,' commended his elderly superior, then practised his formal cough. 'If the girl's not here by ten, Mrs Prentiss, you'll inform me, prompt.' His careful eyes grew flinty-sharp. 'After that, the young madam will just have to take what's coming to her. . . .' His expression politely invited questions, but expected none. Mrs Prentiss nodded in agreement, and the trio dispersed to their respective duties. It was only then that Mrs Prentiss had the thought that something might have happened to Betty Collins that wasn't of her own doing.

Although the common land on Heydon Berrow was closer by far to Brookfield Farm, the grazing on Lakey Hill was so much better that it was worth the extra trouble of driving sheep there, even if it did take more than half the morning. For one thing, apart from the quality of the grass, it was easier to find shelter for putting up lambing pens when the time came; what's more, the fair sized coppice at the brow of the hill provided a natural sanctuary for the beasts should there be sleet or snow. But Dan had more than just a working fondness for the hill. The view it gave over Ambridge and the rolling farmland all about was a joy to see, especially in spring or early summer, and there was a peace to be found there that few other local spots possessed. The edge of the wood was an ideal placing for a shepherd, for it gave clear sight of the grassy flanks falling gently away to the hedged-off fields far below. As a boy, tending the sheep on Lakey Hill had been one of Dan's first jobs. Later, as eldest, he had helped his father with the heavier work of ploughing, and in the dairy, while Frank, the youngest, had been sent out to the sheep. But the place had never lost its hold on Dan; it was from here that he surveyed the burly shoulders of the hill and built a dream that one day they, and all the fields beyond, would be his alone to hold and farm, not as Squire's tenant, but maybe as Squire himself. And the memory still amused him that his boyish daydreaming had been interrupted more than once by a scrambling and scurrying in the undergrowth about the trees, a giggling and a cursing, a hurried and unseen escape from the fear of prying eyes. For the coppice on Lakey Hill was hotly favoured as a courting place, especially in summer; and as a more knowing young man, Dan had many a time turned a blind eye to the flurries of romantic excess that had started simply as a picnic on the hill, or an expedition to gather blackberries at the edge of the wood.

But in the bitter chill of a November morning, a sudden movement in the undergrowth would hold a different meaning for a shepherd; more than likely a ruddled ewe caught by her tangled wool amongst the brambles. Dan had mounted the flank of the hill, checking his charges as he went; like his father, he wasn't keen on using the tricks of the Down sheep-herders of the south, putting the ram in with the ewes from early September on. It meant more work, and greater risk in these hardier Midland hills, and the rewards were still there with lambs born at the turn of spring, early March, early to the market and still fetching a good price. For this reason, every ewe, every lamb, was precious. Setting his mongrel collie, Sally, to stay outside the trees, Dan stepped through the sodden bracken into the pathways made by rabbit and by pheasant, to find his sheep. Instead, it was Betty Collins that he found, and she was in a sorry state.

He'd left Sally outside for the simple reason that even her skilled movements might panic the ewe even deeper into trouble. In fact, it was the soft, troubled whimper of the perk-eared bitch as she rummaged around the perimeter of a wild laurel, that led Dan to find the cringing, miserable girl. At first all he saw was a dim, wide-eyed face, deep inside the foliage; it wasn't until she called his name that he realised with a start just who the girl was.

'Mister Archer . . .' she moaned pitifully, 'get me out . . . please get me out. . . .'

'Hold on, Betty,' he said, his voice warm with comfort and good sense; and pulling the springy branches to one side, he clasped her thin shoulders and drew her to him.

Even held tight in his sturdy arms, she couldn't stop shiver-ing; the thin coat she had on was damp and chill, and by the touch of his hands about her, Dan realised that she had little more than her cotton working clothes beneath it. She huddled close, face buried in his chest, her breath coming in short spasmodic gasps; it wasn't until his body had warmed her that her breathing and her shudders eased. Dan said nothing, but waited for her panic to subside. At last she tilted her wan face up to him, and he could see that she was crying, silently.

'There, chuck,' he murmured, 'you'll be all right now. . . .'

Swallowing her tears, she shook her bedraggled head and tried to raise a trembling smile. 'I'm glad you'm here, Mister

Archer,' she whispered, then biting her lip, screwed up her eyes in a brave attempt not to give way to the threatening storm of misery. 'But I in't out of trouble yet. . . .'

'Safe at least, pet,' he said, wondering what she had been through, and what there was yet to come.

She gave a tiny, frightened nod. 'Safe now,' she said, with a quick, involuntary glance past his comforting shoulder, into the heart of the laurel bush. Following her eyes, Dan looked too. A brown stone bottle, tightly stoppered, was set down close by where he'd found her. Curious, he made to leave Betty for a moment, to investigate the simple but ominous brown shape. She clutched at his arm, holding him back, her face desperately pleading.

'Leave it be,' she begged, '. . . it don't matter. . . .'

She had started shivering again; he slipped out of his stiff oilskin and laid it on her shoulders, before completing his purpose of reaching for the hidden bottle. She made no attempt to stop him now, and bowed her head silently in the collar of his coat, as he reappeared from the cover of the laurel, the bottle in his hand. It had no label, and unscrewing the rubber-ringed stopper, he put his nose towards the open neck. Abruptly, he drew back from the pungent tang, head swimming; it was lysol, as powerful and as lingering as carbolic. At arm's length, he tipped it slightly, and a dribble of thick liquid spilled out on to the grass at his feet, showing that the bottle was still full, untouched by the girl's mouth. He looked across to her for confirmation, and she shook her head miserably.

'I didn't have none,' she whispered plaintively, 'not in the end, I couldn't.'

He knew what she said was true; she'd be knotted and screaming in slow agony, otherwise, but he had to be sure.

'God's truth?' he demanded, firmly.

'I said, didn't I?' she retorted, sullen-faced, then added in all innocence, 'Besides, they can put you inside prison for that . . . !'

Dan nodded, his face serious. 'Just for trying,' he said, and

Betty stared at him, wide-eyed with sudden alarm. Suddenly, she burst into a short whinny of bitter, terrified laughter.

'God Almighty!' she protested wildly, 'Haven't I done enough already...?'

'Best get ye back to the Hall,' said Dan. Her eyes were still fixed on the bottle in his hand, and he hefted its deadly weight, cautiously, before pouring its contents into the pile of soil thrown up by a burrowing buck rabbit. The container empty, he slipped it out of sight down another burrow entrance, yards away. Betty watched him, blankly.

'Ready then?' Dan asked, moving back to the impassive girl. She stared at him, unable to find further words of gratitude, not wanting to tell him why what he'd just done was so pointless. As though not caring, she shrugged her bony shoulders, and stared out past the trees, over the misted, frosty fields below the hill, towards the faintly seen gaunt elegance that was Arkwright Hall.

'It doesn't really matter,' she muttered through pinched lips, hopelessly. 'They're going to get rid of me anyway. . . .'

It was almost mid-morning by the time Ted reached the feeding point for the pheasant around Grange woods; with Grit tucked at heel, he approached the accustomed glade slowly, giving that low, insistent whistle that his birds knew only too well. Rooks were there too, settled and waiting high in the nearly barren trees, but as long as Ted stayed close by, they wouldn't dare to swoop down and take the mixture that made their bold thieving such a pleasure. First to come were the hens who'd been left in the wood to 'hold' the pheasants that they'd earlier helped to rear as chicks; without them, the pheasant would scatter carelessly, deserting their feeding ground for those in the other woodlands and unbalancing the shoot pattern that George Nugent so shrewdly maintained. With the old mum hen amongst them to call them in, the pheasant rarely strayed; the other broody hens now did their duty by the keepers in just as practical a way, by laying their season of eggs through to the New Year and beyond, a free perk to the keepers who had bought them first of all to hatch the pheasant eggs during May, in carefully secluded coops. Eventually, the coops had been moved into the coppiced woods, where the undergrowth had been thinned out to form glades and rideways. Come September and the end of rearing, the hens had been thinned out and brought in to lay, though feeding the game birds by hand continued; in this way, each keeper had a fair idea of numbers and which areas had been over-shot or under, whichever the case might be. Feeding wasn't simply a mechanical chore, however; it was a time for Ted to use his eyes, spotting the signs left by predators, old foxey especially.

'Don't think you'm following old foxey, son,' Ted's father had told him more than once before, ' 'cos more'n likely it's him afollowing *you*!'

Keen eyes had shown this to be only too true. On a bitterly frosted morning, Ted had retraced his own footprints and found, set daintily alongside his, the paw marks of a stalking fox; the cunning trail had broken from his not because of his coming, but because foxey's little game had paid off, handsomely. A scattering of fawny feathers amongst the remaining scraps of food, scrabbled, frantic markings in the thick hoar frost otherwise only disturbed by prints from the bird itself, and a melting spatter of bright blood showed what had happened. Ted could only curse quietly, too irritated to admire the skill of the sleek enemy. Somewhere in the bracken sat the fox, gorged and satisfied, washing the blood from its muzzle with meticulous paws. It was a simple lesson, one that had turned classroom advice into living experience, adding to Ted's ever-growing store of keeping lore. But today Ted's wits were too preoccupied to take up the challenge of the wood; he had only one purpose in mind beyond his essential chores – to find Emma, reason with her, and beg for time.

He had barely slept for thinking of what she was asking of him. The business of reading his palm puzzled him; if he understood her right, she was openly asking him to change what was written there – if you blindly believed such nonsense.

When it came to the put to, it was a simple, straightforward matter of choosing: her way of life, or his. For Emma, it was easy. She had no roots, nor needed any, centred as she was within the painted vardo and the family that she would raise inside its snug walls, his childer, pray to God. But she had to be made to understand how it stood with Ted. With him, there wasn't only sister, home and parents to consider, there was his job, its responsibility, the future. If Emma would only try his way, he knew she wouldn't be disappointed; for love of him, and Emma's own beauty, Ted's parents would take to the gypsy as though she were one of their own. Doris would love her as a sister, there'd be no trouble on that score; and Emma had said herself she'd go one better than jump the broomstick, that she'd wed in church. Bright words and glib persuasions tumbled confidently through his mind as he strode swiftly to the clearing, but even as he reached it, he knew he was too late.

The ashes of the fire were kicked clear, and cold. There was no other trace of vardo, horse or dog. Ted could only stand there, sick with longing, and utterly alone.

When Dan had carried the scrunched-up waif, her face tucked timidly against him, into the Hall kitchens, the immediate consternation was quickly got under control once Mister Stokes had been informed. Mary Ann Hudson was given the task of putting the bedraggled girl to rights, and quickly, for now it was to be a matter between the girl and Lady Hester. Doris was there, listening keenly to Dan's plain version of the story; a simple tale of discovery and rescue, without any mention of either the virulent chemical, or of the desperate intention to use it.

'The spinney on Lakey Hill,' explained Dan patiently. 'She must've been there all night, I reckon....'

'Alone?' demanded Mrs Prentiss.

'No sight nor sound of anyone else, no,' said Dan.

'Poor mite . . .' murmured Doris. 'But whatever was she thinking of . . .?'

'Said nothing to me,' Dan responded with a slow shake of the head. 'She knows she's in for trouble, though.'

'And so she should be!' snapped Mrs Prentiss, though if the truth be told, she'd had more a twinge of pity for the crumpled, forlorn child.

Suddenly, Betty had been brought back into the room, and for a moment, everyone had looked at her with quiet surprise. In a plain but clean cotton dress, face and hands scrubbed to a shining pink, and her hair brushed and pinned, Betty not only looked changed in appearance, but in manner as well. Gone was the familiar, hangdog stoop; her chin was up, her back was straight, and there was a gleam of something like defiance in her eye. Brusquely and silently inspected by Mister Stokes, she had accompanied him out of the kitchen without another word; but no sooner had she left than Mary Ann, who had been standing behind Betty, bright-eyed and bursting with her secret, at last had told the others what she knew.

'She's pregnant!' she exclaimed, half-shocked and half-delighted. 'And nearly three months gone!'

Betty Collins faced Lady Hester, and for once in her life, she wasn't afraid. To start with, she already knew the inevitable outcome of this meeting, in fact she'd known it all along; but more than that, when she had told Mary Ann her dismal news, instead of disgust and a tongue-lashing, she had been given a great hug that had left both her and Mary Ann tearful with . . . joy.

'Why, pet,' the glowing kitchenmaid had murmured softly, 'you'm a woman now and no mistake!'

Whatever happened now, she had that pride in her, making her all the more thankful of Dan Archer's own part in the affair. Without him saying so, she knew that the bitter secret now buried up on Lakey Hill would be known to nobody but the two of them. With that behind her, only two painful meetings now remained – this formal interview with Lady Hester, and the more ugly storm she knew she'd have to face from her own mother. But that black moment wasn't yet. She stood, hands clasped together patiently, while her mistress looked at her with cold eyes; at the door, a little way behind Betty's shoulder, Mister Stokes waited warily, hoping that nothing untoward would happen, for he'd sensed the girl's uncompromising attitude and it had left him distinctly uneasy.

Lady Hester sat bolt-upright at her exquisitely inlaid escritoire, the cool light from the tall window by her side edging her stern features into dramatic shadow. She studied the gawky child standing before her, and considered the facts as told to her by Stokes. The girl had been absent from the house all night, without permission, and had only returned after being discovered hiding on Lakey Hill, by a local farmer, the tenant of Brookfield. There seemed to be only two possible causes: either the child, spending a stolen evening in the village and finding herself locked out on her stealthy return, had panicked and hidden herself out of fear of the natural consequences, or she had been caught in the process of running away, a different intention altogether. Although, instinctively, Lady Hester felt sorry for the child, she also knew that discipline towards staff was essential; nevertheless, the facts had to be known, before all else. Clasping her hands, she commenced the interrogation.

'Betty Collins . . . ?'

'Yes, m'lady.'

'What is your age?'

'Sixteen come January, m'lady. The twenty-third.'

'Do you know the meaning of service, girl?'

'Yes, m'lady. Work hard and do as you're told. That's what me Mam said, anyroad.'

'And do you work hard?'

'Yes, m'lady. I do.'

Lady Hester's glance flicked across to Stokes, and silently, he nodded in confirmation.

'But apparently you are disobedient.'

'I only ever done wrong this once, m'lady. Honest!'

'Please don't interrupt. You have been out all night, without permission, and I view such conduct very seriously indeed. Do you understand?'

'Yes, m'lady. . .'

Pausing, Lady Hester scrutinised the pallid face, the modest pose; the girl seemed to be duly contrite. Perhaps, if there was sufficiently good reason, she could be let off with a severe reprimand and a stoppage in her wages; on the other hand, she would be easy to replace, and to make a stern example would help maintain the correct tone below stairs. Relaxing slightly, Lady Hester reminded herself that she didn't yet know the full facts about this childish escapade.

'You will tell me the reason for your absence, girl,' Lady Hester demanded with a moderate coolness.

'I'm pregnant, m'lady, and I didn't know what to do.'

There was a shuddering silence, and even the normally imperturbable Stokes visibly stiffened with shocked surprise. When Lady Hester next spoke, her voice was ice-cold with unconcealed distaste.

'Who . . . is the man . . . responsible?'

'Can't say, m'lady.'

'Do you mean . . you don't know?'

'No, m'lady. I know all right. And I know just when it happened, too, 'cos it was only the once . . .' Betty saw from Lady Hester's rigid features that she may have gone too far, but she felt obliged to add the final important fact. 'I'm nearly three months gone,' she added.

'That's enough, girl!' Stokes rebuked sternly, aware that such shocking revelations could only make matters worse. 'Speak when you're asked, that's all!' He threw a quick glance towards his mistress, concerned for her feelings. In fact the one sordid realisation that hadn't struck home to the indignant butler, had impinged on Lady Hester's moral susceptibilities with breathtaking brutality. She stared at Betty Collins with something akin to horror.

'But . . . you were under age, child!' The girl looked baffled, and her mistress hurriedly explained. 'Under the age of consent. That is a criminal offence – and the man must be brought to justice, we must see to it!'

'But I let him . . .' retorted Betty, her face puzzled. 'He didn't force me, nothing like that – '

Lady Hester was getting impatient with the stubborn girl; didn't she want the protection of the law, the rites of marriage to legalise the unborn child?

'My dear girl,' she insisted vehemently, 'this man – whoever he is, and I insist that he be named – has taken a cruel advantage of your innocence. . . .'

'I wanted him to!' shrieked Betty.

It was the last straw, Stokes could see that; he moved forward smoothly, and took Betty by the elbow, ready to extract her from the room. The girl wriggled, but found his grasp surprisingly strong, as he looked calmly and politely to Lady Hester for her sign of dismissal. It came, not in words, but as a quiet, disturbed gesture of the arm. It wasn't enough, as Stokes's discreet cough reminded her; a judgement had to be made. As she spoke, she turned to the window and gazed out, her attitude casually vague, even ethereal. Sometimes, reality could be simply too much.

'Send the girl away, Stokes,' she said in her tired voice. 'I want to hear nothing more about it. . . .'

'Don't I even get notice?' protested Betty, more than a little aware that a week's wages would help placate her irate mother to a certain extent at least.

'Notice . . .?' queried Lady Hester, looking at the miserable child with weary distaste. 'Certainly not. She will go today, Stokes, and you will arrange for her fare to be paid. That is all. . . .'

She turned back to the window and her desk, firmly putting the incident behind her. She seemed not to hear Betty's last defiant words, thrown at her from the doorway, where Stokes discreetly struggled to thrust the tense girl into the corridor outside.

'I'll tell you someat else then!' shouted Betty raucously. 'It happened right here, in this house, right under your bloody nose it did!'

There was an explosive smack of hand on face, a wail of pain and anger rising to a shrill scream.

'You old bastard!'

'Excuse me, my lady,' murmured Stokes politely to his unmoved mistress, and closed the door with a near silent click that finally terminated all sight and sound of the sobbing girl. With peace re-established, Lady Hester sighed gently, and taking up her pen, began to make up a guest-list for her usual New Year's Eve party and first-footing. It would be held at the house in Chester Square, she decided thoughtfully. Town was, after all, so very much more civilised. . . .

CHAPTER TWELVE

DORIS HAD said not so much as a word at home about her brief skirmish with John, especially to brother Ted. When her mother announced her plans for Christmas, there was apprehension and excitement too, in Doris's mind; but in spite of that, she raised no objection.

'I thought on asking the Archer boys, William,' said Liza to her comfortably settled husband, reading the *Echo*.

'Just as you wish, Mother,' came his quiet answer.

'Both of them?' questioned Doris, continuing to lay the table for their evening meal. Today was her half-day off, and it always pleased her to help her mother set table for the family. Liza Forrest threw her daughter a quick glance, but Doris seemed unconcerned.

'Can't very well ask the one without the other, can us,' said Mrs Forrest, firmly. 'Wouldn't be fair or proper.' She watched, arms akimbo, as Doris laid down the last fork, then gently confronted her daughter, a faint smile of teasing amusement on her lips. 'Unless you'm got a preference, my pet . . .?'

'They're Ted's pals, not mine,' answered Doris with a pert twinkle. 'Why should I welcome the one any more than the other, Mam?'

Liza looked at her daughter with a smile, but her eyes were serious. 'That's not for me to say, pet, is it. . . .' She opened the cutlery drawer at the end of the table, and took out serving spoons. 'But you knows my mind well enough, at any rate. . . .'

'It'll do both those lads good to be with family,' declared Bill Forrest, turning the page of his paper. 'But I wouldn't be too certain that young John'll come, mind.'

His wife nodded, knowingly. Doris tried not to look put out, and asked, mildly, 'Whyever not, Dad?'

Her father peered at her over the top of the *Echo*, then at Liza, then back to Doris, thoughtfully.

'Got ideas of his own, I dare say....'

'And friends of his own, too,' asserted Liza, adding meaningly, '. . . in Borchester.'

The market town wasn't many miles away, and most of the Ambridge farmers sold their produce there, and not just on market days, either; several wives would take in eggs and vegetables in season, sometimes even daily. On market days, no one expected the men to return home before they'd had their ale and an hour or two of working gossip, but only one or two stayed there until the public houses closed their doors and after. Walter Gabriel was one, and John, not even admittedly a farmer, was another. More than that, even, both John Archer and Walter Gabriel paid visits to the busy little town that were nothing whatsoever to do with work; what those merrily furtive journeys entailed, Liza would never bring herself to talk about, not even with her husband. But she knew, as every woman in the village knew, that John Archer was a wild one who wasn't past seeking low company for his amusement. A handsome lad, they'd all admit, shaking their heads, and very different from his brother Daniel.

Doris, too, had heard many a tale about the wild lads, especially from Mary Ann Hudson who always seemed to know more than she'd willingly let on. But to Doris, Walter was the wicked one, leading and provoking John the sad hero into unseemly scrapes. Granted he was hot-blooded – Doris knew that for a fact, only too well, and still wondered half-guiltily what might have happened if she hadn't been carrying a certain basket on the day they met so fatefully in the drive-way – but this would surely make him all the better a man to hold, once he was wed as surely he must be in due course of time. And with the right woman by his side, he'd soon come to terms with this rumbustious nature, Doris was sure of that. On the other hand she half-sensed the heart-ache that he'd bring to any girl who'd willingly take up with him, but wasn't that very heart-ache part of loving? Daniel, now; he was a lonely man, but there was a warmth in him that Doris had touched upon the once. If he had had but a part of John's bright fire, what a husband he would make! And if John had but one ounce of Daniel's application, what a man to be sought after *he* would be!

'His pals in Borchester won't give him such a Christmas as we would,' murmured Doris, deliberately offhand.

'Then Ted shall ask them,' said Mrs Forrest, putting an end to further discussion. 'For I'm sure they'll make no celebration of their own. . . .' There had been a closeness since her shared childhood with Phoebe, mother to the Archer boys, and even now that they were full-grown into manhood, Liza Forrest couldn't but help feel the need to foster them, albeit at a distance. The one so shy, the other so wild, it would be tragedy to their father's name if they should remain bachelors for all their lives; but the house had seen all too few women since Phoebe Archer died. The farm wasn't doing so badly that it couldn't afford a housekeeper, everyone knew that; but no one had been asked or even tried, and small wonder with such a one as John about the place. Without a woman to take care, living-in apprentices or pupils couldn't be thought of, and even casual help, such little as was available, held back from being fed from a kitchen that was more a barrackroom than a home. With Frank gone abroad, and parents both passed on, the sense of family at Brookfield no longer existed – a sad state of affairs at any time, but all the more so at this first Christmas in the empty farmhouse. Liza Forrest wasn't going to let that happen, and if she had her way, it would be the *only* year that Brookfield didn't itself glow with Christmas cheer. But that was her secret, nodded to only by husband William; springtime would come soon enough, but until then, the bond between her children and Phoebe's must be kept warm, at least.

So it was that on Christmas Day, after church Dan and John Archer arrived, boot-stamping in the powdery snow that had started to lay in the Forrests' yard, to be greeted by the family, and tankards of hot punch made tangy with Mrs Forrest's own blend of spices, held as tight a secret as her husband's feeding mixture for his pheasants. Ted had himself not long finished his rounds, and thankfully, for it would blow even colder, he claimed. His father would take the afternoon stint, unchallenged by his Liza, for she knew all too well the truth of his announcement to all and sundry, that 'poachers don't sleep on Sundays or feast-days, and neither must I!' John, spick and span as ever, was the first to drink to this, for Bill Forrest's was the sharpest eye he knew, and if John was to even hope to court Doris on the sly, his only chance was if her father wasn't there.

'Down with poachers!' cried John gaily, then added with a wink, ' – and here's to absent friends – Willie Ashford!' This brought a laugh, even from Ted, who didn't seem himself by a long chalk. Dan, relaxed by the warming drink, let his wary glance slip from his brother, well separated from Doris but watching her bright-eyed, towards Ted, his friend. For a week after he'd nabbed old Willie, Ted had been on top of the world, bright and lively as a pair of magpies. But something had changed him, and Dan couldn't think what.

It had been there, a shadow between them, when Ted had brought his mother's invitation for the brothers to spend the whole of Christmas Day at Riverbank. At first, Dan had been reluctant to impose, and it had been Ted who'd insisted; but the old spark wasn't there, rather a more forced, stolid cheeriness that wasn't far removed from anger. After Ted had gone, John remarked that it was as though the young keeper had grown into an old man overnight, and laughingly prescribed Polly Harper as the cure. Dan, bitter at John's quick acceptance of the Forrests' hospitality, and aware that the challenge over Doris still lay between them, snapped angrily at his brother's lewd wit, but wondered secretly. He was almost certain that Ted wasn't going with any village girl, though it was a subject that Ted never talked about, and neither did Dan; but there was the matter of Betty Collins, too, and again Dan wondered.

It was young Tom's bright voice that broke Dan's sombre train of thought, abruptly.

'How about this then!' the boy demanded, thrusting the fork of polished hazelwood under Dan's nose. 'Ted give it me, for Christmas.'

His mother looked at him from across the room and waggled her head, disapprovingly. 'Just you take care, my lad,' she said firmly. 'I'll have no playing with catapults in this house.'

'He'll take care, Mother,' said Bill Forrest, with a quiet glance at Tom, 'won't ye, son?'

Tom nodded, and Ted chipped in with a grin and a mock-hard punch to the boy's ribs. 'He better had. Knock his block off otherwise, I will . . .'

'You and whose army!' cheeked Tom, sparring up to his laughing brother.

'Haig's,' chuckled John. 'Could've won the war twice over with tack like this,' he said, and twitched the catapult from Dan's fingers to examine it himself.

Tom moved with it, possessively. Offering it to Dan for his opinion had been an act of comradeship, an acknowledgement of the bond between Ted and Dan that Tom too, was allowed to enjoy in his boyish way. John, though likeable enough, was something different again; for one thing, he was forever staring at Doris on the sly, and for another, whenever he tried a rough and tumble, he never let Tom win once. Suddenly, John swung the primitive weapon straight at Tom's startled face, pulling the sturdy rubber taut, one dark eye squinting threateningly and sighting the boy's nose as target. 'Now I've got you, Tommy!' joked John, and flicked the released leather pebble-holder just short of the boy's tense face.

Tom paled, but didn't flinch. Abruptly, he snatched the prized catapult back from John and retorted angrily, 'That's stupid! Mam said it in't to be played with in here. Give it us!'

'Hey up, Tom . . .' said his brother, with a cool glance at John, who was still smiling, '. . . he was only teasing ye.'

'Put it away son, I would for now,' murmured Bill Forrest,

and Tom reluctantly obeyed. It was his mother's voice that brightened his sullen face into eagerness again.

'Shall us all eat then?'

Seated at the laden table, warmth, friendship and good food swept all the shadows from everyone's mind, but Dan's. He hadn't seen so much delicious grub since that last Christmas with Mother, and for a moment the sheer generosity and open kindness moved him to tight-throated thinking of how it might have been had this been Brookfield, with Mother and her beloved Ben at top and tail of table. As though reading his thoughts, Mrs Forrest gave him a soft, knowing smile and urged him to more crackling from the pork, while Doris, who had also noted the downward glance and the deep, swallowed pause in Dan's eating, brightly passed him the lemon-tanged apple sauce with a pretty smile. After that moment, only the cheeriness remained; he even felt his bitterness towards John ease from him, for Mrs Forrest had skilfully arranged places so that Doris, young Tom, and Ted sat across the table from Dan and John, with herself at Dan's elbow, where she could bring him out if needs be. The helpings were massive, and the grub was unbeatable; succulent, thick slices of pork; richly-browned roast spuds, flakey but not too dry inside; greens and whole carrots, the apple sauce and piping hot gravy, all seemed to have no limit. On then to the gleaming richness of the Christmas plum pudding, in spite of everybody's protestations of being too full to eat more, with the exception of young Tom, who would probably be sick before the evening was out, though it was he who triumphantly found the silver tanner in the pudding. The meal cleared away, and the women-folk washing up in the scullery, the men were left to themselves. Bill Forrest was quickly away out, true to his word; John, finding a pack of cards, suggested a quick game of brag, but neither Dan nor Ted were keen. They chatted lazily together while John tried to make his peace with Tom by showing him how to play Blind Man's Patience.

Soon Doris and her mother returned, laden with bowls of nuts and raisins, fruit and drop-cakes, and nobody refused.

Doris sat at the piano and jauntily persuaded Ted to sing, after a pretended moment of reluctance and a request for suggestions.

'No marching songs, eh . . .' said John brightly, and for a tiny moment there was a flicker of past shadows in the room. But Ted's songs came mainly from his father, and he sang them robustly, with a dry, knowing humour. 'Jim the Carter's Lad' was followed by the cheery disasters of 'The Rest of the Day's Your Own'; and it wasn't until after young Tom's fine treble had finished harmonising with Ted in 'Just a Song at Twilight' that Dan remembered that there was still work to be done back at Brookfield, before he could take his ease completely. The cows would be bawling for feed and milking, if he left things to ride, and he wasn't one for that. The others understood, and made no attempt to delay him, but John wasn't slow to let Dan know where the advantage lay.

'I'll stay, old son,' he volunteered cheerfully.

Ted's shrewd wink told Dan that he needn't worry, that Doris was in safe hands, but urged by young Tom scampering at his heels, he went to the scullery door with his mother, to see Dan off, and it was then it happened.

'It's cold supper,' Mrs Forrest was informing Dan pleasantly, 'but that's no reason to be late coming back to us, my son . . .' Both she and Ted saw Dan's cheery face change, and wondered. Ted turned, but too late to see what Dan had seen, half-glimpsed through the sitting-room window: Doris, a bunch of mistletoe shielding her face, being kissed long and passionately by John.

Those few staff left at the Hall, not having local homes to go to, had the evening to themselves for their own merrymaking. There had been an earlier, formal giving of presents and exchange of good wishes between the Squire and the domestics, but that tired ritual was long over, the bright golden guineas compared for newness and bitten for quality, and now the kitchen, the food, and a discreet amount of wine were there for Mister Stokes and his underlings to enjoy. Even Merrick was observed to laugh; Mrs Prentiss not only received but demanded her rights beneath the mistletoe; the new lad, Donald, performed a shambling but highly comical dance to the ragged accompaniment of squeezebox and spoons, played by Joe Lees and Merrick respectively, and Mary Ann tried to introduce her own version of Blind Man's Buff, involving much squealing, fumbling, and kisses as forfeit for being caught, which Mary Ann continually was. The laughter and the simple pleasure spilled like the cracks of light slipping past the blind-drawn kitchen windows, into the yard outside, and across the drifting, wind-whipped snow to the rear terrace overlooking the gaunt, snow-etched gardens and the ornamental lake. A solitary figure, well-wrapped and stark against the lambent snow, paused and listened, then moved closer to the kitchen quarters to observe more closely; head inclined as though caught up in a secret amusement, the figure quietly entered by the servants' door, only to be confronted by the huddled figures of Mary Ann and Tetsall, kissing murmured compliments to Christmas. A gasp, a rapid shuffling and a stifled giggle, heralded a rapid retreat back into the more public merrymaking in the kitchen proper; Tetsall, ever-imperturbable, paused formally in the half-open doorway and gestured cheerfully with his battered, berried wand.

'Merry Christmas, Master Anthony, sir. . . .'

A perky grin, and then he was gone and the door firmly closed. A small skirl of female laughter filtered outside, but Anthony now moved quickly on, his curiosity quite deflated.

For him and for his parents, the day had not gone well. Lady Hester, denied the bright gaiety of a party that would have deadened, for her at least, the pain of Christmas without Harry or Andrew, rose late, suffered lunch with polite silence, and retired to her room almost as soon as evening fell. The headache she pleaded was nonetheless real for being convenient, but Father's withering scorn hadn't helped.

'Certainly, if you must, my dear . . .' he had said, with a thin smile that called her coward. He and Anthony had eventually eaten a cold-cut supper alone, separated by the length of the vast mahogany dining table, without a word being exchanged. Father had eaten just as he shot or hunted, brusquely, savagely, with cleancut, economical movements aimed at bringing about immediate and effective results. His food elegantly destroyed, napkin precisely rolled and reinserted into his silver napkin ring, Father had risen, still silent, and moved as though called by ghosts to the total privacy of his fire-lit study. Anthony, alone and restless, had gone to the saloon, the old family room where the glittering Christmas tree had always stood when they were children. It was empty now, and cold, despite the fire that burnt so brightly in the grate. In desperation, he had gone out into the snow; the silence there at least was natural.

But even the snow was dead. The gaiety of the servants only seemed to screw the coffin tighter, and he had returned at last to the saloon, determined to purge the feeling of decay, with brandy – more than one, if necessary. He had barely poured it when the door opened, and Father entered. He saw Anthony, but made no acknowledgement, moving instead directly to the fireplace where he stood staring down into the flames, hands clasped behind his back. Anthony paused, uncertain whether to observe the protocol demanded, or to follow his father's manner and be silent.

'Yes, I'll have a whisky, Harry. Large one, what?'

The light, companionable request cutting across the brooding room at first froze him, then almost choked him with despair. Instinctively, he poured the familiar measure, hand fighting to control its tremor, eyes straining to focus on the glass. Father spoke again.

'Damned good weather for tomorrow's shoot, eh?'

Without answering, Anthony brought the charged glass to his father's hand, and it was only then that the older man realised the cruel, bitter truth. Standing before him was the soft face of a weak boy, not the hunter's scan that mirrored Harry's favourite bird, the kestrel. He stiffened slowly from his casual stoop, his face rigid with disapproval, challenging Anthony's very presence with his chilling stare.

'Must you be here . . . ?' the cold voice whispered.

Its effect on Anthony surprised even himself. For the first time in his life he felt defiance of the man before him, a determination not to be swept aside.

'To the New Year, Father,' he said, and raised his glass in solemn toast. The older man made no movement whatsoever, but his eyes blazed.

'I've been riding about the farms,' Anthony continued, quietly relentless. 'Talking to the tenants.' He paused, and sipped the brandy, savouring its fragrant fire as he held his father's gaze across the rim of the hand-cut goblet. 'It seems that Wickham is holding back . . .'

Lawson-Hope said nothing; he seemed immoveable as rock, but for a barely perceived tightening of the lean mouth. Anthony plunged on. There was no turning back now.

'Something should be done,' he insisted calmly, 'before they start to go downhill . . .'

Sitll no reply. The only sound seemed to be the whispered crackle of the burning logs, and the deep, stern breathing of the older man.

'We have to think of the future, Father,' his son persisted earnestly. He wasn't considering the estate as an inheritance, at that moment; it was part of something bigger, the broader issue of a community in bond to feudal monopoly, the outcome of two hundred years of life and soil husbandry, man, beast, crop and village. Change was coming, Anthony was sure of that; unless they could sense and guide its mood, that change would surely go against them and produce only conflict and a slow destruction. His father had known this once, even tentatively acted on it; but now he was turning his back on any sort of change, and this was utterly wrong. 'What you've done already for the estate, *has* to be maintained!'

At last Lawson-Hope spoke, eyes hooded, voice cruelly implacable. 'It was never meant for you,' he said, with searing precision. 'Go your own way. University, or London, I don't care, it means nothing to me at all.' He drank, staring at the dumb-struck boy, then sneered, 'Inevitably, you will inherit . . .' his voice dropped to a saddened whisper, '. . . if only by default.'

He gulped the final measure of whisky back and set the empty glass upon the marble mantlepiece with crisp brutality.

'Until then, you will kindly not interfere. . . .'

And he walked out, blindly.

It had almost been Dan's decision not to go back to the Forrests' home, for fear of what his bitterness might make him do. But the determination not to let John get away with courting Doris unchallenged had grown into an obsession by the time Dan had finished settling his cows, and without more ado, he'd returned to Riverbank and its homely warmth, but with an edge to him that made the others wonder. He wasn't to know that Doris, after that one stolen kiss under the pretence of seasonal right by John, had made certain she was never alone with him again for long.

Her mother, returning to the sitting-room from having seen Dan off, was quick to note the suddenly tense atmosphere in the room; it was with some relief that she found Doris constantly making excuses to help her in the kitchen, especially when more sporty party games were suggested by John, or more innocently, by young Tom. She asked Doris no questions, but more than once caught her troubled frown in John's direction; there was obviously something between the two, and Doris wasn't happy over it, but it wasn't for mothers to interfere without good reason. John had made his mark and was now content to wait, to all intents and purposes the perfect gentleman; it was only the occasional secret glance at Doris, aimed at not letting her forget the quickening excitement that his kiss had roused in her, that gave his game away, and then only to the girl.

But when Dan returned, there was a definite change in Doris; she seemed almost too eager to draw him into a more festive mood and, wondering, Dan let himself thaw out. John prided himself on knowing the ways of a girl in such a situation, and decided it was for his benefit, to convince him that taking Doris wasn't to be thought of as yet another easy conquest. He found Dan's eyes studying him questioningly, and returned the look with a slow, arrogant smile that claimed the victory as though the prize was already his. Dan read the meaning with a frown, and John was pleased – only to find that Doris was persistently elusive to the point of irritation.

Confused, but playing the gentleman more than he'd ever done by way of being asked by Doris to fetch her another glass of spiced punch, Dan began to wonder; had the kiss he'd seen in fact been freely given? At the punchbowl, he managed to murmur a casual question to Ted.

'John been behaving hisself, has he?'

'Fit to bust,' chuckled Ted, with a nod to his sister, sitting casually but safely close to her mother. 'Doris an't given him a look in at all . . .'

The news filled Dan with a quiet fizz of elation. For all John's ladykilling ways, perhaps the game wasn't as cut and dried as he'd like to make out. But then the thought flicked through his mind that the attention that Doris was paying him might well be meant to lead his brother on, as a discreet answer to that earlier kiss. With her parents and brothers present, Doris would hardly make a bold show of willingness towards John; was her laughter as she leaned to Dan to take the offered glass for him, or for his sharp-eyed brother? Somehow, Dan had to know, but the opportunity didn't come until the evening was nearly over.

The supper of cold meats, cheeses, pickles and fresh bread eaten and cleared, the gathering – now complete again with the return of Bill Forrest – bubbled into a medley of games and child-like tricks and treats. A couple of games of Newmarket were played, and then 'I spy', until Mrs Forrest's suggestion to 'hunt the thimble' gave the lads a chance for innocent horseplay. The good-humoured rough and tumble of Tom, Ted, Dan and John all scrabbling for the precious treasure under the loose covers of the unoccupied settee ended with the Archer brothers grabbing and holding it simultaneously, laughing and breathless.

'A draw!' cried Mrs Forrest.

'Has to be a winner,' declared Ted, getting to his feet, cheerful and unthinking. 'You saw 'em – you choose, Doris!'

Doris hid her alarm behind a shy laugh. 'Oh, Ted – I couldn't!' she said, shaking her head.

'Why not, pet?' said her father, shrewdly. 'Go on – you be the judge . . .'

The thimble, still held by the fingers of each brother, was presented before her, for judgement. With the briefest of hesitations, she chose quickly, touching his fingers with all the grace of a born princess: John. His bright eyes staring into hers, he seized her hand and kissed it with a swagger of mock gallantry. But when his head came up from the gesture, it was to find Dan being given the sweetest and lightest of consolation prizes – a kiss on the cheek that seemingly by accident brushed against his mouth. Not to be outdone, John lunged forward.

'Me too!' he exclaimed. 'Fair's fair!'

But Doris drew back, blushing, and John's clumsy purpose was shouldered aside by Dan, face laughing but eyes steely cold. 'Easy now, John,' he said. 'Y'can't go having two bites at the cherry. . . .'

John had no option but to concede, but his smile was like that of a dog fox, waiting. 'Just remember I was the winner, that's all . . . Slogger,' he needled, hoping that the boyhood nickname would score, but there wasn't even a flicker of reaction from Dan.

'Early to rise in the morning,' declared Bill Forrest with paternal good humour. 'What say a quick night cap, lads, and then home to bed?'

The drink, and the hint, was soon taken, and farewells made in the lantern-lit hallway and porch. Doris, standing a few steps up at the foot of the stairs, and conveniently shielded by her parents, seemed to have withdrawn from any further chance of physical contact with either of the brothers. Ted saw John's blazingly demanding glance go out towards his sister, and half frowned; but then he realised that far from meeting or returning that bold stare, Doris's eyes were set instead, wonderingly, on Dan. There was a moment's answer in the young farmer's cheery face, then with a blunt 'Goodnight!' he and John left, and Ted closed the door after them. When he turned to Doris, she had gone to help her mother.

In the scullery, setting the small pile of dishes down on the wooden draining board, Liza Forrest stepped deliberately in front of her daughter, and silently demanded an answer with shrewd, comforting eyes; but Doris shook her head and broke away, shyly.

'Mam,' she pleaded softly, 'I don't know my own mind myself. . . . Don't ask me. . . .'

The mile and a half to Brookfield was soon covered with a matched, brisk stride that left neither brother breath for conversation, even if they'd had anything brotherly to say. The scrunch of crisp snow beneath their boots, the occasional slip on icy grass, and the thin whisper of the keening wind were the only sounds to punctuate their sullen journey home to the cold, unwelcoming farmhouse. It wasn't until they had entered the snow-drifted yard and Dan had closed the gate after them, that either of them spoke of what was burning in their minds.

'John,' said his brother, standing in the centre of the yard, 'if you want Doris, you're going to have to flatten me first, y'know that.'

'No contest, mate. It's sorted already.'

'Y're a liar,' said Dan, standing his ground as John turned to confront him. 'I'll believe that when ye marry her . . . not before.'

'It'll be too late then, Slogger,' sneered John.

'Oh aye?' queried Dan harshly. 'Like with Mary Ann Hudson . . . and Betty Collins?'

There was a pause, as John shifted his feet, poised to strike but holding back. His voice was thick with anger. 'You berk,' he grated. 'That was Sam! Told me himself, didn't he, boasted he was the first to score with that scraggy kid!'

'Not if you got there first, tup.'

'It was never on, mate. . . .' He strutted forward, crowing his taunting laugh into Dan's grim face. 'But it will be, with Doris.'

'You've still got to walk over me, I said.'

'Any time, mate!'

'Now,' said Dan. 'Tonight.' He waited until John had nodded curtly in agreement, before adding, 'And winner takes all.'

John stared at his brother, surprise over-riding his mounting anger. 'You serious? The farm as well?'

'The lot,' said Dan grimly, unbuttoning his top coat.

John followed suit, more slowly, his mind racing at Dan's rashness. 'What about the loser then?' he demanded, narrow-eyed.

'He gets out, don't he,' stated Dan. 'Right out, clear out of Ambridge. For good. Brookfield wouldn't hold both of us.'

'Done!' rapped John, then laughed. 'You bloody fool . . .'

'Shake on it,' insisted Dan, hand outstretched. John's hand hesitated, then went out to his and gripped it, briefly but firmly. It was the last time their hands ever met in friendship.

'In here,' gritted Dan, and led the way into the barn.

CHAPTER THIRTEEN

THEY FLUNG their coats down into a corner, and stood for a moment, sizing up the space and the shadows all about them. With half the barn door propped open, the pale glimmer of the snow outside reflected faintly into the darkness of the barn, as though there was a waning moon, cloud-high. The dim light didn't satisfy John.

'Light a lamp,' he said, laying his flat cap on to his folded coat.

'Not in here,' grunted Dan, nodding towards the loose hay scattered on the otherwise tidy floor, and the wall of hay beyond, cut into chunky parapets where kerves of the wilted green had been carved out for feeding. 'Too dangerous . . .'

'Always the bloody farmer, aren't you,' muttered John, and lashing out, struck his brother a welt-raising blow high on the cheekbone. Dan only grunted, and shaking his head, moved in, arms swinging, fists clenched like hammers. He had no defence, and wanted none; his only purpose was to reach and strike down the one man who stood between him and not only Doris, but an unshared stake in the land he had fought for all his working days. John was no boxer, but he knew the style; he knew something of the strength of Dan's right hand, as well, and had no intention of hanging about waiting to be hit by it. On his toes, hit and dodge, that was the way. And as for Queensberry rules, you could stuff those with your Sunday dinner! As though to make that point viciously clear, he lashed out with one steel-tipped boot and caught Dan a numbing blow on the left knee-cap to bring him pitching forward in agony on to his knees. As Dan struggled to get up, John pounded the bowed head before him with short, grunting blows, knuckle on bone, before exploding into a breathless gasp as Dan threw himself hard into his brother's midriff, hurling him back into the smothering wall of hay. Now they lashed out at each other with blindly random fists, desperately trying to find and strike the heaving form that was their target, almost immediately lurching apart, gasping and coughing from the choking hay dust raised by their floundering. Somehow John got the heel of his boot against Dan's ribs, and with a mighty, thrusting heave, flung him thudding backwards into the door post. He had barely clambered to his feet before Dan was at him again, more warily now; John tried the stabbing kick again but missed, and Dan, managing to grab at the lunging foot, threw John staggering off balance. With surprising speed, Dan followed up and swung a massive, flailing blow at John's undefended head; ears ringing and eyes smarting with the searing pain, John was pitched sprawling to the ground, half-stunned and helpless.

Grim-faced, Dan lumbered forward to pin his wiry antagonist to the dusty floor, but John, snatching up a handful of loose kerf, hurled it blindingly into his opponent's eyes. Dan fell back, pawing at his face, desperate to clear his sight, while John, dodging to the left, stumbled and nearly fell against a short pitchfork propped against the wall of hay. Steadying himself, he clutched it; the smoothly worn wooden stock came to his hand like rifle and bayonet, and it was no longer his brother that groped towards him, but a faceless enemy advancing murderously from distant trenches. Dan, still half-blinded, never saw the killing lunge that missed him by inches as he slipped on a twist of hay and stumbled to one side; the wicked, twin-horned spearhead shuddered deep into the wall of tight-packed binding hay, and held there; for a brief second, John hands fiercely wrenching to free the wooden shaft, was poised open and vulnerable – and in that moment, Dan saw clearly and struck home.

The first crushing blow caught John squarely on the side of his face, splitting the eyebrow and smashing him with stunning force against a stall partition. Again Dan struck, his leg straddled to throw all his weight into the crippling punch. This time it was the left fist that knuckled deep into the half-conscious face, jerking it agonisingly to one side, bringing an involuntary groan of pain. But, propped up by the wooden wall behind him, and by some deep-burning obstinate defiance, John wouldn't go down, despite another bone-shuddering punch that left him numb and helpless. Gasping for breath, Dan held back, looking to strike the finishing blow; barely able to see the burly frame of his brother looming over him, John pawed the air with feeble, hopelessly uncoordinated fists. Again Dan hit home, but still John would not fall. Knees buckling, he forced himself upright before putting all his last strands of shattered strength into a final, desperate blow. With a moan of effort, he swung, wildly, but missed; then, as Dan shuffled back a pace, John slowly toppled, to fall sickeningly on to his battered face and lie there, still and unmoving.

Chest heaving with effort, Dan crouched, and turning his brother over on to his back, looked down at that bloodied, pitiable mask. John coughed, heaving with bright blood from his nose and broken teeth, and Dan could barely choke back his misery at the sight.

'For God's sake, John – say *enough* . . . !'

In the silence of the barn, punctuated only by the desperate cross-rhythms of their rasping breath, Dan clenched his fist and prayed that he wouldn't have to strike again. To go on would be no victory, but he knew he had to have his answer if the challenge was to end. At last it came, in a choking, angry whisper.

'Keep your bloody . . . farm . . . Slogger . . .' John coughed, and slumped into welcoming oblivion.

It was greed that caught Ernie Ashford out in the end; greed, and the wrong-headed idea that he was as clever as his old man, Willie. The fact was, to be a top poacher you had to be able to think like a keeper, and vice versa. Willie did this, knowing for instance that poaching the same patch twice in a week was both asking for trouble and not likely to produce much apart from a bunch of waiting keepers. Similarly, George Nugent wouldn't shoot over the same ground twice inside a week, even less frequently if he could get away with it. They were two of a kind, and well-matched. Ernie was nimble, right enough, but he had little brain; with his Dad behind bars he had even less. So, having but the previous week caught up a fair number of birds with both purse net and wire snare in Station Wood, he went there again certain in his own mind that Bill Forrest and his lad would be expecting him elsewhere, at a different place entirely. Another thing went against him too; luck, they say, like the inherited, sly skills of the tinker and the poacher, runs in families and in seasons. And this season was a bad one for the Ashfords.

As it happened, he might have got away with it, but for the fact that Ted Forrest had stopped to pass the time of day with Constable Jim; the lane running uphill from the ford below Grange Farm towards Riverbank was steep enough to take the puff out of most bicycle riders, and sooner than be caught out of breath, Jim Gregory welcomed the chance to dismount with dignity and almost by accident, get up his strength to finally conquer the wearying incline.

'Morning, Ted.'

'Morning, Mister Gregory. Cold enough for ye?'

'For brass monkeys, I reckon. Dad not at home, is he by any chance, lad?'

'He's over at Ten Elms.'

The burly constable settled his helmet more comfortably adjusted its strap, and then gave a quick upward brush to each side of his Kitchener moustache. 'Bit far from the line of duty, that is. Give him a message for me, will you?' he demanded affably.

'Certainly I will,' answered Ted automatically, but his mind wasn't on what was being said. Ted had learned soon enough that a keeper has more eyes than one, and more than one ear to listen with as well. He had been listening to what was all about them, as they paused on that lonely incline each tiny, normal sound registered and was noted as being in place, each natural movement seen and mentally accounted for, except for one. When he and Jim Gregory had first started their casual chat, a pheasant had clattered close by among the trees, and from the bare branches, a pair of rooks had flown off, irritated by these rare intruders. Now, for no apparent reason, a pigeon had fluttered from the line of trees, *towards* the lane, before seeing the two figures there and veering fast away, dipping and dodging down towards the river-bank below. The less-trained eyes of the policeman hadn't noticed the bird, or what it meant, but he had seen Ted's reaction and sensed that something odd was up. Without the slightest sign of excitement or alarm, he continued the conversation in his slow, friendly drawl; seen from afar, he showed no indication whatsoever of being on the alert.

'Seen something, boy?' he asked Ted quietly.

'There's someone in the trees back there,' murmured Ted in reply, his eyes apparently gazing into the grey haze hanging over the river. 'And I reckons I knows who it might be. . . .'

Jim Gregory nodded. 'I'll ride on a bit then cut across,' he said. 'On the left, y'reckon?'

Ted nodded. 'See you then, Mister Gregory,' he said, and gave a cheery wave as the constable mounted up and heaved the cycle into straining motion up the hill.

In the woods, not far from the lane, Ernie saw the two figures part company and sensed that it was time to move on, without ceremony. He had laid enough traps to be getting on with, and he would return that night to take up the catch. What he hadn't bargained for was that he only had one line of retreat, and that was along his line of snares. Moving surprisingly swiftly for all his shambling gait, all his senses tuned to possible pursuit just as any animal, he glided nimbly on then paused; from the trees towards the top of the hill, clumsy movements in the dead bracken told him that Jim Gregory was on foot and lumbering across. Behind him too, there came a quieter, less brutal sound of skilled movement, and then the running of a dog. Turning, Ernie knew he must reach the deepest thickets where he could hide from hounds, if necessary.

He broke into his fastest, flittering run and, eyes keenly ahead, forgot what was at his very feet – his own wire snares. In an instant, his boot had entered the loop, it tightened, and held, long enough to pitch him headlong. By the time he'd scrambled to his feet again, the silent dog was upon him, followed hard by Ted. At Ted's quiet command, the dog sat and watched, tongue lolling, as Ernie sat down on the frosted soil and casually and deliberately removed the offending loop of wire from his boot; Ted was still chuckling when Jim Gregory came upon the scene, and when the constable was told, he laughed out loud. Ernie wasn't amused, but was still perky enough to try to wriggle his way out of being run in.

'I could have you, Ted Forrest,' he said with a brave show of righteous indignation, 'putting down wires to trip up innocent folk like me!'

'Don't go being so chipper, my lad,' grunted Constable Gregory drily, 'we can have you for trespass, if nothing else!' He rummaged in the many pockets of Ernie's loosely flapping coat, and came out with two more unused wire loops, ready attached to sturdy pegs for setting into the ground. The wires were set long, head-high for pheasant. 'Nasty,' the bobby said. 'Could do yourself an injury with those . . .' Ernie shrugged in practised resignation, and Gregory turned to Ted with a nod of thanks. 'Good for you, Ted,' he said. 'I'll take over now, shall I?'

'Fair enough,' responded Ted, then had a twinge of conscience. 'You wanted me to take a message to my Dad though, didn't you?'

'That's true,' grunted Gregory, then flicked a sober glance at Ernie, standing dejectedly at his side. 'I was going to remind him that our Willie's due out, back end of next month. Pity you won't be home to greet him, Ernie . . .' At least he had the grace not to laugh.

It was infuriating; intensely so, in fact, decided Lady Hester. On a day when she had woken with a piercing headache, everything was going wrong. Tense-faced, she sat before her dressing table, studying her perfect but slightly drawn face in its mirror and trying to waft away the mood that threatened her by savouring the delicate, refreshing fragrance of cologne touched petal-light upon her throbbing forehead. Even this passive effort brought on a disturbing tension, and no wonder. One didn't expect to get one's way in everything; but Randolph was usually so considerate, while Anthony had never before gone against her wishes in his life. Today, however, was different. She hadn't been often faced with open rebellion, least of all from Anthony, but she had seen it in his eyes and now she was feeling thoroughly upset.

It had begun with Randolph. He had declared, quite unexpectedly, that he wasn't going to Scotland after all.

'There's enough sport here,' he'd insisted, dismissing her surprise at his decision, with a curt hand. 'I shall stay.'

Her first surge of apprehension had been for Anthony. With only two weeks to go before he went up to Oxford, a bout of seclusion with his silent father was the last thing that was needed to put him in the right spirits for university life.

'You'd best take Anthony to London,' Randolph had said, drily, as though reading her mind. 'There's nothing to amuse him here. . . .' With that, he had gone down to the gun room to discuss arrangements for the first shoot of the new year, with Nugent.

Despite the thought of having to make several necessary changes to the plans she had already made for her prolonged stay at Chester Square, the idea of having her son with her as escort pleased her enormously. He had style, latent as yet perhaps, but a month in town would make him blossom; even in that brief month they could be seen at concerts and the opera together, and there would be charming encounters for him with other young people. He needed that touch of 'beau facile' that only London could give, and who knows, he might come to like its qualities so much that it would be to London he would turn during his vacations, not the country. The house in Chester Square needed young life within its walls, and Anthony would grace it admirably.

But he had rejected her bright-eyed invitation out of hand, bluntly, almost as though angered by it.

'No, Mother,' he had said, politely but firmly. 'Thank you, but I'd rather stay here.'

'But my dear,' she had persisted sweetly, 'January is so . . . dismal. Hardly anybody visits at all, in winter.'

'I've rather a lot of reading to do,' he said, with a distant smile, 'and besides, I'd like to meet more of the tenants on the estate.'

She stared at him, hurt and curious. What was he thinking about? There was no role for him to play here, not for years yet. Perhaps he didn't understand that the estate, with its relentless gearing to those sports in which Randolph so proudly excelled, was merely a source of income, a rural backdrop to be occasionally enjoyed as a respite from the more earnest pleasures of cosmopolitan life. He must learn never to take it seriously, or he would end just as his father was, rooted in hunter, rod and gun, with never a thought for the real world that existed so excitingly outside his countrified boundaries. He obviously didn't yet know of his father's latest decision; she would tell him, and then he would take the chance she had to offer.

'Your father isn't going to Lanark after all,' she murmured. 'Perhaps you didn't know that . . . ?'

It had come as a surprise to him, obviously, but it had made no difference. 'Don't worry, Mother,' he said gently, 'I shall keep out of his way. Besides,' he added drily, 'we each have our own interests.'

She had flared, angrily, something she wouldn't forgive herself easily. 'Anthony,' she snapped, chin lifting prettily to cold hauteur, 'I shall insist – '

'I hope you will not, Mother,' he had responded calmly, but with a flat deliberation. 'I can't see either of us enjoying that sort of situation.'

It was all she could do to retain her composure; then, with a sense of longing for the boy-babe who had been her dearest child, she realised that the boy had become a man, and that the steel that Randolph had never seen was there, coldly gleaming, behind Anthony's steady gaze.

Gracefully, with a polite petulance, she had tried to wheedle him, but he was adamant. In the end she had withdrawn from conflict and dismissed him with a bright kiss and a smile of understanding, all the while seething with hurt pride and anger underneath.

'You must do as you think best, my dear,' she murmured, and pausing in the doorway, he had nodded, and was gone.

Lily Summers, summoned and curtly given her orders, had seen the set of her mistress's mouth and the tiny vertical frown between her perfectly plucked eyebrows, and was wary of trouble. Bringing Doris to Lady Hester's door as she had been told to do, Lily gave the girl a straight glance and warned her, firmly.

'She's in a mood,' she half-whispered, brusquely, 'so watch your *p*s and *q*s. . . .'

Doris had entered, tensely, and presented herself only to find Lady Hester greeting her with a pleasant, almost radiant smile.

'Doris.'

'Yes, my lady.'

'Miss Summers may have told you that I shall be staying at the house in Chester Square for several months, commencing in the New Year . . .'

'Yes, my lady, I had heard,' responded the respectful, quiet voice.

Lady Hester looked at the girl and was pleased; yes, she'd do well in town. 'You will be coming with us,' she stated amiably. 'We leave tomorrow.'

Doris could only look at her, eyes wide, her mind in a terrible confusion. To leave tomorrow – for several *months* – that was bad enough; but to have to go to *London!* Suddenly, she knew it couldn't be done. And whatever the consequences, she had to say so, now.

'I'm sorry, my lady,' she whispered miserably, 'but I don't like London,'

'Nonsense, girl!' exclaimed Lady Hester, her bright smile

edged with clouds of anger. 'It's a wonderful city – an education for a child like you. You'll quickly get used to it. You may have this evening free to tell your parents . . . they should be highly delighted for you . . .'

She turned away, dismissing Doris with a gentle wave of her ringed hand. Lily, her face set in a warning frown, stepped forward to usher Doris out, but the girl evaded the hand on her arm, and met the cool eyes staring at her from the mirror, unflinchingly.

'I'm honoured by the invitation, my lady, but I'd rather you took somebody else . . . please.'

Her mistress whirled to face her, her anger boiling over, flaring in the beautiful eyes, flashing from the bared, delicate teeth. 'It is an *order*, girl – *not* an invitation!' The exquisite hands clasped into an angry knot of entwined fingers. 'You will do as you are told!'

'I'm sorry, my lady. I just can't . . .'

By now Lady Hester was virtually trembling with rage; though her hands remained locked together and her face seemed a frozen mask, her voice was like a whiplash.

'Can't? Won't? Are you trying to *spite* me, girl?'

'I wouldn't ever do such a thing, my lady.' Doris bowed her head for a moment, miserably. But she looked up sharply again, eyes defiant, as Lady Hester spoke.

'Then we shall have no more arguments. Is that understood? That is settled!'

'No, my lady,' answered Doris politely, though her knees felt like water. 'It's not my place. If you please,' she added hesitantly, 'Mary Ann Hudson'd be better there than me.'

Lily Summers' face was impassive, though she flinched inwardly at the sight of the thin smile tightening across her mistress's lips. Then Lady Hester turned to her, eyes questioning.

'Mary Ann Hudson . . .?'

'Kitchenmaid, my lady. A good worker, very clean . . .' She wanted to go on to say how the rosy cheeked girl was altogether too fresh with the men, but she held back. Lady Hester's smile broadened and softened, a dangerous sign to those who knew her well, and turning back to Doris, she nodded, graciously.

'Very well, then . . . it shall be Mary Ann Hudson.'

'Thank you, my lady,' murmured Doris gratefully.

'You will take a month's notice, child,' said Lady Hester, succinctly, and the interview was over.

Chapter Fourteen

'There's someat about this morning,' growled George Nugent ominously, 'that ain't right. I don't like it.'

'Ah,' agreed Henry Adsall, squinting up at the weather, ' – and it in't just the weather, either . . .'

It was to be a rough shoot, without beaters, the six guns flanked by the keepers and their dogs; the aim was to raise the game as they walked and shoot pot luck. Anything was fair game – pheasant, pigeon, rabbit, hare – and protocol would be kept to the minimum. Bill Forrest could remember being told that it was an old way of shooting the dead year out.

'We could do with a new 'un,' observed Henry, and the head keeper agreed with a brisk nod.

'Next shoot'll be nineteen twenty,' he said, lighting up his pipe yet again, forced to shelter his match in the haven of Bill Forrest's jacket, an improvised wind-break against cold gusts of dying December. 'Pray to God it'll be a better year than this last!'

'First year of peace, weren't it . . .' muttered Ted, stamping his feet into the frost-hardened turf.

George Nugent gave him a shrewd look, and biting on his pipe, grinned wickedly. 'Time you was getting your oats, young feller,' he growled, and the older keepers laughed.

'Lost your chance with Mary Ann Hudson, an't ye,' Henry Adsall nudged, with a wink.

'She won't go short,' grunted the head keeper, and he laughed again, but this time only Henry joined in. Not knowing how things stood, Nugent nevertheless sensed something the matter in the Forrest household, and knew them well enough to be bluntly inquisitive.

'You an't had a poke at her already, lad, have ye?' he asked. 'Not sending her off to go pop, are they?'

'Not of my doing, anyroad,' responded Ted, trying to make a joke of it; he met his father's eyes, and turned away, afraid to let his anger flare. If folk had to be told, let it be someone else that did it!

'Guns're coming,' called Henry, who had paced a little way off, and could see the approaching car lurching up the track.

'You done enough already, son,' commended Nugent, indicating the vague direction of Borchester, invisible and miles away. 'I'd sooner have old Willie and his lad inside any time, than you spending your time picking cherries!' He nodded knowingly to Bill Forrest. 'You an't got a bad lad here, y'know, William. . . .'

'Not bad,' smiled Ted's father, 'considering, that is.'

'He can flank me this morning, anyroad,' grunted Nugent, and Ted warmed to him, for this was a compliment indeed, of far greater value than mere words. Bill knew it too and, pleased, moved across to stand with Henry. The Squire and his party of guns – no ladies today – were out of the car now and walking across the crisped white grass. Nugent stood aside, turning away apparently to check that the breech of his gun was empty, but it was a dry deceit to hide his quiet undertone.

'I've pals in Norfolk,' he muttered offhandedly, 'that tells me it's a grand place for a young keeper what's well thought of. . . .'

'Is that a fact?' replied Ted carefully, wondering what was in Nugent's mind. Did he know about Doris already; did everyone? Patiently, he waited while the grizzled keeper squinted carefully along the shining barrel, seemingly intent on only that.

'Some places got a future, lad,' he growled, then looked Ted straight in the eye, shrewdly, '. . . and some places haven't.'

'Need a good character for Norfolk, a feller would . . .' Ted seemed to think aloud. His mind asked different questions, however. Was a gypsy as welcome in Norfolk as she would be here?

'Once Ernie Ashford's nailed in court tomorrow,' said

Nugent, 'a feller'd have no trouble placing hisself. That is,' he added to his dog, sat quietly at heel, 'if he so wanted. . . .'

'Mister Nugent,' grinned Ted, half-embarrassed at the pleasure given to him by the older man's generous advice, 'you're a great bloke to work with, did y'know?'

'Don't go calling my shots for me, that's all, lad,' chuckled Nugent, and they both moved off to place themselves in the line of guns.

Walter had only just finished bagging the coal slack from the dusty railway siding, when from his vantage point on his wagon he saw the gleaming car from the Hall roll sleekly into the station yard and draw to a halt. Taking the chance of a breather, he watched idly as Alfred Tetsall stepped out and opened the passenger door for Lady Hester; Walter had no liking for the wooden-faced Brummie, and mentally compared him to a tin soldier, forever standing at attention, eyes front and nose in the air. Lily Summers came next, following Lady Hester into the gloomy recesses of the station's ticket office; it was then that Walter came alert and, first scratching his head, then resettling his battered trilby on his coal-grimed forehead, gave a small whistle at the sight of Mary Ann Hudson. He had never seen her in the coat she now wore, and she looked a proper treat, especially all rosy-cheeked with excitement as she was. He frowned slightly as he saw the bright glances she kept giving Alfred, busy taking out the mountain of luggage and cases from the car's boot. The overcoated chauffeur now slipped into the station, obviously to try and rouse Clem, the porter. For a moment, Mary Ann was left guarding the luggage, and Walter took his chance, coming up behind her and giving her waist a quick cuddle and a squeeze. Mary Ann gave a stifled squeal and whirled about, arm raised to retaliate; but seeing Walter her face lost its anger and rippled into a broad, embarrassed smile.

'Walter Gabriel, you wickedness!' she exclaimed softly clutching at her hat and looking all about to make sure they weren't being observed. 'Don't . . .!'

Aware that she was playing the lady, he stood back slightly, and looked her up and down with blatant admiration, giving an appreciative chuckle and a wink. 'By Jim,' he said, 'but you'm a pretty sight. But what am you up to, me love?'

Suddenly Mary Ann's face fell, and she bowed her head slightly. When she looked up at him again, he could see an unaccustomed sadness in her eyes. 'Going to London, in't I,' she said, then paused before going on, quietly, 'Miss Summers's maid, I am. . . .'

'Eh?' exclaimed Walter, puzzled. 'What's the matter with young Doris then? Sick is she, or what?'

Mary Ann shook her head, miserably. 'Her ladyship give her a month's notice.'

'Did her now . . .' muttered Walter, wonderingly. 'What had her done to deserve that, for heaven's sakes?' The thought half-flicked through his mind that maybe John Archer was in some way responsible, but as he'd seen nothing of him since before Christmas, there was no way of telling.

'Disobeyed the mistress,' confessed Mary Ann, then added bitterly, 'just 'cos she asked not to go to London. . . .' While Walter considered this, her face brightened. 'I got picked instead!' she cried, bubbling with excitement once again. 'In't I lucky?'

Walter frowned. This was bad news and no mistake. 'Do Dan or John Archer know, d'y'reckon?' he asked, and the concern in his face communicated itself to Mary Ann.

'I dunno, pet,' she murmured. 'But I daresay Mister Bill Forrest'll tell 'em soon enough. . . .'

She saw Walter stiffen slightly as his eyes went past her, and turning, she realised that Alfred Tetsall had returned. Clem and his trolley were close behind him, whistling as tunelessly as ever. While the bird-like porter gathered and piled the luggage ready for taking through to the platform and the incoming guard van, Alfred stood close by Mary Ann, carefully making a show of his magnificent leather gloves, all the while staring hard at Walter and the blotches of coal dust smeared on to his weathered face.

'I hope you're not bothering this young lady, son,' he said grimly. 'Shove off.'

'He's an old friend,' Mary Ann cut in quickly, before trouble could develop, 'come to say goodbye. . . .'

'That's right, me old pal,' agreed Walter with a warning twinkle in Alfred's direction. 'You wouldn't be thinking of objecting, would ye . . .?'

Alfred shook his head, insolently unimpressed by Walter's implied threat of earthy retribution. 'Good riddance to bad rubbish,' he said, and closing the car boot with a precise thud, turned to follow Clem and the trolley back inside the station. 'I'd come on, doll, if I was you . . .' The shiny peak of his driving cap gleamed as he nodded pointedly towards the railway station. 'Y'know what she's like . . .' He put his gloved hand possessively under Mary Ann's elbow, and steered her firmly towards the grimy-bricked entrance, and Walter noticed the small flutter of delight in Mary Ann's pert face.

'Good luck to ye, pet,' he said, not moving to interfere. 'Write us a letter, eh?'

'You come up to London,' Mary Ann called back from the door held open for her by the chauffeur. Her eyes flashed knowingly at Walter, a snapshot of past pleasures. 'I'll show you the sights,' she grinned cheekily, then gave a little wave and disappeared inside. Walter had raised his grimy trilby in a jovial salute; by the time it had been resettled on his head, he was already wondering who'd they get to replace Mary Ann and Doris, and what sort of jolly wenches they might be.

The first drive had ended close by Marney's farm, and the line of guns had wheeled and paused to consider the bag so far, before driving on around the west flank of Lakey Hill, across back of Sixpenny Farm, with the eventual sweep to end at the lake behind Arkwright Hall. Old Herbert and his black retriever Gyp were picking up, and as Nugent came towards him, the old man nodded, cheerily.

'Not bad, Mister Nugent,' he croaked. 'D'y'reckon?'

'Pretty fair,' agreed the head keeper, his keen eye taking in numbers, for this was all that counted with the Squire. It was rough sport, but that didn't mean that the guns wanted just to blaze away to no account; sizing up what had been taken, Nugent decided it was just as well he was steering the next stage of the drive around towards the windbreak of tall elms between Meadow Farm and Sixpenny. There were both pigeon and pheasant there, and with luck the guns'd pick off a tidy few, enough for the Squire to be content before the party went inside for luncheon. He had just started to make his report to the Squire, when young Ted Forrest called from the flank, pointing towards the not-far-distant trees. In a wind-blown flurry of scattering wings, the precious birds there were rising, well out of range, and swinging even farther away, to the thick sanctuary of Blossom Hill Wood. The Squire saw, and stiffened in surprise and anger.

'What the devil!' he barked, and turned on Nugent, cursing silently at his side. The belt of trees cleared of birds, there'd be little left to shoot but rabbit or hare; the remaining drive would be utter failure.

'Have you left some fool or other down ahead, Nugent – ?' grated Lawson-Hope, eyes blazing.

The grizzled keeper didn't reply immediately, for he was listening to a faint ring of sound carried to them standing as they were downwind from the trees.

'There's someone there all right, sir,' he growled, his hand clenched tight about the stock of his gun. 'But not with my knowledge.'

'Can you hear that, Bill?' queried Henry Adsall, hardly believing his ears. Bill looked uncomfortable, and glanced surreptitiously towards the Squire who, like a pointing gundog with his nose to the wind, faced the drifting sound with a fiercely intent, hawk-like face. The voice they could all hear now was a single tenor, richly singing.

Suddenly, out of the dipped shallow of the long field stretched before them, came one figure, then another closely following; even from where the watchers stood, they were aware of the cheerful wildness in the movements of the approaching pair, but it was full ten seconds before they realised that the second figure was female, trilling out bursts of giggling laughter as a counterpoint to the words of the ribald song.

'When this bloody shoot is over . . .
Oh, how happy I shall be . . .
Rolling Polly in the clover . . .
Once for you, and twice for me. . .'

The voice rang out, high and true, in sweet mockery of the black hymn sung with such plaintive resignation by warfare-sickened heroes, sparse years ago.

'Well I be jiggered,' whispered Old Herbert, and turned to huddle over his pipe, the lighting of it serving to hide the cough of laughter lodged tight in his throat. A gesture from George Nugent held the other keepers in their place; it wasn't for them to act, only on the word of the Squire himself, and he was at the forefront of the listening group, rigid as a statue. Like Old Herbert, he and the keepers had recognised the strutting walk of dapper John Archer; but neither young Ted nor the Squire knew that the girl with John was Polly Harper.

Someone amongst the visiting guns had realised that the imminent scene was strictly a domestic one for Lawson-Hope to handle, and as a group these men stepped casually out of earshot, determined to ignore the confrontation. As John stumbled to a halt some ten yards short of the Squire, it was obvious that both he and Polly were, to put it politely, half cut. Clinging together happily, eager to balance each other's every shift and sway, they beamed upon the Squire and his keepers like a pair of visiting angels.

'Polly, you slut,' said John, eyes glittering, 'it's the bloody Squire. Say hello nicely to the gentleman!'

Giggling and helpless, Polly attempted a brave curtsey, and tumbled over on to her backside. Gathering up her skirts with ostentatious modesty, she stayed at John's feet, her arms cuddling his knees, her pretty but bedraggled hat untidily askew, there was nevertheless in her face something that few men could resist; not wantonness, but a warmth that denied all bitterness and offered only complete friendship, total trust. Ted saw it and remembered Emma, while all but the Squire had memories of their own. He saw only a limpid-eyed girl and a ghost from the past, and his mind was numb with misery. John thought he recognised Ted's pain, and laughed.

'Don't look so worried, Ted, old son – it's not your sister.' He laughed, bitterly. 'I've sworn off Doris, mate – *and* this whole bloody place!' he shouted, glaring teeth-bared at the Squire, who still seemed not to hear. His blankness made John rage all the more.

'Your bloody guns . . .! the wire-taut figure howled. 'It's all you're bloody good for, in't it – killing! Sending good lads to the war. Sticking bloody wreaths on their graves. Sending 'em up to heaven with a bloody brass band!'

The whole company was frozen and listening now, even the visitors. There was an anguish in John's cracked voice that touched all of them, but it was wasted on the one man he so desperately wanted to hurt. The Squire, safe in his empty shell, heard nothing and saw only his own private nightmare, summoned up by that ridiculous parody from the trenches. Not a single word of John's ejaculated hatred could etch any deeper than the two lost faces forever fading out of reach, their sad laughter perpetually slipping into shadow. What other men might have lost was meaningless because it was unknown, outside experience. Nothing was left but empty rooms, and a silence where there should have been voices.

'What would you ever bloody know . . .!' bawled John, racked with his own sad agony. 'You never even saw 'em *die*!'

'Get off my land,' the desiccated face at last uttered.

'Your bloody land!' sneered John, scathingly. 'My brother's got more feeling for the land in his left boot than you've had all your life! You own it – use it – but it's him that works it and makes it bloody what it is!' Suddenly he knew he had bared a nerve, and drew the razor of his anger slicing across it, without pity.

'It isn't even yours. It's theirs – and they're both bloody *dead*!'

For a timeless moment, the figures on that frosted hillside stood silent and unmoving as mourners about a grave; then, as though the intruders had never even existed, Lawson-Hope looked over and beyond them to the waiting trees. John stared at him, still held by Polly's arms and swaying, the cocky smile slipping slowly from his face.

'Nugent,' said the Squire, 'things should've settled down by now. We'll move on.'

'Sir,' Nugent answered, but hesitated for a moment, wondering what was to be done about John and his girl, set firmly in the way. Checking the open breech of his gun to see that it was loaded, the Squire looked up, and following the keeper's gaze, seemed to see the two figures for the very first time. He gave a curt gesture, then moved forward past them as he spoke. The line moved with him, leaving John and the kneeling girl isolated in their wake.

'Adsall!' he rapped, eyes searching only for a quarry to be killed.

'Squire . . . ?' responded the second keeper, briskly.

'Get those two out of here and down to the road, and warn them they've been trespassing. Next time they'll be up before the Bench!'

The line moved relentlessly away, leaving the keeper slowly approaching the intruders. They were laughing, hopelessly; John was on his knees with Polly held giggling to his chest, and she looked up wet-eyed as Adsall stood sternly over them.

'Squire didn't even know me,' she said, wiping the foolish tears from her tired eyes.

'Course he didn't, pet,' giggled John, helping Polly to her feet. 'I mean, we're not even his bloody tenants any more . . . are we!' And he laughed all the louder, knowing that Henry Adsall didn't understand.

CHAPTER FIFTEEN

IT WAS Bill Forrest who had told Dan first of John's last escapade, and then about Doris. He had met the young farmer coming from the cow shed, where Dolly could be heard lowing restlessly in her stall. Her time wasn't long due now, but typically, she wasn't going to make things easy for herself. Bill knew the signs well enough, but he had more important things to speak of.

'Cooked his own goose good and proper, has John,' the keeper said shrewdly, noticing the still livid bruises on Dan's face and the scabs on his broken knuckles. 'And not just with the Squire. . . .'

Dan shrugged. 'It'd be like him to go out in glory,' he grunted. He gave a slow look at the keeper, and then explained. 'We've come to an agreement, John and me,' he said. 'He won't be coming back.'

Bill Forrest nodded. 'Just as well,' was his response to the news, and then he had told Dan about Doris being dismissed. Dan listened, frowning. Apart from the injustice of it, he knew that another position in service could be hard to come by, especially if Lady Hester took it upon herself to be vindictive. Doris was in a spot, and no mistake.

'What's she going to do then?' he asked Doris's father.

'Work her notice,' was the curt answer. Then Mr Forrest paused, idly scratching away an unseen flake of skin from his calloused hand, his eyes turned away from Dan. 'She could get another position, away from here,' he said, 'but me and Mother'd rather she stayed in these parts. . . .' Dan didn't answer, and the older man went on, now staring uncompromisingly into Dan's thoughtful eyes. 'It's about time she was wed, us reckons,' he declared quietly, and waited for the young man's reply. It hadn't come quickly.

'There's John between us . . .' answered Dan at last, his face troubled.

'She heard about this business with Polly Harper,' retorted the keeper. 'Our Ted told her, said she ought to know. And you'm just said as the rascal's gone off out of Ambridge, in't that a fact?'

Dan nodded.

'Well then,' said Bill. 'Besides,' he added, with a tightening of the mouth, 'Ted's got ideas of his own, y'see.' He sensed rather than saw the question in Dan's face, and continued awkwardly, 'He's done well for hisself here. Time he was moving on, mebbe . . .' He paused, but couldn't hide the pride in his voice. 'George Nugent reckons he can help place him on one o' the big estates in Norfolk.' Dan still didn't answer, and Ted's father insistently made his point again. 'Us wouldn't want to be losing both on 'em,' he sad, 'not with our Tommy still such a lad. . . .'

Dan himself got on well with the boy, and he knew how tightly bonded the whole family were. Ted was a hero in the youngster's eyes, and if Doris was to leave home as well, there'd be no telling how he'd take it. But that still wasn't the right reason for putting the question to Doris; it had to be for his own sake, not because of her kin and their problems. And asking her promised to be a greater ordeal by far than even fighting John. Besides, sooner or later she'd be bound to find out about John leaving; if she was still sweet on him then she'd put all the blame on Dan, and that'd be the end of everything.

'You know how I feel,' muttered Dan, 'but it in't easy, Mr Forrest.'

'I can't do it for ye, son,' was the dry reply. 'Just remember she finishes come the end of the month, that's all. And it's about then – end of the season – that Ted'll be making his move, all right?'

'It's in my mind, don't worry,' Dan replied firmly.

'Well don't go thinking about it for *too* long, son,' said the older man, then nodded towards Dolly's stall. 'Going to have your work cut out today, I reckon: Good luck with her, eh. . . .' With that, they had exchanged a friendly nod of parting, and Bill Forrest had moved off about his business, to feed his pheasants along the woods of Ten Elms Rise.

That had been hours ago; now Dan's thoughts were only on Dolly and the fix she'd got herself into; true to form, she was the last of the Christmas calving, and just to be okkard, her calf was coming backwards. She always made a fuss, of course, but Dan had discovered the worst not long after she had come to the softening of the bones. Instead of the freedom-seeking muzzle, the hind feet, upside down, had been the first to emerge; even just from the hips Dan could tell it was a bull calf, which wasn't going to make things any easier. He'd be a winner if he came out safe, Dan realised that, but now, half pushed out, with Dolly bawling and restless to get done, they had reached the danger point. Dan's mind was both quick and cool as he set up the block and tackle with practised hands, from the stall beam overhead. With the calf stuck midway and coming out all the wrong shape, the umbilical was almost bound to rupture. If it wasn't out soon after that, the calf'd be dead, and all poor Dolly's efforts wasted. With the block and tackle, Dan could still only do so much to help, alone; but two hands were all he had, and they'd have to do for now.

He was just slipping the rope nooses over each of the calf's protruding rear legs, when the help he so desperately wanted stepped inside the cowshed doorway. Taking in what was happening at a glance, Master Anthony was already unbuttoning his jacket as he spoke, quietly but urgently.

'Tell me what I can do, Daniel,' he said, flinging his coat on to a nearby stall partition. 'Is it a breech?'

'Not as bad as that,' grunted Dan, 'but it's coming backwards and she needs all the help she can get.' He indicated the chain on the block and tackle, which was now firmly linked to the slowly shifting calf; for once, Dolly had decided to co-operate, and was lying down, though still protesting.

'Take the strain . . . gently,' Dan said. 'While you do that, I can ease the chest through without the guts getting squashed all over the place.' He crouched by the limp form of the emergent calf; Dolly was beginning to push again, and Dan looked back over his shoulder to the youngster poised and ready to take the strain. 'Here it comes then,' the farmer muttered. 'Just take it easy, that's all.' He grinned, feeling the slippery form between his hands begin its desperate journey into daylight. 'No pulling his legs off, eh. . . .'

'I'll try not to,' came the nervous but smiling reply. 'It's Dolly, isn't it?'

'Aye,' said Dan, 'it is. Steady. . . .'

Anthony could see the danger if Dolly became too restless, and he frowned. 'Her head,' he warned.

'Don't fret, lad,' grunted Dan irritably, 'her head's safe tethered, I know her tricks!' Suddenly he remembered what Anthony stood for, and his own position, and muttered apologetically. 'Sorry, Master Anthony. . . .'

'Don't be silly,' said his grave-faced assistant. 'You're the master here. . . .' There was a trace of perspiration on his face; not free to reach his handkerchief, he wiped his face against his shirt sleeve. 'Are we winning?' he demanded tensely.

Dan was frowning; there didn't seem to be enough movement. 'The cord's broken for certain, b'now,' he muttered. 'There's only minutes – no time to waste. Heave!' he ordered, then felt a prompt response under his firming hands. 'That's it – ah!' All of a rush the slimy, gawky bundle was out and free, but still they weren't done.

'Is it alive?' cried Anthony, leaving the pulley chain, and moving to Dan's shoulder.

'That's up to us,' grunted the farmer, deftly slipping off the ropes from the bull calf's back legs. 'Help me put him over that gate, come on!'

Without thinking of himself, of his crisp shirt or immaculate riding breeches, Anthony grabbed hold as best he could and matched Dan's practised heave. Its rear legs over the gate bar, and its nose nearly on the floor, the stretched-out body

184

looked as though it was ready for the abattoir, and Anthony questioned Dan with a hard glance.

'Got to make him breathe, an't we,' explained Dan, curtly. 'Rub his back, hard!'

Anthony responded vigorously, hands slithering along the bull calf's spine and ribs; his eyes were fixed on Dan, kneeling head down at the animal's flopping head. He had picked up a single, long-stemmed straw, and with deft, steady hands, slid it up the calf's nostril. For a long second, there was no reaction whatsoever; then the calf shuddered with a mighty sneeze, and then again. Dan stood up, face impassive, but Anthony's eyes danced with triumph. 'We've done it!' he cried, laughing, and helped Dan ease the now-struggling bull calf to the ground. It bawled for its mother, and Dan took up the warm body in his arms, to lay it down close by.

'Dolly'll do the rest,' he said cheerfully, then flashed a quick glance at Anthony, who was regarding his soiled shirt with some amusement.

'Here,' said Dan, handing him a fistful of clean straw. 'Rub y'self down with this. We'll make a farmer of ye yet. . . .'

They moved outside, into the yard, and paused there; Dan, uncomfortable at how to resume his proper station, could only offer a clumsy hospitality.

'There's a drop of whisky in the kitchen,' he said, half-hesitating. 'Not much, to be honest. . . .'

'Enough for two, I'm sure,' grinned Anthony, clapping Dan on the shoulder. 'Let's go in . . . !'

They were barely across the yard when they heard the call of Constable Jim's brusque voice, commanding and urgent.

'Master Anthony, sir!'

They turned to see him struggling with the fastening of the yard gate, his bicycle thrown down outside. And when they saw his face they knew that something was desperately wrong.

January wasn't such a bad month, thought Ted Forrest to himself as he strode along the lane that would take him home to Riverbank; not if you allowed for a good season and the success that Ted had had over nabbing both the Ashfords. More than that was the praise he'd received from George Nugent, and the offer of an interview for the Norfolk job. The Squire hadn't objected, it seemed, and Alexander Wickham had written Ted a character reference that, with Nugent's shrewd comments to flavour its formal prose into glowing life, had all but won him the position already. Dad was all for it, Tommy full of amazement at the thought of Ted keepering over an estate of thirty thousand acres, and even Mam had admitted a tearful pride at such advancement, at his young years, too. The only shadow over the year had been Doris's misfortune in crossing Lady Hester; but with only a week to go before her notice would be worked off, she was cheerfully looking forward to being at home with her mother, certainly until she might find other work. If only Dan could see his way to saying the word, thought Ted, wryly; Doris would surely say yes, he was certain of it, but she had to be asked! Another shadow flitted through his mind, sweeter yet more infinitely sad : Emma. It was she that had brought him both luck and love; from the moment she had given him the tip that nailed old Willie Ashford, the good fortune had run on, clear to the time when Ernie had been caught, just off of this very lane. Suddenly a guilty thought checked his pace, and without waiting to think twice, he stepped off the road, under the wire fence, and into the thickets of Station Wood.

He had been hereabouts many times since Ernie had been caught by his own snares, but this was not a feeding wood, and therefore less well attended. But thinking about the nifty little poacher had reminded Ted of what he hadn't done – lifted the remaining wires. It was a daft mistake, one for which he'd kick himself when it came to clear them now, for more than likely there'd be carcases limp and rotting in the killing loops. But it wouldn't take long, and might even be easier without Grit trotting along at heel. He was a fine dog, but still liable to get excited by the sight of fallen game; it would save trouble too, if he wasn't there to nuzzle any dead rabbit caught by the snares, and pick up the deserting fleas. Ted smiled; he prided himself on keeping a clean dog, something he'd enjoy showing off in the wilds of Norfolk. He found himself now on a familiar path, and looking keenly ahead, saw the game-trodden runway broaden into a forest ride. At the same time he felt the ground tremble, and heard the swiftly rippling sound of approaching hoof-beats coming towards him; he knew it would be the Squire on Trumper, and he halted, ready to tip his cap in customary respect. It was from here, too far away to interfere, that he saw the gleam of danger; in that split second he was helpless, and when at last he did move, it was too late.

Round the gentle curve of the ride came Trumper, at a fast canter that was safe enough; on his back, Squire Lawson-Hope crouched low to avoid an over-hanging branch. Neither horse nor rider saw the scattering of snares along the ride ahead until the searing agony caught and held the horse's front fetlock, cutting to the bone, bringing him to his knees, and pitching his rider headlong into a sickening fall. The force of the stride had not only drawn the wire tight enough to spurt blood from flesh, it had torn the holding peg clean from the ground; but a rear leg had stepped inside yet another wickedly effective noose, and the horse, neighing with shrill pain at the terror of this unseen attacker, somehow scrambled to its feet, rearing and kicking viciously over the body of its fallen master. Lawson-Hope was sprawled, still and unmoving, beneath the screaming menace of the horse, its hooves thudding down on to the leaf-strewn ride and missing him only by inches. Again it reared high over him, blood streaming from its savaged fetlocks, a majestic demon flailing at invisible enemies. Ted took the only chance that he could see to dash forward and try to drag the Squire clear, but his scrabbling foot slipped and he fell, wide-eyed and helpless, as those terrifying hooves came lashing downward yet again. In that last split second, as he saw the ring of bright silver gleaming about the bloody bone, he knew at last the truth of what Emma had once seen : then the scimitar edge of bright horseshoe scythed into the frail temple of his brain, and he slumped, a lifeless shield, across the unconscious body of the Squire.

This was how Constable Jim Gregory had found them; the horse, quiet now and grazing, the Squire stirring fitfully but still concussed, and the awful horror of the broken boy. A quick, heart-pounding examination was enough to show that there was little to be done, other than briefly tend the Squire and cover the other's shattered face. Then, stolidly clinging to the formal ritual of evidence, Constable Jim had taken out his notebook and jotted down the facts as he had found them. His mind concentrated on the clumsy phrases to be carefully pencilled down with regulation exactitude; they were not required to show any testimony of grief.

'From my knowledge of the deceased, I was able to identify him as Edward George Forrest, underkeeper to the aforesaid injured person, Mr Randolph Lawson-Hope. I then proceeded to make known the facts to all parties legally concerned, namely Mister Anthony Lawson-Hope, son of the injured person, and those persons being the next of kin of the deceased Edward Forrest.'

The page ended with an impulsively scribbled motif, thickly pencilled over to hide its lack of relevance to the coroner's enquiry.

'R.I.P.'

CHAPTER SIXTEEN

TOM KNELT on the grass, the hours-old lamb cradled awkwardly in his arms. Twisting his head he tried to look down into the flickering glass alley that was the creature's eye, but it was snuggled so closely that he had to be contented with its tight-curled warmth, tucked hard against him. The boy looked across to Dan, and laughed for the first time in weeks.

'He tickles,' he said, grinning down at the lamb again. 'Do he have a name yet?'

'Not yet,' smiled Dan. 'You give him one. . . .'

He watched Tom's face grow thoughtful, but not so serious that it hid the flush of pleasure that seemed to radiate between him and the creature that he carried. It was all of six weeks now since Ted had died; in that time the family at Riverbank had bonded even more closely together, but Dan too had been drawn into their grief, only to find that Tom had set him in the place that Ted had once occupied, that of brother, rather than uncle or family friend. Dan had willingly taken the boy under his wing, not cosseting him, but placing him in the way of living things such as Dolly's rumbustious bull calf Joker, and now, the first of the March lambs. In those first weeks of numbing loss, the boy, blank-faced but obedient, had followed Dan about like an automaton, his dark-ringed eyes always close to tears. Now, with the bustling March wind buffeting his hair and skin, there was new colour to his cheeks and a quick curl to his mouth that brought an answering boyishness to Dan's normally stolid features.

'He looks like a Spotted Dick,' grinned the happy youngster, stroking the black-dappled kinks of wool. 'But I'll call him Smuts.'

'Fair enough,' responded Dan, then added with a nod towards the plaintively bawling ewe close by, 'Best let him go for a bit. His Mam's wanting him, see?'

Responding to the call, the lamb was now wriggling to escape; Tom let him go and watched cheerfully as the tottering, spry-legged offspring reached its mother and immediately dived beneath her flank, thrusting for the milk-flushed udder, and wagging its upturned rudder with furious delight. The boy turned, laughing, back to Dan, but found the young farmer staring past the scattered sheep, down the gentle slope of Lakey Hill, to a black-clad figure walking steadily up towards them. The boy stood now, eyes bright with happy recognition.

'It's Doris!' he cried delightedly. 'And she's got a picnic!'

Dan stood his ground as the excited boy ran from him down the hill to greet his sister; reaching her, he took the cloth-covered basket from her and raced with it back up the hill to Dan, with Doris gaily following.

'I said she would!' exclaimed Tom. 'She's brought the grub. And lemonade!'

'Find us a place to sit then,' suggested Dan, 'and we'll tuck in. Over there,' he indicated, pointing to the shelter of the trees. Tom was already scampering off when Doris arrived at the brow of the slope and gracefully settled on the ground, her sweet face flushed and sparkling.

'Oh,' she murmured, 'but I'm puffed!'

Dan sat down by her, but not too close. She noted his glance at Tom, still moving perkily towards the trees, and smiled. She could accept his shyness now, but knew his real feelings. There was a safety in him, a comfort that had shown itself in so many little ways since the funeral; not only to her but to her Mam, even to her father, determined not to break except in the darkness of the bedroom, with Liza's arms tight about him. She had heard their soft sad murmurings, and easing their grief had kept her own tears at bay for nearly two weeks after standing over that rain-gusted grave and watching the plain coffin slowly covered. It had been on Dan's broad chest that she had finally wept; he had said nothing, but quietly stroking her tight-drawn hair, he had at last soothed those deep-wrenching sobs into silence. She had looked up at him then, eyes brimming, her trembling mouth asking for love. He had kissed her, softly but briefly, and she had found peace, at last. But even then they couldn't think only of themselves; there had been Tom, so utterly lost without his hero brother that his mother had despaired of the terrifying misery in his pale, gaunt face. It had been Dan who had been the rock, the strong arm, the offered hand that Tom had at last turned to, and today, after what seemed a lifetime, Doris had seen her young brother come alive with excitement once more.

'He's happy,' Doris said, following Dan's eyes. 'Really happy. . . .' She turned back to Dan, her soft eyes glowing. 'What happened?'

'I let him watch the old girl drop her lamb,' Dan muttered, shrewd-eyed and thoughtful. 'Seemed to mean someat to him, like finding out there's a secret to the seasons . . .' He paused, awkwardly; he was saying more than he was used to, but words seemed easier now with Doris. 'Could be the turning point, I reckon. Like a fever,' he explained, thinking of animals and their simple ways. He found her eyes blazing at him, bright with a fondness that forced him to drop his own glance and seek a sober refuge in the mourning that she wore; black woollen shawl over the plain black blouse tightly collared at that soft-curving neck, the heavy black skirt springing so fulsomely from her womanly hips. Suddenly she was crouching closer to him, and he couldn't move away.

'I don't like wearing black,' she said, putting her face firmly into his line of sight. 'Even for love of our Ted . . .' And she kissed him.

'Come on . . . !' the breeze carried Tom's eager call down to them from the trees where he'd been perched, watching them with innocent curiosity. 'I'm hungry!'

They broke apart, laughing, and Dan helped Doris to her feet. They stood close together, and his arm was round her waist, as she looked up at him, a soft challenge in her eyes.

'Well, Dan Archer,' she said, her mouth twitching with

amusement at the pickle he was in, 'what've y'got to say then?'

'Can't make any promises before summer,' he growled, but his shrewd eyes glittered.

'If you think I'll be kept waiting for Christmas to come and us not even engaged –' Doris flared prettily, but Dan's dry decision cut her protest short.

'After harvest then,' came the quiet declaration, and she nodded contentedly. Then he put his strong arms about her, and lifting her, whirled her in a slow circle, all the time setting his lips to hers. When at last her feet touched the ground, she held on to him, laughing and dizzy. 'That seals it, does it, my love?' he demanded, and she nodded again, gazing out past him over the gentle slopes below to the sun-bright rooftops of distant Brookfield Farm, her future home.

'Could be Old Herbert's right, y'know,' he chuckled, and she looked at him, puzzled and smiling. 'He reckons as a good wife makes a good harvest,' grinned Dan, and ran Doris laughing up the hill to join young Tom.